I need you to save me

BOOKS BY GENICIOUS

The I Need You Series

I Need You To Hate Me
I Need You To Love Me
I Need You To Save Me

Standalones

Sins for Cigarettes

I need you to save me

GENICIOUS

First Edition

HTTPS://GENICIOUS.COM

For those who still wish upon shooting stars.

PROLOGUE

Ace

My life flashed before my eyes many times. Yet never once have I been surprised or wistful and reminiscent. I accepted it like one would accept an inherited fortune from a long-lost family member. With arms wide open and readiness.

After all, I've surrendered myself to a lifetime of trouble with everything I've gotten involved in.

The fighting.

The illegal clubs.

And all the consequences that came with the above.

However, each time the reaper lingered around the corner, the universe has decided my time isn't up yet. It chewed me up, got a taste of what kind of devil I'd be in hell and spat me right back out where I belonged.

If someone had asked me a year ago whether I would take it all back, I would have said no. There's only one thing I regret, only one thing I would change.

I've been brought up to know that every mistake, every action I take is a learning opportunity. It's what made me who I am—formed the roots of my being and urged me to do better.

But now, as I stare into the eyes of the woman I love with a sharp pain puncturing my chest, I realize that perhaps if someone asked me the same question now, my answer would be different. I would take it *all* back if it meant the reaper would hold off a little longer.

In the few seconds I stare into Calla's eyes, eyes that brim with tears while mayhem explodes around us, I find a secret lurking behind them.

A secret she had no right to keep from me.

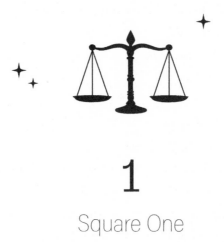

1

Square One

Calla

What is unconditional love?

Some would say it's to love someone no matter what. To give your all to someone but also to know your worth. Some believe that only children—souls that haven't been tainted by the ugly world—deserve unconditional love. Some don't believe in it at all and say all love has conditions.

I think that if you find the right person, unconditional love is possible.

Tears stream down my face in endless waves. I can't stop the vicious cycle now that it's started.

"Ace!" I call out to him one last time before they take him. My voice shakes. It's almost undecipherable, but my own ears recognize how much raw pain it carries.

He turns his head, glancing back at me, and in that moment—in that small flicker of time—I witness everything that I'm about to lose.

My entire world. My stars.

Us.

My heart stops.

My world collapses.

I turn into a distorted mess.

I've always lived by the saying that everything happens for a reason. The universe throws obstacles my way every day, and it urges me to overcome them, to learn a valuable lesson. But right now, I'm having a hard time grasping what the reason for this is.

Is the universe only trying to balance the right and wrong? Or is it telling me, pushing me to see that there's no future for me and Ace? It terrifies me that after finally beginning to be comfortable with the possibility of *us*, it can all get ripped away from me in a matter of seconds.

Everyone's stares are like a million glass shards in my back. I don't look around. I keep my head down, too afraid to meet anyone's gaze. It's human nature to be curious, so I can't blame them for the most common instinct. But the weight of everyone's gaze on me remains uncomfortable and heavy.

I emerge from the grand airport doors, gasping for fresh air, desperate not to suffocate.

I stumble toward the police car, catching a glimpse of Ace already seated inside. The raging sun obstructs my view, casting a blinding glare that obscures the interior. Amidst the shadows, I barely discern his head slumped over his broad shoulders. At the last minute, his head jerks up, and he looks out the window, searching for me.

I blink, and the patrol car fades into the distance.

My hands tremble as I reach for my phone. It takes three goes to type in my passcode, and my thumb hovers over Nik's contact for a few beats. There's no one else for me to call that can help in this kind of situation, and Nik would want to know about this.

Wouldn't he?

Over the last few months, Nik and Ace have become close. They have this weird brotherly bond I didn't think would ever be possible considering how their relationship started.

Considering that *I* was once involved with Nik.

I still can't grasp how blind I was to what remained directly in front of me. How strikingly similar the brothers are, if not in their personalities, then definitely their appearances.

My thumb hits Nik's contact. The phone rings, and rings, and rings.

My hands continue to tremble with each passing second. There's no answer, only the deep, professional tone of Nik's voice as the call swerves to voicemail.

My entire body shakes as I succumb to a panic attack. I squat outside the airport, burying my head in my quivering hands. People hurry past me, dragging their suitcases behind them. All of them stare. But no one stops, no one asks if I'm okay, no one offers any help. The insidious bystander effect. Everyone assumes that someone else will step up and offer assistance. No one wants to risk getting into trouble, so they do nothing at all.

An airplane passes over me, and its deafening rumble blocks everything else out.

Breathe in.

Breathe out.

The stupid breathing exercises my therapist suggested I do are hopeless when everything hits rock bottom all over again. They don't work.

How can everything go from such a high to such an inescapable low?

"Calla." My dad approaches me with apprehension written all over him. His entire body is stiff, like he was struck by lightning. Like he knows and has already accepted that he's losing me, and he doesn't care as long as there's balance in the world. In *his* world.

I look at him, at the void swimming in his eyes. I want to scream, *why, why, why*. After everything I told him, after I'd bared myself vulnerable, why now? Why has he waited this long? How did he continue to talk to me on the phone and over FaceTime, acting like everything was normal? Like he wasn't about to crush my world.

Although I'm angry, I don't blame him for what he did. How could I?

He's only doing what anyone else in his position would. My father has been a cop for more than twenty-five years. That's more than half of his life. He's always lived by the rules. By the law. His religion is the law. And when someone is *that* dedicated to something, there's very little you can do to change it, to alter the way they think about the decisions they make.

His mouth opens like he wants to say something but doesn't know what. Or he has nothing to say to me, which is understandable. I decide to relieve both of us of the awkwardness, at least for the time being. "I need some time."

I can't face him now. I'm not sure to what extent our relationship will change because of this. Does he understand the depth of my feelings for Ace?

How, without Ace, I feel like I'm merely on the edge of survival, simply existing in a world that seems like it's not meant for me, instead of *living, thriving*. It's like trying to navigate a pitch-black night without any stars to guide me.

Despite everything we've been through, or maybe *because* of everything we've been through, Ace makes me want to be a better person, and I believe I do the same for him. They say to find someone who brings out the best in you, but I didn't know what that meant until him.

Right now, I need to get a hold of Nik. I don't know where they took Ace or what's going to happen.

My dad nods and trudges for his car with his head down, leaving me alone. Even though it's what I asked for, somehow it makes me feel a hundred times worse. I didn't expect him to apologize for what he's done, but him being unable to say anything at all somehow hurts me even more.

Everything that I've been afraid of is happening.

I just got Ace back in my life, and we were doing better

than ever before. I'm unable to wrap my head around how the world can take that away from me—from us. Haven't we suffered enough?

What do I do now?

A blatant choice stares me right in the face. My dad or Ace. It shouldn't be difficult. I should pick family, my blood.

Shouldn't I?

But I can't. Especially not after how much pain, forgiveness and growth Ace and I have endured to get where we are today. We sacrificed so much. Overcame the most difficult times to find our way back to each other.

So where do I go from here? I can't stay in a house with my dad, knowing that he's rooting for the man I love to go to jail, and I can't possibly leave and go back to Switzerland, although there's only a couple of months left of my contract. What will this mean for my career? I've only just begun to feel like I'm heading in the right direction.

And now...now I'm lurching down a hill at full speed with nothing to slow my fall.

2

Revisiting the Past

Calla

The taxi drops me off in front of a garage. It's large and spacious with the metal door halfway open. I wipe at my face, hiding the remnants of the tears and then run my fingers through my hair. I'm sure I still look like a total mess.

I duck to avoid hitting my head as I slip under the door and step inside the shop. Four cars, ranging from vintage Mustangs to the everyday Honda sit in each corner of the shop with their hoods up.

The smell of grease and steel hits me hard.

From the lack of people and noise, I assume it's empty, but then metal clanks onto the ground, echoing through the shop, and a grunt follows. I twist my head in the direction of the sound.

A pair of black work boots catch my eye as they appear from under a red Jeep, followed by a body sliding out beneath the vehicle.

Nate.

He's changed so much since the last time I saw him, back when I visited my dad last year. Gained some size. With his square shoulders and the biceps slightly swelling underneath his navy-colored button-up shirt, Nate looks more of a man now and less like the boy I knew through my adolescence.

A sheen of sweat covers his forehead, and he wipes it with the back of his hand, smudging some grease above his eyebrow.

When he realizes it's me, his eyes widen. "Hey, Cals!" He stumbles toward me. "I'd give you a hug, but..." He motions to his work shirt smeared with black grease.

"That's okay." I force a small smile.

"What are you doing here?" His forehead crinkles in confusion, the sun lines more prominent now.

I doubt my dad would have told Nate I was coming to Idaho, considering he planned this turmoil. I still don't understand how he knew Ace would be with me. Or how he even knew that Ace and I were together again. I specifically didn't tell him that detail via our calls, accepting that it would be a recipe for disaster.

And a *disaster* it is.

Scenarios race in my mind like a movie on fast-forward, constantly changing and shifting, but nothing makes sense. I'm not surprised. My dad has always been the one for grand plans, and he's committed to his job. I guess this was his grandest plan yet.

Has he been keeping tabs on me while I was away in Switzerland? He's never been one to do that. He's usually accepted my want for privacy and solitude, but a lot has changed since I told him what I knew about *that* night. Since I told him the man I'm in love with took away the person that meant the absolute world to the both of us.

"I need someone to talk to."

Nate scrutinizes me from head to toe, like he's trying to piece a puzzle together, but he would never figure this one out on his own. I doubt anyone would.

"Of course. Let me finish up here, and then we can go back to my place. It's only around the corner."

I nod in agreement. Nate studies me for a few beats longer before packing his tools away and locking up the garage.

He fishes in his pockets for his keys and then motions for me to get into his pick-up truck. When I climb inside, the scent of aged leather and motor oil greets me, hauling me back to my childhood memories of riding in my father's Jeep.

"New stereo?" I point to the dashboard where a sleek, modern stereo system catches my eye. The vibrant display lights up with various colors, delivering the truck's classic interior with a modern touch.

Nate chuckles, his eyes glinting with amusement. "Yeah, had to upgrade the old one. Gotta have some tunes for the road, right?"

The drive fills with mellow country music, and I gather

my thoughts. I don't even have time to think about Nate listening to country music, I simply accept the fact that he's changed.

How am I going to reveal this secret to Nate? And is that even the right thing to do? I mean, look what happened after I told my dad.

Will Nate's reaction be similar to my dad's?

Will he hate me for choosing Ace? Look at me differently? Especially considering he's never been a fan of Ace in the first place. Nate's always thought something is off about him, and I guess, in a way, he was right.

Only a few minutes have passed when we arrive at a corner house.

Rich-turquoise paint clings to the exterior, a white wooden door stands tall, accompanied by the square windows that punctuate the façade. Wooden stairs matching the front door lead up to the cozy porch, and a round table only big enough to seat two nestles to the side with matching chairs.

Nate unlocks the door and motions for me to go in first. I wring my hands as I follow him and step through onto a beige rug. The inside of the house is almost identical to my dad's—the same color pattern and layout. Perhaps that's what happens when someone spends so much time with another person, they become a clone of them.

Nate motions for me to take a seat at a round table. I take the chair out and sink into it.

"Drink?" Nate asks.

"Just water, please."

He nods. Once he places the glass of water on the table, his gaze lands on me. "What the hell happened, Cals? Is it your dad? Did something happen? I saw him this morning, and he seemed fine. A little on edge, but otherwise fine…" Nate rambles off, clearly reading my gloom expression.

I shake my head. "No, nothing like that. It's about my mom's accident."

Nate creases his brows. "Did your dad find out who did it? Who the other driver was? Is that why your dad was on edge? Was there a breakthrough in the case?" He fires question after question, not leaving me with enough time to provide any answers.

Inhaling a breath, I allow the words to surface. "Ace is the one who caused the crash," I tell him. "He was driving with someone else in the car that night."

Confusion surfaces on Nate's expression, followed by what I can only imagine is shock. He stiffens suddenly, his shoulders becoming rigid.

"Ace caused the accident," he repeats, but I assume he meant to phrase it as more of a question.

I relay the events of that night yet again, and it seems easier this time around. I'm not sure if it's because I'm telling Nate and not my dad, or because I'm working on auto-pilot now. Words flow out of my mouth like a river, tumbling in a steady stream without me having to think of them. I don't bother to sugarcoat the events. I tell the story exactly how it happened, or at least how I *think* it happened, mingling my own memories with what Ace told me.

When I'm done, Nate seems to be shade paler. He begins shaking his head as if he doesn't know how to process what I've just told him. In truth, it does sound crazy. It sounds like a made-up story, but it's my life.

I give him a moment and allow the silence to ripple through the small space between us. I'm not sure how much time passes. It could be a minute, or it could be ten. I'm lost in my mind, wondering what they're doing with Ace, how he's reacting to all of this.

Finally, Nate shifts in the seat, bumping both of his elbows on the wooden table and staring at me like he's been possessed. "Well, fuck me," he finally says. "I don't even know what to say."

I swallow hard, waiting for what's about to come.

"How did you expect your dad not to do everything in his power to get justice? Ace committed a crime. He took an innocent life, your *mother's* life." He emphasizes that word like I haven't been thinking about it every day since I found out. He shakes his head again.

"My dad said it was too late to do anything...but I guess he found a way."

"You should've known he wouldn't stop trying. You know what he's like. Goddamn it, Calla..." He digs his palms into his forehead. "No matter what he says, he'll always seek justice for those who've been wronged. He'll always want to put the bad guys behind bars. There's no gray area for him. Your dad only operates in black and white."

It doesn't surprise me that Nate holds clear perceptions

of my dad's views on matters. It shows how much I've drifted from my dad since I left for college. Or perhaps the distance began forming upon my mother's death.

"Seems like you know him more than I do these days," I admit.

My attention is drawn to the sound of the wooden door creaking open. A woman with a mane of burnt-orange hair gracefully steps onto the rug near the entrance, her hands burdened with grocery bags. Struggling to close the door behind her, she remains oblivious to our presence.

Nate shoves his chair back, causing an unpleasant screech against the wooden floors that sends a shiver down my spine. He rushes to her side and gallantly retrieves the bags. "Hey, you're back," he exclaims, planting a swift kiss on her mouth.

My eyes widen. Nate has a…girlfriend? Despite our occasional phone conversations, he's never mentioned being in a relationship, leaving me to wonder why he has kept it a secret. A wave of joy floods over me as I realize he's finally found someone special.

Her vibrant yellow dress dances around her as she turns and notices me. A brief moment of confusion flits across her face, quickly replaced by a warm smile that lights up her plump mouth and creases her dark-brown eyes at the corners.

Uncertain of what to do, I stand and wait for Nate to introduce us. "Nina, this is Calla. Calla, this is Nina, my girlfriend," Nate confirms, positioning himself awkwardly between us before retreating to the counter to unload the shopping bags.

Nina approaches me and envelopes me in a surprising hug.

So she's a hugger.

The gesture doesn't feel as awkward as I'd anticipated. The scent of cotton candy and oranges surrounds her, an unusual combination that somehow works perfectly for her. "Nate told me so much about you. I was wondering when I'd meet you."

Returning the smile, I shoot Nate a silent look that says *how dare you put me in this situation*, and then I proceed to lie through my teeth. "He told me so much about you too, it's lovely to finally meet you."

Just as I utter those words, my tightly gripped phone rings in my hand. Nik's name illuminates the screen.

"I have to take this," I announce and rush outside onto the front porch, stumbling over my own feet in my haste.

"Sweetheart. Long time no talk," Nik greets me. Although we ceased any romantic connection, he still uses the endearment, and strangely, I don't mind it.

Cutting straight through the bullshit, I waste no time. "Nik, Ace is in trouble. I didn't know who else to call."

"What do you mean?" His tone fluctuates immediately, the calm replaced by an indestructible brotherly bond.

"We arrived in Idaho, and my dad was there. They took Ace."

"Who's they? The cops?" Nik questions.

"Yes, they were waiting for him. My dad made it clear I'm not going to be able to see him until the trial. I'm not sure what's going to happen or what proof he's dug up on Ace.

Would my confession to my dad be enough to convict him?"

It can't be. Can it?

And what if it is? How will I live with the knowledge that Ace is in prison because of me? I had years to come forward and didn't. Some would think I chose to turn a blind eye to the crimes he committed. I chose to allow him to continue with his life without bringing the authorities into it because a big part of me believes that he's already suffered enough for his mistakes.

"Fuck…" He pauses, and then his voice muffles like he's covering the microphone and talking to someone else. A thick fog of guilt forms around me for reaching out to him. "I'm about to go into court with a client, but it shouldn't take long. I'll get the first flight out. Where are you now?" Nik asks.

"I'm with a family friend. But I'm going to get a hotel room for the night." I can't go to see my father. At least not yet. I have nothing to say to him, and I doubt he wants me there either.

How can we move forward from this?

Deep down inside, I already know the answer.

There isn't a way to move forward. Our relationship will forever be tainted. That's something I came to terms with when I chose Ace. Because that's exactly what I did, isn't it?

"I'll call you when I land. Don't do anything stupid. Stay put. We'll sort this out," Nik assures me.

"Thank you." I breathe into the phone, unsure if he hears me before the line goes silent.

3

Temporary Distraction

Calla

Following the phone call, I remain on the porch enveloped in a profound silence while the turmoil raging within me echoes. The chaos is so overwhelming that I struggle to find a single word to describe what I'm feeling. A part of me ponders whether Ace and I will ever get out of this seemingly endless cycle where we are good for a while, maybe a week or a month or sometimes longer, but eventually something happens that sets off one firecracker and then another.

It takes me a while to gather the courage to return inside. When I finally open the front door, I manage to utter, "I should get going."

Nate's curious gaze lingers on me, silently asking if everything is alright.

I shrug, uncertain of the answer. I consider going to the station alone to find out what's going on with Ace, but I'm not sure if they'll let me see him considering I'm not his legal representative or family. I also haven't figured out what to say to him yet.

All I can say is that I'm here for him no matter what, but will that be enough?

"You should stay for lunch," Nina says from the kitchen where she's unpacking the groceries. "I was just about to make fajitas, and Nate says that I always cook enough to feed an army."

"She does," Nate chimes in to persuade me to stay.

The last thing I want right now is to stay and have lunch with Nate and his girlfriend and act like everything is okay, playing house, when it's far from that. But Nik instructed me to stay put, and there's a part of me that trusts him—trusts that he can fix this. So I plant a smile on my face. "Sure," I say, hoping that this meal will serve as a temporary distraction, even though deep down I know it won't.

Over the next few hours, I try to play the role of a respectable guest. I join in a conversation about mundane topics like them getting a dog. I can't wait for the moment when Ace and I can discuss getting a dog over a meal rather than being consumed by uncertainty.

"Nate wants to get a poodle, but I've always wanted a border collie," Nina shares.

I cough, a bit of pepper stuck in my throat. I reach for the glass of water to my right and gulp it down. My cheeks burn at the mention of a poodle, recalling how Nate's family poodle tried to hump his leg while Nate and I did the deed for the first time. I avoid looking directly at Nate as I shake my head and say, "Don't get a poodle."

Nina laughs, turning to Nate. "See, babe. Calla agrees with me."

Throughout the meal, Nate's eyes remain fixed on me. I'm not sure whether it's because of what I told him earlier about Ace, or because he didn't tell me about Nina. Regardless, it's not something I'm willing to get into in front of her—someone I just met.

My life is too screwed up for strangers to even begin to understand it.

Otherwise, Nina seems nice and a perfect match for Nate.

Nina and Nate. Their names even have this weird, cute flow.

She's a part-time kindergarten teacher, and in her spare time, she enjoys gardening. Nate built her a garden out the back, complete with a greenhouse. It took him a month from start to finish, and she's more than eager to drag me out after I help her clean up lunch and show me.

Youthful fruit trees bearing apples, oranges and peaches adorn the outskirts of their spacious backyard. A picturesque greenhouse stands proudly in the center, its frame painted pristine white. We stroll along the garden path, basking in the sunlight that seeps through the cracks in the clouds.

Nina opens the door, inviting me to step inside. "It's not much yet. I'm still in the process of planting and organizing," she confesses with a nervous laugh.

"It's beautiful," I say.

The floor boasts a stunning sunset hue, accentuated by a captivating terrazzo pattern. The overcast day fails to do it justice. Wooden shelving lines the interior, displaying a mix of empty pots and some already bursting with greenery.

"I've always loved plants," she shares. "But I never had the space to nurture them until now."

As we continue to walk around the greenhouse, Nina points out different plants and dives into their care and maintenance. I listen, trying to take my mind off everything else.

"It's amazing. I'll definitely have to come back to visit and check on the plants," I remark when we step out of the greenhouse.

Nina smiles. "I would love that, and I'm sure Nate will too."

I bid my farewell around four in the afternoon, declining multiple offers to stay the night. I assure Nate that I have someone waiting for me. "I'll call you later," I promise, although deep down, I'm uncertain if I'll actually make that call.

He appears happy and content with the life he's built. He doesn't need the weight of my burdens. I wish he'd told me about Nina, but I guess we aren't close enough for him to feel comfortable sharing this part of his life with me. I get it. We've been family friends our entire life, but as soon as those boundaries were crossed, we were done. I resented him for breaking up with me before college, but I soon learned that it was a blessing in disguise.

Nate regretted his decision wholeheartedly, but it was too late.

Truth be told, the only reason why Nate and I continued to talk is because of my dad and convenience. Like now, I only went to see Nate because I needed someone to talk to. How selfish is that?

Maybe if I'd picked up the phone more than once in a while and called him to ask about his life, I wouldn't have been caught off guard by Nina's presence. But I shouldn't solely blame myself for that. Communication goes both ways.

I hail a taxi and hand the driver a twenty-dollar bill when we arrive at a nearby hotel.

Stepping inside, a dimly lit lobby with an empty front desk welcomes me. A bell chimes above as I stand there, suitcase in hand. An orange-hued light flickers above my head at the same time a teenage girl ambles from the back, her head buried in her phone.

I pay for a room with two beds, keeping in mind that Nik will be here soon. Will he want to stay here? It's the least I can offer, especially since I've dragged him into a mess again. How will Ace react when he finds out I've called Nik for help?

Will it cause tension? I don't want him to dwell on it more than necessary or make a big deal out of it when it isn't.

Turning the shower handle, I adjust the water temperature. I let the water warm up and quickly shed my clothes, discarding them on the bathroom floor. I step beneath the cascading water, and the intense heat stings my skin, but I resist the urge to lower the temperature.

I revel in it.

It fails to fully distract my mind from the mayhem. That won't happen until I find out what comes next. I feel powerless, and the inside of my cheek is raw from the nonstop chewing. On top of all that, my head throbs as if it collided with a concrete wall multiple times.

I lose track of time as I stand under the water, my thoughts consumed by the chaos swirling inside my head. My phone rings abruptly and shatters the stillness. I turn off the tap, grab a towel from the rack, and step out of the shower. My hands tremble as I dry them. I attribute the shakes to the immense stress that has plagued today.

Glancing at the caller ID, Nik's name flashes on the screen. With a sense of urgency, I swipe to answer the call.

"Calla, I just landed. Text me the address of where you're staying, and I'll meet you there. I might be a while, I'm going to stop at the station first and find out what's happening," Nik informs me in a rapid succession of words.

"Okay," I respond, overwhelmed. I begin to pace around the room, unable to keep still. "Should I come with you?"

"I don't think that's a good idea. At least, not until I know the details of the situation. You probably won't be allowed to see him today."

Nik's words hang in the air, heavy with uncertainty. Should I brace myself for the worst? It certainly seems that way. The urge to insist on accompanying him to the station tugs at me, but I know my presence may not be much help.

"Calla?" Nik's voice veers me back to the conversation.

"Hmm?" I respond, my mind still clouded with worry and fear.

"I wish I could tell you everything is going to be okay, but I can't. What I'll say is that I'm going to do everything in my power to fix this."

As his words sink in, I release a long, shuddering breath. "Thank you," I manage to rasp before he hangs up.

I have no room left for tears, and there's no point for them. They can't do anything for me. For Ace. For us. I need to get my shit together and find out what I *can* do to help.

I swing the hotel door open. Nik holds his briefcase in one hand and a black duffel bag in the other.

I meet his eyes. "How can this happen? My dad said it was too late to bring any action against him," I say before he even manages to get a word out.

"Hello, sweetheart," Nik greets me.

"Seriously," I continue, frustration evident in my tone. "How is this happening?"

He sighs, and I stand to the side to let him pass. "He's using the excuse that Ace wasn't in the state for the last two years," Nik states. He sets his briefcase onto the square coffee table and the duffel bag on the floor before turning to face me again.

"Can he do that?"

"No, but..."

His pause provides the answer I'm searching for. The gravity of the situation shines in his eyes.

"What's the worst-case scenario?" Desperation fills my steady voice.

"Calla—"

"Worst-case scenario, Nik," I insist, my heart pounding. I need to be prepared, to brace myself for the worst possible outcome. I can't afford to cling to false hope and be crushed by disappointment later.

"If they find him guilty of driving under the influence, or even driving recklessly when he caused the accident... fifteen years. But he was underage when the crime occurred, and they don't have proof unless he incriminates himself..." Nik explains, his words heavy with the weight of the truth.

I already know that Ace will want to confess, to take responsibility for everything.

"We have a good case. On top of that, almost seven years have passed since the accident. The statute of limitations is five, and Ace has been out of state for the last two. The judge will take that into consideration. There's no way this should escalate to a trial," he adds, his voice trying to offer some reassurance.

But I can barely comprehend his words.

Fifteen years. The enormity of it slaps me in the face with full force.

I try to imagine my life fifteen years from now. I would be nearing forty. The thought of that brings a shudder up my spine, but I push through it.

Fifteen years from now, I hope to have some stability in all aspects of my life—my job, my relationships. Perhaps even have my own publishing company that contributes to society like no other, but for that to happen, I have to put some hard yards in now.

I want to have a family, children—even though the word terrifies me now. But is it because my life has been nothing but chaos?

"I'm going to file to get the case moved to New York, since that's where Ace resides on paper. It'll be easier for him, and if he gets bail—which I'm certain that he will—he can continue with his life while we sort this out," Nik explains, bringing me back to the room.

Moved to New York.

But my home isn't in New York anymore. It's in Switzerland. And so is my career at least for the foreseeable future.

What am I supposed to do?

Give it all up?

Or should I return to Switzerland and act like the man I love isn't about to face his biggest obstacle yet?

There is no easy answer, no clear path forward. I'm torn between my love for Ace and the life I've built for myself. The word "consequences" lingers in my mind, reminding me that no matter what choice I make, there will be sacrifices.

4

Inevitable Consequences

Ace

This moment is inevitable, an unavoidable result of my actions. Throughout my life, I've been ingrained with the belief that every choice carries consequences, and there exists a higher power that seeks to restore balance to the wrongs committed.

Some may call it karma, others, God. The name itself holds little significance, it's a different expression of the same underlying principle.

Now, the day has arrived for to me atone for my crimes, to set things right. I'm prepared to face whatever comes my way. I deserve it all, and I'm done hiding behind a shield I show the whole world. I'm not the man everyone thinks I am, but that carefully crafted image earned me my reputation.

If only they knew the depth of my cowardice. Weakness

isn't encouraged, it's something I've learned to hide because nothing good can materialize from flaunting it.

The officers throw me into a chilling holding cell, and yet, paradoxically, my body feels aflame. The metal bars resemble icy blocks, but I grasp them, pressing my forehead against their cold surface, hoping to suppress the raging fire.

Two others occupy the cramped space with me. A disheveled man with his reddish hair matted and unkempt, who looks higher than the Empire State and keeps muttering to himself. The other guy is on the brink of collapse, a walking embodiment of imminent alcohol poisoning, his form trembling with each labored breath.

There's no denying that I deserve to be here, but the look on Calla's face when she realized the officers were taking me away still lingers in the back of my mind. It was as though she thought I had something to do with it. As though she thought I'd set this up.

Don't get me wrong, I've considered it on numerous occasions, especially after college. The notion of approaching her father, confessing my guilt as the drunken driver responsible for his wife's tragic accident and asking him—no, *begging* him—to put me behind bars. Although I'm sure begging wouldn't be needed in that situation.

There were times—a shit ton of times—after I left Bridgevale, that I was sure Calla would change her mind and tell her father.

Every day for more than four years, I waited...but it never happened.

The burden of guilt coils tightly, a relentless spiral that will haunt me for the remainder of my days. Yet, I'm too self-ish, especially in the last couple of months when everything has been going so well, to even consider turning myself in.

"Why is he in here?" I hear one of the officers ask Calla's father, who looks worse than most people in here, even the ones behind bars.

His dark hair, with some gray peppered throughout, remains unruly, and his bloodshot eyes droop, like he hasn't got any sleep for at least a few nights or even weeks. Or perhaps it's the eyes of the man who hasn't slept properly for the last seven years since his wife died.

My gut twists. There's an invisible rope around it, tightening each time I think about how many lives I've ruined. There's nothing I could possibly do to get rid of that feeling. No amount of punishment will eliminate the guilt in my mind. I have to live with it.

Some days are easier than others. *Easier*. That word comes with a grain of salt, maybe a fucking mountain of salt. The truth is, it's far from easy. It's just certain days, when I'm with my family or Calla, I hate myself a little less.

How long has Calla's dad been plotting this? How long has he been waiting patiently for the perfect opportunity to arrest me in the state of Idaho—the exact place where all of our lives changed.

I shift my body as close to the metallic bars as possible, trying to eavesdrop on their conversation without drawing direct attention to myself. But honestly, who the fuck cares at this point? It's not like things can get any worse than they already are.

"He's a murderer. He took away my wife," Calla's father's voice rings with a gravelly tone, mingling anger with an underlying trace of everlasting sadness. No matter how many times those words are spoken, the pain will never truly dissipate.

Silence follows. I turn my head, slowly observing their expressions. The officer looks at me, but not with disgust, more with a look of apology. I can't comprehend why. I'm guilty as charged, yet his expression implies he might believe differently.

Determined to catch the next exchange, I strain my ears, but the words drown by the sudden, raucous snoring coming from one of my cellmates.

Fuck me.

With two swift strides, I close the distance and deliver a shove to the snorer's ribs with my foot. He grumbles and shifts to the side but remains undisturbed in his slumber.

"What proof do you have?" I barely hear the officer ask.

"My daughter's confession," Calla's father responds.

And soon mine too—if given the chance.

The dim lighting within the cell grants me a glimpse of the subtle exchanges between Calla's dad and the other officer. Her father holds the title of sheriff—or at least used to, judging by the waning authority he commands over certain officers. The other man doesn't treat him with the respect one would expect. Instead, I sense a tinge of pity in his gaze.

What am I missing? Why is this officer acting as if he's superior to the sheriff? Could it be that Calla's father resigned...or worse, has he been forcibly relieved of his duties?

"I need to speak with my client."

I shoot up from my seat at the sound of the familiar voice. Just as I thought, my brother stands confidently against the front desk, exuding an air of superiority. Clad in one of his impeccably tailored suits, he's as polished as ever, despite the seven-hour flight he must have endured. Not a single wrinkle stains the fabric.

What the fuck is he doing here, anyway?

And then it dawns on me. Calla must've called him. If he managed to arrive so promptly, it means she must have dialed his number the moment they took me away in the patrol car.

Though it shouldn't, it rubs me the wrong way that she called him. Nik and I set our differences aside, or rather, our striking similarities when it comes to our taste in women. I know Nik and Calla still communicate on occasion, and I can't expect them not to, since they are both a big part of my life now. Yet, the engulfing jealousy, stemming from the fact that she instinctively turned to him, constricts me like a vise.

I clench my fists, attempting to rid myself of the feeling. When it comes to Calla, my feelings intensify, and I act on impulse. It's something that I'm learning to control, though it's not something that comes easy.

"I'm sorry, but I've been advised that he's not to talk to anyone today. If you want to return in the morning…"

With those words, I realize the officer is new here and they are about to get an earful of lawyer jargon on how it's his client's right to have a lawyer present, and if they want to keep their job, they will immediately allow him to converse with me.

I don't even bother to listen to the remainder of the conversation. I sit back and wait for an officer to come and get me and lead me to a room where Nik will be waiting for me.

Barely two minutes pass before I'm guided through a dimly lit hallway and into a tight, windowless room. A table and two chairs occupy the space—one of which my brother sits in, a composed expression adorning his face.

He lifts his head from the indigo folder spread across the desk, meeting my gaze. He nods, a greeting and acknowledgement in one. It's a look that lets me know he's here to once again get me out of the mess I'm in.

It's not vicious or even a look that says I'll owe him. That's not his style. I know he means well, and yet an urge to lash out at him surges within me, to demand that I don't want him here.

But I resist.

Instead, I swallow my pride and the jealousy that has risen from my gut into my throat and take a step forward.

Observing the scene, the officer pulls out a chair for me. Without stating a word, Nik gestures toward the restraints on my hands. The officer sighs in response, seeming resigned to the situation, and proceeds to uncuff me without engaging in any argument. One more look from Nik, and he leaves, closing the door behind him.

"We have to stop meeting like this. If you wanted to catch up, you could have just called me instead of getting yourself arrested."

Hah.

"I didn't ask you to come," I remark wryly.

"Ah, yes. Calla called me," he states, confirming what I already knew. Is he trying to rub it in my face? "So tomorrow will be simple. During the hearing you'll let me do the talking. I'll do my best to get this case thrown out. If and when the judge decides to move forward, I'll make a motion to move the case to New York, where there'll be an arraignment. At the arraignment, you'll plead not guilty and then—"

"No," I cut him off.

"What do you mean 'no'?" Nik asks.

"I'll be pleading guilty."

At first, there's no reaction from him. He stares at me, his expression devoid of emotion. Then he sighs, like he knew this was coming all along but had hoped he was wrong.

He glances down at the paperwork in front of him and drags his hand over his face. Dark craters dwell under his eyes. It's no news that he's married to his job, even more so in the last year.

I wonder if it has anything to do with Calla. We haven't talked about his relationship with her, but I know he was in love with her. Or he thought he was.

Is he still in love with her?

Over the short time of knowing Nik, I've realized that we have a lot more in common than just our shitty sperm donor. One of them being we both keep our cards close to our chest.

"As your lawyer, I wouldn't recommend that. And as your brother, I think you're a fucking idiot," he finally says without holding back.

I've had time to think about my decision. A whole lot of it, and I'm not shifting on it.

"How about this…" Nik begins. "You plead not guilty if and when it gets to your arraignment, and I'll let you take the stand at the trial. The jury can decide whether you're guilty or not."

I know he's only saying this to prolong the situation. For me to change my mind before the trial commences. There's no way any sane lawyer would let his client take the stand knowing the client is guilty.

Nik isn't planning to allow me to do it either. But I let him think he's won for now.

"I'll think about it," I reply, allowing him to believe there's a chance I might change my mind.

5

Blood & Ethics

Calla

The night brings little rest, failing to give me the break I desperately need. Nik assured me earlier this morning that the outcome of the preliminary trial will be favorable, that there's even a glimmer of hope the judge might dismiss the entire case due to the lack of evidence or the muddy issue of the statute of limitations.

This best-case scenario seems highly improbable and is a mere flicker of possibility.

If the case isn't thrown out, Nik will file a motion to relocate the case to New York, where Ace's work is based. He assured me there's no reason for Ace not to be granted bail, but Ace would have to remain in New York for the duration of the trial, which could stretch on for weeks or even months, depending when it begins.

How will this situation impact our relationship? What consequences will it have on my work? And what awaits us at the trial? These questions spin relentlessly in my mind, like industrious spiders tirelessly weaving their intricate webs. But those aren't the issues I should be focusing on just yet. We just need to get through today first.

"Coffee?" Nik offers, nudging a mug toward me as I shuffle into the modest kitchenette still in my sleep tank top and shorts. My hair must be a mess from all the turning and tossing I did last night chasing sleep that never came.

I nod, accepting the striped mug from the counter. The heat pours through it and into my hands while the cream eddies inside.

"Thank you." These words hold a double meaning, conveying my gratitude not only for the coffee, but for everything else as well. For him showing up time and time again when I need his help. When his brother needs his help.

"Calla..." Nik begins.

"Really, Nik," I interrupt, wanting him to understand how appreciative I am that he's here. I doubt Ace would say any of this. He's still working on communicating his feelings. "Less than a year ago, you didn't even know you had a brother, and now you're doing everything you can to help him, even though I'm sure your morals are saying that you should be working on the other side of the law."

I often wonder about the internal battle Nik must be facing. From the moment I met Nik, he has always shown ethical behavior—a rare find in this world. But what constitutes ethical behavior in this situation? Is it right to help his brother, who has committed a terrible crime? Or would it be more ethical to withhold aid and let Ace suffer the consequences of his past actions as a teenager?

Nik's dark brows furrow, but he offers no denial. All he says is, "He's my brother. And even though blood isn't always everything, in this case, it is for me."

The rest of the morning blurs by in a haze. I feel as though I'm operating robotically, striving to gather my composure and endure this part of the day until I can see Ace.

Within a few hours, we find ourselves in a taxi, making our way to the small courthouse nestled in the heart of the town. Throughout the ride, I stare out of the window, fidgeting nervously. I toy with my fingers, pick at the lint on my sweater, anything to distract myself.

This place, my childhood home for eighteen years, now feels unfamiliar and estranged. I ache to escape from it and never look back.

We drive past a family—a mother pushing a stroller, with the father following closely behind on the footpath. Above me, envy circles like a vulture ready to swoop. Ace and I have casually discussed starting a family, but those conversations were lighthearted. We pondered and imagined what qualities our future child would get from both of us.

We sat at a small table in a cozy café with a fireplace crackling in the corner and soft music seeping from the speakers. Steam rose from our cups of hot chocolate. We were still settling in each other's company after the New Year, taking things at our own pace, even though some might've considered it going too fast. Glancing out the window, I admired the snow-capped mountains in the distance. They added to the serene atmosphere.

Two young girls burst into the café, their snow-covered boots leaving tiny footprints on the wooden floor. They wore matching outfits and held hands, giggling at some shared amusement. Their infectious laughter reached our ears, and their parents followed closely behind. It was in that moment Ace turned to me and said, "I can't wait to have kids with you."

His words stirred deep emotions. Warmth enveloped me like a feathery cloud, but at the same time, an overwhelming feeling of guilt surfaced. My mind raced back to a few months ago when I believed I might have been pregnant instead of Mia. I hadn't shared that thought with Ace, but I shouldn't feel guilty about it either.

Smiling, I responded, "I can see you being a girl dad."

"Oh really?"

"Totally. You'd suit purple nails and a face full of makeup."

He laughed. "I know. Ellie has already attacked me with the nail polish. Seriously Calla, I can't wait to start a family with you," he said. "But for now, let's just enjoy this time together and take things one step at a time."

The courthouse is a brick building identical to others in the area. Vines gracefully climb up its sides and around the windows. I used to walk or drive past it, believing it to be the place where justice prevailed. I even entered its double wooden doors a few times with my dad, his authoritative uniform provided me with a sense of importance.

Now, my perspective has shifted. I see it as a place that tears apart souls and changes lives, indifferent to the pain it inflicts. Nik leads me into the courtroom, and to my surprise, there are numerous people present. Unfamiliar, condemning faces glance up from the back seats—some belonging to the public, while others are hungry journalists ready to cover the story.

Of course, I should have known the media would some-how get a whiff of Ace's arrest. I hoped for a few more days of privacy. My dad is here too, seated near the front, but he isn't wearing his uniform.

I drop my gaze, afraid to look at him, afraid of what I'll find in his expression, but I imagine it would be disappoint-ment, resentment, and confusion. Confusion at how I can be here for *him*—for Ace.

Nik squeezes my shoulder. "Take a seat, sweetheart. Everything will be alright," he says before leaving to join Ace.

Everything will be alright. I hope that part ends up being true.

My gaze lands on Ace as I find a seat at the back, not wanting to draw any more attention to myself. He's watching me—watching the way Nik and I interacted.

Even from here, I notice the dark circles that have formed under his eyes and the disheveled hair. There's no doubt in me that he hasn't slept, and how could he at a time like this?

The prosecutor begins by outlining the case against Ace, meticulously detailing the events of the night I wish had never happened. As the prosecutor speaks, I watch as Nik listens intently, takes notes, and occasionally confers with Ace.

When it's Nik's turn to speak, he rises, fixes his tie, and addresses the courtroom.

My ears ring loudly, drowning out the words, and I struggle to comprehend the magnitude of the situation. Anxiety grips me, and I hold my breath, awaiting the judge's response.

"After thorough consideration of both arguments and acknowledging that the motion was filed within the statute of limitations, I conclude there's enough evidence to move forward. Let's arrange a date for the upcoming hearing."

My heart sinks.

6

Nostalgic Reminders

Calla

It hits me hard. I'm not entirely sure why, since I've mentally prepared myself for this moment—for the worst-case scenario. I suppose a tiny flicker of hope was still buried deep within me. Maybe that flicker of hope hasn't completely faded away.

Silence submerges us until we step outside.

"Care for a day trip?" Ace asks.

My eyebrows crease. He doesn't seem overly concerned about what he's just gone through. Unless he's trying to put on a brave face for me. Or maybe he just wants to pretend that his life isn't falling apart once again.

But whatever the reason, that makes two of us. I would give anything to go back to our time in Switzerland, when it felt like everything was flowing smoothly for once.

"A day trip? To where?" I play along, meeting his gaze, perhaps both of us are aware of the unspoken intentions behind our words.

"I still have to see Dean, and I thought we could reminisce before I have to go to New York. I'm not sure if you've been back since college, but a lot has changed in town."

Reminisce.

I haven't set foot in Bridgevale since graduating. The thought of returning sends jolts of excitement through my veins. Intertwined with the thrill is also an unexpected swell of anxiety.

When I left, I vowed to never return to the place that shattered my heart in unimaginable ways. I lost nearly everyone I loved, and I was certain that town, or my presence in it, was cursed.

But my perceptions have changed. *I* have changed. And it might be intriguing to see how the town has transformed, to revisit the place where everything between Ace and I began. And maybe I can forget about the madness the last couple of days has brought us.

"Okay," I finally reply, embracing the idea.

We accompany Nik to the airport in a taxi since there's a car-rental place right across from the airport. Ace suggested we rent a car for the next few days to avoid relying on taxis throughout our stay.

Nik settles in the front seat, giving Ace and I privacy in the back. It might just be me, but there seems to be a slight awkwardness among the three of us. Like there's some kind of elephant in the room none of us are willing to address.

It's the first time the three of us have been in the same space since...I can't even recall when.

Nik's phone interrupts the silence, and without hesitation, he swiftly reaches for it and answers the call. So it's not just me who's feeling the tension.

While Nik engages in conversation with one of his clients, Ace leans closer to me. "Did you and Nik stay in the same place last night?"

I look at him, trying to gauge the situation. Is he mad?

I swallow. Take a breath. "Yes."

"In the same bed?"

I glare at him, incredulous. Is he serious? "No," I retort sharply.

He nods. Once. That's it.

Before the tension between us can escalate further, Nik's phone call comes to an end. He must sense the unease in the air, because as he turns toward us, a playful smirk tugs at the corner of his lips.

"Ah, Calla and I had a lovely sleepover," Nik says, his voice dripping with sarcasm. "We built a fort, had pillow fights, painted each other's nails."

I can't help but crack a smile at his witty remark, grateful for the lightheartedness he injects into the moment. It serves as a temporary relief from the tension.

"Well, I'm glad you two had a memorable night."

Nik raises an eyebrow, his smirk widening. "Oh, you have no idea. It was a *wild* time."

"Fuck off." Ace chuckles.

It's moments like these that remind me of the bond they share, despite the complicated circumstances.

When the taxi drops us off, we say our goodbyes to Nik. He mostly talks to Ace about the trial, but just as we're about to leave, Nik unexpectedly turns to me. It all kind of happens on instinct. He leans down like he's going to brush his lips against my cheek, like he's done a hundred times before. But this time, everything feels different. He shouldn't be doing this. Maybe it would be okay if we didn't share an intimate relationship previously, but we did, and that changes everything.

In that fleeting moment, realization dawns upon Nik's face. His expression tightens, his brows furrow, and he abruptly pulls back, clearing his throat.

"Old habit," he mutters under his breath. "See you later, Calla." He nods to me before retreating.

His behavior is a lot different to how he acted last night and this morning. Like our entire dynamic has shifted with Ace's presence. It almost makes me feel like we were doing something wrong when it was just us in the hotel room, though nothing happened.

Ace doesn't bring up the incident as we rent a car.

The entire drive to Dean's club is silent but not awkward. Not like it was in the taxi with Nik.

A single glance in Ace's direction reveals he's deep in thought. It could be the weight of the charges brought against him and the impending trial, the recent incident with Nik, or perhaps the flood of memories this familiar route awakens.

Maybe it's a combination of all three.

The road ahead is so familiar yet unsettling. It holds a significance I can't ignore. It was this very road that led me to Ace, the catalyst for both my happiness and turmoil. When I first drove along this path, full of anxiety, I wondered what my housemates would be like, what college would entail for me, and whether I'd be able to overcome all of my mental barriers.

"Are you still set on convincing Dean to get a license and set up a legal club?" I break the silence.

Dean was our college chancellor, but in his spare time he formed an underground fighting club.

Ace nods resolutely, his eyes reflecting determination and concern. "Of course. I know he makes a lot of money doing what he does and helps kids who need to take that anger out somewhere, but we both know the consequences that come with it. And I don't want him to get caught up on the wrong side of it like I have."

"He's been doing it for so long though. What makes you think that you can change his mind? You've already talked to him about it before, and he brushed you off," I express my doubts.

"To be honest, I have a feeling his mind won't be changed. But I have to try. That way, I can say that I've done everything I could."

"Do you feel responsible for him because he..." I'm not sure how to phrase what I want to say without overstepping boundaries or stirring up painful memories.

However, I need to stop beating around the bush with Ace. We're both adults, and we should be able to talk about sensitive topics without the other person shutting it down.

"Because?" Ace prompts, although he probably knows what I'm about to say.

"Because he acted as a father figure at times when you didn't have that?"

Ace releases a deep sigh, the weariness clear. His father is a delicate topic, and I'm never sure how he will react when I bring it up. That man caused Ace and his family so much mental and physical trauma. He's still a catalyst for Ace's actions, even if Ace denies it.

I wonder how he feels knowing that his father kept in touch with Nik and continued to be somewhat of a father figure to him while only coming to Ace when he needs money.

"Dean helped me a lot throughout college. Both academically and mentally. If I hadn't met him back then, I'm not sure where I would be now. I owe most of my success to him in a way."

I understand what he's trying to say. Dean recognized Ace's potential and was the one who encouraged Ace to pursue his fighting career. And maybe that's why Ace thinks he owes his success to Dean, but in my opinion, he's wrong.

Ace is the true architect of his success. From his fighting career to his business, he's the one who climbed to where he is today with perseverance and hard work.

I see his unwavering motivation when he's training, when he takes phone calls and meetings about his company, always striving to improve it. Yes, Dean might have nudged him in the right direction, but no one can make a person do something that requires that much time and incentive.

Ace parks the car in front of the familiar brick building, and my mind instantly veers to the first time I came here five years ago. It feels like forever ago. So much has changed since then, yet the surroundings seem frozen in time.

This is the same club I witnessed Ace fight in for the very first time. It's where we had our first argument but made up almost instantly.

Like you and me.

"Did you want to come with? I won't be long," Ace offers.

"I have some emails to catch up on," I reply, although I only have one or two that will take all of about five minutes. I don't want to intrude, so I'll read a book on my phone or something.

He nods, leans over, and touches his lips to mine, and then he's gone—disappearing into the building.

Thirty minutes later, Ace returns, slamming the car door harder than necessary. "Hungry?" he asks abruptly, starting the car and beginning to drive in the direction of the setting sun.

"How did it go with Dean?" I ask, though I think I already know what the answer will be.

Ace shrugs, disappointment and resignation evident on his face. "Like I thought it would."

"He isn't interested in pursuing a license and making the club legal? Is there a reason?"

"He says he doesn't have the funds, but I've offered him money, and he doesn't even want to consider it." Ace's frustration seeps into his words.

That seems...a lot more reasonable than I thought it would. Not everyone would readily accept financial help, especially if it comes with a sense of indebtedness. I know I wouldn't.

"It's not your job to make sure he does the right thing. You did everything you could, but in the end, it's his decision."

"I know." Ace exhales in frustration, tightening his grip around the steering wheel for a moment before he releases it. "I thought maybe hearing about what happened with me would make him think twice, but all he said was that he knows what he's doing and accepts the consequences."

I toy with my fingers in my lap. "Would you have listened to anyone if they came to you and tried to tell you to change your ways?"

Without hesitation, he responds with a firm, "No."

"Exactly. The only way some people learn is by going through the situation themselves and making mistakes."

Ace sighs. It's a sound that carries a sense of acceptance.

Moments later, Ace parks the car in front of Brody's cafe. Talk about a drive down memory lane. The café appears quite empty, as expected for a small town in the middle of the afternoon.

The entrance is still that pasty-blue that needs to be repainted since it's peeling in some spots. Ace holds the door open for me, and I enter, instantly getting a whiff of cinnamon and nutmeg. A young guy, likely a college student, with mousey hair and a tee that displays an alien with red eyes, works the front counter. By working, I mean standing by the register and swiping left and right on his phone.

I recall Brody being quite lax on how Mia and I spent our time during work hours as long as we served customers promptly and received no complaints.

Although I stayed with him and Mia for a while in college, I didn't see much of Brody. He was around physically, but his mind was always elsewhere.

"Order for me. I'm starving." Ace plants a kiss on my lips that lasts a second too long to be considered casual. There's a lingering need behind it, but it's hard for me to dissect it further.

"Are you okay?" I ask, realizing it's a futile question. I quickly rephrase, "Are *we* okay?"

His brows pinch together for a moment, and then he nods, forcing a crooked smile into his words. "We're okay," he reassures me.

I settle into the booth at the back.

Cracks spider across the aged leather seating. I glance at the limited menu but already know what I want, so when the guy from the counter comes to take my order, I fire away.

The food doesn't take long to arrive, maybe because we're the only ones here who've ordered something other than drinks. I ordered Ace the biggest meal, because the man can eat, and when my plate of pancakes land in front of me, with strawberries and whipped cream, Ace chuckles.

"What?" I ask.

He shakes his head, a teasing smile on his lips. "You can't tell me that you didn't order those because of the memories."

"What memories?" I stab my fork into a soft pancake.

He arches an eyebrow at me as if saying, "Come on, Calla." It's one of the most unforgettable moments of our time together in college. By *unforgettable*, I mean defining—perhaps even a turning point in our relationship. It was one of the very few times I've lost my temper, and Ace ended up wearing his breakfast pancakes instead of eating them.

After scoffing the better part of his food, he finally looks at me. "We'll leave tomorrow?" He phrases it as a question, looking for my confirmation.

"I want to visit my mom's grave before I go." I twirl my fork between my fingers. I'm not sure why it's something I feel like I need to do, but it's haunted my mind since I stepped foot off the plane in Idaho.

Home.

That word doesn't mean anything to me in the form of a physical place. Home for me is a person. And he's sitting right in front of me.

"Okay. I'll come with you." Ace wipes his face with a napkin.

I swallow. Should I tell him that this is something I was hoping to do alone?

I decide against it. I have no inclination to explain the reason why I don't want him to come with me, at least, not right now when we're doing such a good job of ignoring the issues once again.

Before we rise from the table, Ace hesitates. "There's somewhere else I want to take you." His voice holds a hint of anticipation. "Tonight."

7

Perfectly Imperfect

Calla

Nightfall descends by the time we leave the café, and the road is nearly empty. Our headlights deliver the sole source of illumination for the rough road ahead. We drive in silence, a shift that might have once unnerved me, but now it provides a sense of comfort. Perhaps it's a sign of our deepening connection that we can simply exist in each other's presence without needing to cram it with conversation.

The only sound is the music trickling from the speakers. It's so quiet that I barely hear it.

Only a couple of minutes pass when Ace parks by the curb, cuts the engine, and turns to look at me. He's waiting for me to realize where we are.

Peering through the window into the darkness, only the

tree shadows lurk on the edges of my vision. Despite this, there's a rush of familiarity, whether from Ace's gaze or another source, and I know I've been here before.

Opening the car door, a flash of memories invades all at once.

In an instant, I know where we are. The scent of pine trees, the crispness of the breeze on my skin, and the sound of branches crunching beneath my boots as I step out of the car trigger nostalgia to brush against me in every sense. I didn't realize how strong the feeling would be when visiting this place again.

I turn to Ace as he follows suit, gets out of the car, and shuts the door behind him. His expression holds emotions impossible to decipher.

"Tell me what you're thinking."

A contemplative pause follows. "I've been wanting to come back here for the last five years," he says as he looks at our surroundings, taking it all in.

"Why haven't you?"

"Life got in the way. Priorities shifted. And it wouldn't be the same without you." He offers me his hand, and I gladly take it.

We stroll through the opening amidst the towering trees, their branches reaching out like welcoming arms. My eyes drift to the lake, and I'm transported back to the time when I walked the same path back in college to meet Ace on the pier. Déjà vu hits me like a bolt from the blue.

Our first kiss.

Our first time.

It's as if time stood still in this town, preserving every detail exactly like I remember it.

What's it like to remain in a place that's so stagnant?

Do people who spend their entire life in one place wonder what it's like to live somewhere else? Or is that just a handful of people, including me?

I can't imagine remaining in one place for my entire life. Years go by so quickly, and people often find themselves in a monotonous routine. They forget to live, but there's a whole world out there waiting to be explored.

In the distance, the water lies peacefully, and if there were a full moon, the glow of it would spill on the glass-like liquid. But tonight, the darkness steals the night. The only radiance is from billions of stars above. I take one long glance into the sky, and a flicker of movement catches my eye.

A shooting star.

From every direction, the chorus of cicadas plugs the air, their relentless shrill echoes around us.

Goosebumps dance along my skin as the universe quite literally rewinds time for us to when everything was less complicated. When Ace and I were only kids.

When we were both trying to come to terms with what our past meant for us.

Hand in hand, we walk along the pier to the deck. The closer we advance, the more I notice Ace planned to bring me here and has strategically set the deck up.

Pillows and blankets scatter the weathered wooden surface, mirroring the night of our first time. As corny or cliché as it may sound, it was probably the most magical moment of my life. The night I lost myself to him beneath the shimmering stars.

But this time, there's more.

Lamps flank our pathway, shimmering a yellow ambiance. Strings of lights snake around the four pier poles, and it truly feels like a fairytale. He's gone all out, and I have no idea when he had the time to organize all this for us. Was it before my father put him in handcuffs? After?

I can't stop staring at everything. At the place where I used to seek solitude and would always run into Ace. I guess some people would call that fate.

And I can't stop staring at Ace himself. Despite our differences and the challenges we've faced, I'm still so in love with him, to the point where it hurts.

"God, Ace. Why does it feel like you're going to propose?" I joke, trying to mask my overwhelming emotions with humor. Tears crave to escape.

Ace has always been unpredictable. I never know what to expect, and it reminds me that behind everything—behind that hard exterior that he puts on for the world—is a soft heart. A glimmer of the person I fell for.

He doesn't laugh at the joke like I expect him to.

Turning to face him, the truth spirals in his face. It's overshadowed by something else. The way he looks at me with both regret and immeasurable tenderness... No one else could ever make me feel like this.

"Oh, you are?" I go on teasing him when he doesn't reply.

At times like these, I wish I could read his mind just to know what's going on in that twisted place.

He rakes a hand through his hair. "Fuck, I don't know. When we had this trip planned, I was going to, but it doesn't seem like the right moment now."

I'm beyond speechless. Perhaps I didn't understand...

Before I have the chance to pose a question, Ace continues. "I don't know when it became clear to me. It might have been after our first kiss, or after our first proper conversation when we were working on our assignment in my room, or maybe it was when I took you to my father's cabin, but I know sometime almost five years ago, I realized the only person I want to spend the rest of my life with is you. When we were in Switzerland, everything was finally falling into place, and I thought this trip would be the perfect time to have a full-circle moment. But now..."

I know what he's thinking but doesn't say. *Now it's more complicated than that.*

It's become a thing with us. When everything gets too good, too comfortable, it doesn't last long. After everything that's happened, I'm always expecting the worst, which isn't a healthy way to live.

"My feelings for you will never change. But I hoped to do this when we were in a good place. Although it seems like whenever that happens, it doesn't last long," Ace says like he's reading my mind.

Throughout the years of knowing Ace, I've become

accustomed to many of his moods and feelings, but never have I seen this side to him. If you didn't know him, it would be difficult to spot. He's skilled in concealing his emotions, but now he's bearing all his emotions as clear as day.

I can read him like an open book, and I take it all in before he slams it shut once again. The man standing before me is outstandingly apologetic and vigorously candid.

"I don't know how I can stand before you right now and ask that of you," he says.

"I don't care what's happened in the last couple of days. It still doesn't change my feelings about you. It doesn't change anything about *us*."

"It should. It doesn't make sense that you can just forgive the person who took away everything from you. It's fucked up."

So everyone keeps reminding me. But what if it's not that simple?

I fell for Ace before knowing the full extent of our past. And when you fall for someone, it becomes easier to forgive them for what happened before them. Even when it caused tremendous hurt to you and those you love.

There have been countless moments where I wished it wasn't the case. Where I wished I'd find a way to *unlove* or perhaps even *hate* him. But that day never came, even though Ace himself sometimes endeavored to push me to that point.

"Truth be told, I'm not sure if I forgive *that* person for that night. I don't know if I ever will. But that doesn't matter, because you're not *him* anymore. You've learned from your mistakes, and that's what matters to me now. And if that makes me fucked up, so be it."

He shakes his head, but his shoulders sag, indicating that my words brought him a sense of relief. It still astounds me that after all the obstacles we've overcome, and everything we've been through, he still thinks I can change my mind about him in the blink of an eye. It's like he doesn't understand that my feelings for him are as strong as his for me.

And even if I wanted to, I don't think I could change my mind about him. We're like two binary stars—bound to each other, appearing as a single point from a distance. But together?

Together we're a cosmic phenomenon. Destined in one another's existence.

Ace takes a step closer, and the heat of his breath hits my cheek. He leans his forehead against mine.

We stand like that for what seems like eternity, but no matter how much time passes, it never feels like enough. We're teetering on the edge of losing each other once again.

How far am I willing to go to prevent that from happening?

What sacrifices are we both prepared to make this time around?

"What did I ever do to deserve you?" he asks.

I lift my head and cup his cheeks, guiding his gaze to meet mine. "You're you. And even if you don't ask me today, I want you to know that my answer will always be yes. It's always you. It will always be you. No matter what happens, that will never change."

A smile edges the corners of his lips and elicits one of my own.

Without warning and without any hesitation, he drops down to one knee and takes my trembling hands in his. They're warm against my cold ones. My body slightly shakes more from the nerves than the temperature.

Ace looks up at me like no one else ever has. As if he's looking at his whole existence. Molten, charged eyes lock me in place, rendering me unable to move even if I wanted to. I'm utterly consumed. Hypnotized because I know what's coming next.

There's only been a handful of times when I've felt this way around a person before, and all of those times have been with Ace. It's like whenever I'm with him, there's always an increased amount of oxytocin coursing through my body.

In this moment, it's increased tenfold.

"I can't fucking imagine a life without you. As soon as we crossed paths, I knew I'd never be able to look at another person the way I look at you. No one could come close to making me feel even a fraction of what I feel for you."

His words impale the air, and my heart races.

"I fucking love you, Calla. So fucking much. Will you marry me?"

The words that I didn't expect to hear at this point in our relationship—or perhaps ever, seeing as our relationship will never be considered normal—leave me breathless.

"Yes," I respond without hesitation. Squatting down to

his level, I cup his cheeks in my hands. "Yes," I repeat. "A million times yes."

A grin spreads across his face. Leaning in, he closes the remaining distance between us, claiming my mouth with his. He dips his tongue in, and my own meets it.

"I can't wait to make you my wife," he murmurs against my lips.

I smile through the kiss, and it's the best feeling. Fire erupts in my bones, he grounds me and sets me alive all at once.

A cool droplet grazes my hand, followed by another. Ace and I both lift our eyes to the sky where a dark cloud looms directly above us. More drops land on my forehead and cheek, and Ace gently brushes them away with the pad of his thumb, but the rain intensifies.

Within seconds, it's pouring, a blanket of rain drenching the world around us.

"Fuck. Well, this isn't how I've planned this. The forecast said it would be clear skies today." Ace rises from his knees and tugs my hand urgently. "Come on."

I let him pull me up, but instead of making a beeline for the car, I tug on his hand. "Wait."

I'm already drenched from head to toe, my wet clothes stick to my skin like a second layer, and the rain keeps pouring. Coldness seeps into my bones, but I step forward into Ace's arms and meet his mouth with mine again. The kiss is wet and nothing like I imagined it would be, but the raw moment holds significance.

It's a moment we'll remember for the rest of our lives.

Ace pulls away first and brushes a strand of my soaked hair back. "I'm all for getting you wet, but we better go before it gets too dangerous to drive."

Laughter bubbles over, and I let him tug me with him. We start off in a fast-paced walk and then we're running through the forest, maneuvering around trees. Like nothing else matters.

This moment is so us. It's flawed, unpredictable, and probably not the way most people hope or even imagine their proposal to go. But nothing we've ever done has been right, so why start now?

It's perfectly imperfect.

8

Talk to Me

Calla

Thunder crackling jolts me awake the following morning. I didn't sleep well, constantly tossing and turning throughout the night, unable to find rest. Of course, that has been normal for me since I can remember.

Rain relentlessly pounds on the roof of our hotel room. I finally squint my eyes open. As they adjust to the morning light, I notice Ace is already awake. With nothing but sweatpants on, he stands by the four-panel window. His gaze fixed on the distant horizon where the eye of the storm rolls in.

He has a commanding presence, like a deity orchestrating the chaos. Shadows dance along his back with each lightning strike, forming stark patterns that I marvel at. My eyes trace the contours of his spine, drawn to the curve that leads to his ass.

And *oh my...* Do they make sweatpants for men differently to accentuate that area?

I reach for my phone on the metal black bedside table. With a single click, I capture a photo of him. It's become my mission to take more photos of us to one day look back on, because at the moment, we barely have any.

I catch the glint of the ring on my finger—a reminder of last night. I smile before realizing the situation we are in.

Everything good is always tainted by how screwed up our life is.

If I hadn't attended therapy for the last five years, I'd be on the verge of a mental breakdown once again. After all, I'm engaged to the man who's on trial for taking my mother's life. But somehow, I've become numb to that fact.

That is so fucked up.

Anyone who doesn't know me would think I'm a total mental case. And maybe those who know me think that too. Like my father.

"Can't sleep?" I swing the blanket off my legs and become accustomed to the chilly air circulating the room.

Ace twists to face me, his expression stoic. "Haven't been able to for a while."

This makes sense considering the events that occurred in the last twenty-four hours, but is it purely because of that, or is he suffering from nightmares again?

I know what it's like to experience them. I had them for the longest time after my mom's death. I would even avoid closing my eyes so I wouldn't fall into that trap. Eventually, I overcame them. It took years of therapy—of trial and error—but I haven't experienced a nightmare for months, and even when I do, I've learned not to allow them to consume me.

It's not just me who had a rough time with them after the *accident*. Ace found himself trapped in the vicious cycle too. It wasn't until I first stayed with him for a few weeks that I noticed he fell victim to them too.

Is that happening again? And if it is, will he speak about it with me, or anyone for that matter?

"You can talk to me, you know." I hope he would. I hope this won't be a repeat of everything we've been trying to avoid over the last few months.

"I know that, Calla," he replies, but I hear the closed-off tone to that statement. Like he's saying *I know that, Calla, but it's not that simple. I know that, Calla, but you know I won't.*

The ring on my finger hasn't magically resolved anything between us overnight. While it symbolizes we'll go to any length to find our way back to each other, it hasn't fixed the core of our issues. Miscommunication.

Raising my head, I meet his gaze, sensing that he's suggesting there's nothing more to discuss.

He takes a deliberate step closer.

Still nestled in bed, I'm leaning against the headrest. My legs remain exposed covered in goosebumps. At first, it was from the cool temperature in the room, but now, it's from the way Ace's gaze slowly trails from my face, down past the blanket still wrapped around my chest and settles on my uncovered legs.

"Ace." His name leaves my mouth. I intend it to be a deterrence, but it slides out more like an invitation.

"Calla," he mimics my tone and takes a final stride that places him by the edge of the bed, only inches from me.

My body instinctively responds to him before he even touches me. My breath quickens, my heart skips a beat, and my toes curl involuntarily. Even after all these months with him, I'm *still* unable to come to terms with it. I'm still rapt by his presence.

Craving to reclaim my power, I shuffle, rising on my knees on the bed directly in front of him. The pastel-pink camisole I'm wearing has ridden up, exposing my stomach to the cool air that washes over me once again.

I bite my lip to stop myself from shivering, but Ace's gaze fixates directly on my mouth. He raises a dark eyebrow, as though I've set him a challenge.

And by now, I know I'm his favorite pursuit.

I refuse to let that deter me, to make me pause, because a man like Ace will jump at any opportunity to bend you to his will. While I'm sure many wouldn't complain about that, I love testing the boundaries with him.

And I know he loves it too.

Prowling closer toward the edge, I set my hands on his firm shoulders. "It feels like you're shutting me out again."

He tilts his head like he's puzzled by my confession. We've vowed to be honest with each other, and I'll be damned if I don't speak my mind around him.

Ace secures his large hands around my wrists, softly

pressing his thumbs into my pulse points, attempting to regain some control of the situation, no matter how minor. It's remarkable that we mesh so well together in certain aspects, while in others we clash like fire and ice.

Our shared need for control due to our past is irreversible. No amount of therapy can fully mend the damage that has been inflicted. But we both know when to surrender to one another.

"I'm not," he assures me. "Let me show you how open I am with you." A cheeky grin that I'm *oh so used to* dances upon his lips and threatens to lure me in. I refuse to succumb to it.

I hold my ground. "I'm serious. I know the last couple of days have been hectic. For the both of us. And maybe that's why I think we need to talk about what happened."

Until now, I've been waiting for Ace to bring it up on his own, but he hasn't.

"I didn't set this up, if that's what you're getting at. I didn't know your dad would be at the airport waiting for me. I didn't know that I would be spending the first night in this town behind bars. I didn't do this, Calla."

I sigh, relief splashing over me as I exhale. I was afraid Ace had set this up and kept it from me. And perhaps the fact that I even entertained the idea is a reminder that, despite our progress, we still have a long way to go in terms of trust.

"Then how... How did he know?"

How did he know we were coming here?

"That's the million-dollar question, love. Maybe you

should talk to him," Ace suggests.

I shake my head, unable to come to terms with the situation. Talking to my dad after what he did and how he handled this is the furthest thing from my mind. Guilt gnaws at me, a consequence of what I've potentially caused by clearing my conscious and telling my dad the truth in hopes he would accept me and Ace.

Could my dad have approached this differently? I wonder whether it would have made a difference if my dad had warned me he was planning this instead of pretending everything was fine each time we spoke on the phone. Would that have changed the bitterness flowing through my veins?

I can't say for sure, although it probably would have caused me more stress.

Ace notices my mind spiraling and perhaps attributes it to my unwillingness or inability to come to terms with what he's told me.

He releases one of my wrists and cups my jaw, his thumb resting lightly against my neck. "I've become accustomed to you over the last few months." He drags his thumb down painstakingly slow, causing me to feel every touch.

Every ridge.

Every pulse under his finger.

"The more time I spend with you, the greedier I become. And it might be selfish of me to say this, but I wouldn't have done anything that would break us apart after I spent so much time getting you back."

I hold my breath as his forefinger tails the same path of

his thumb, gliding down the hollows of my neck, tracing my collarbones, igniting a fire in the places that were once touched by the coolness of the room.

"You belong with me. You're mine, Calla," he tells me earnestly. His other hand, still intertwined with mine, skims over the ring on my finger.

"Yours." All negative thoughts leave my head, and I redirect my focus on *us*. "We'll figure this out."

A brief sadness flickers across his face, though it could be my imagination. It only lasts a second, and then his eyes glaze with need. "Now stop being a tease and spread your thighs for me, love. I'm dying to please my fiancée."

9

It's You, Love

Ace

Her cheeks turn rosy at my command, and my cock throbs in my pants. She knows what she fucking does to me. She shatters my barriers, drives me insane, turns the whole world upside down.

My fingers trail lower, lingering on the opening of her camisole, and she sighs, parting her lips that are always attractively swollen in the mornings, and all I can think about is them wrapped around my cock.

At the same time, she adjusts her legs on the bed, following my command. She's still on her knees facing me, and the only thing covering her beautiful body is that indecent camisole and matching pink panties.

Although nothing would bring me greater pleasure than ripping the garments off her and seeing the way her eyes crease with reprimand but also a hint of that sweet sigh of desire and surprise, I take my time instead.

Calla clutches my shoulders with both of her hands, her nails digging into the flesh of my skin as my fingers skate over her camisole, trekking over her bare stomach. She leans into me, and an immense blaze sparks in her eyes. The look she gets when I'm about to have my way with her is pure frenzy.

"And here I thought you wanted to talk," I playfully tease her.

"I-I do." Her voice is airy, and she tries to concentrate. Her eyebrows pinch together as she attempts to recall what our conversation was about. I love that I'm able to distract her and take her burdens away even if it's just for a few seconds. A few seconds where her brilliant mind goes blank since all she can think about is having me.

Her defenses slip, and I seize the opportunity, gliding and skimming my thumb over her panties. A distant moan escapes her parted lips, and she pushes herself into my hand, chasing the release only I'm able to provide her with.

"So talk," I say, purely for her to humor me as I continue stroking her through the material, listening to her instinctive moans flowing.

Calla sends me a look saying she knows exactly what I'm doing, and I gift her a smirk in response.

"Talk, right…" She clears her throat and tries to gather her thoughts. "Are you still having the nightmares?"

She's persistent, I'll give her credit. It blows my mind how she can still think clearly when her pussy is cupped in my hand and dripping wet through her panties.

"Not regularly." I don't elaborate, and the concern wells up in her eyes like a bright beacon.

I release her sex and inch my fingers toward the sides of her G-string, sliding them over her smooth thighs. Once they aren't in the way, my gaze drops to her throbbing pussy. It's glistening wet with arousal. I'd be lying if I said that seeing her like this before I've even had the chance to touch her doesn't bring me satisfaction and an ego boost. It would do so to any man. We're all creatures who need to be wanted—*needed*.

A soft moan escapes her mouth once again, and it goes straight to my dick, which is so hard it's becoming painful. The need for release intensifies with each passing second. But she squeezes her eyes shut. "Did you have one tonight?"

"Fuck's sake, Calla. Is this what you want to be doing right now? Talking about whether I had a little nightmare?" I slide my hands under her cami and cup one of her breasts. It fits immaculately in my palm. Her skin is soft, hot and smooth everywhere I roam.

She possesses a power over me I can't resist. She's the destruction I'll actively seek time and time again. She's the only one I'll willingly fall to my knees for, even when it means crawling through miles of broken glass and burning coals.

I sound like a fucking addict, and I am. Do you know how intense my withdrawals were when I was away from her all those months? Ferocious to the point where every day I felt physically drained. So disruptive that when I would get into a frenzy, nothing could take my mind off her. I had to pretend I could control myself, that she wasn't slowly eating away at my mind, that I wasn't lusting for another hit of *her* like she was fucking heroin to me.

Her nipple swells under my touch, and all I want to do is to wrap my mouth around it and suck until she can't think clearly anymore. Until she can't ask me these needless questions and instead allows her body to take over.

Calla's eyes—bright and enigmatic—fly open.

The way she looks at me is pure fire, her expression vividly chastising. She pushes down on my shoulders with both of her hands, positioning me so I'll sit to her right, on the edge of the bed. Despite her strength not matching mine, I willingly oblige.

She proceeds to shimmy out of her panties completely, disposing them on the floor below us.

Fuck.

The expression on her face satiates with intent and determination, like she's about to get exactly what she wants. And goddamn it, even if I were a fucking priest, I'd be completely damned by now.

She climbs over me, positioning her bare thighs on either side of me. The scent of her shampoo is intoxicating.

She's goddamn intoxicating.

I skate my hands over her thighs.

Calla swats my hands away. "I'm worried about you. Especially after what happened in the last couple of days, and you're not the one to speak your mind so it's hard for me to know what you're going through in there." She taps one finger gently against my temple.

I groan. She won't drop this until I give her the reassurance she seeks.

She needs to know I'm not on my way down again. But the truth is, I've never been entirely up and thriving. I've seen a therapist a few times, and in hindsight it helped to an extent, but I have no desire to see one again. They aren't for me. That isn't to say they aren't for everyone, but something about talking to a stranger about everything fucked up that's happened to me isn't appealing. I don't care for it. I'd rather peel my own fingernails off than have a shrink, dressed in their pristine outfit, ask me another fucking question while money drains from my wallet.

"I'm fine. The only thing I'm worried about is how all of this will affect us."

There's no telling how long the trial will span out or what the outcome will be. I still own my apartment in New York, but Calla's job requires her to be in Switzerland, at least for a few more months. I would never ask her to give up her career for me. She needs to do what is right for her. Especially when I may jeopardize everything by pleading guilty to my crimes. But that's a conversation for another time.

I'm sure Nik has already told Calla the possibility of that happening. Deep down, I know she won't stand in my way when it comes to doing what I believe is right, even though a part of me wishes she would. But will she regret giving me a chance? Does she feel like she wasted her time on me when I'm probably going to fuck it all up again?

Calla runs her hand over my cheekbone, her skin is warm. Soft. "We'll get through this. We always do." Her voice is sincere, and it seems like she truly believes her own words. If it wasn't for the haunted look in her eyes, then hell, she might've made me believe her too.

But we both know this will be the most difficult challenge we'll have to face. After all, the fucked-up reality of this situation is that I'm on trial for causing her mother's death.

If Calla chooses to stay with me through this, then she'll be pushing her father away further and further each day. He's the only family she has left.

How can I sit back and watch her do that?

How was I selfish enough to ask her to marry me when my future is so uncertain? I could spend the remainder of my life behind bars, and even though I may have accepted that, nothing will prepare me for when I have to say goodbye to Calla once again.

When the news of my trial and our engagement reaches the media—I give it a few days—Calla will receive backlash along with me. And although I've learned not to give a fuck about what the tabloids say about me over the years, Calla will. No matter how hard she'll try to deny it. The tabloids are something I can't protect her from.

"Promise me you'll talk to me if anything bothers you or you just need to let some thoughts out," she says.

I'm not going to lie to her or make a promise I'm not sure I'll be able to keep, so instead I say, "I'll try."

Her brows tighten as she considers my reply. It feels like

a million thoughts race through her mind in less than a few seconds, and then her features smooth out, and she gives me a small, genuine smile. "That's all I can ask from you."

A weight lifts off my chest. I appreciate that she doesn't push me into submission, but I also know she requires me to work with her and not against her. It's like we're in a constant battle to keep the balance scales level. Push and pull. Give and take.

"Jesus, Ace, is this conversation turning you on? I swear that thing has grown more with each word I've said, and it's getting pretty hard to ignore when it keeps digging into my thigh."

She adjusts herself, and the movement of her on me only makes my cock pulse with need.

I chuckle, suppressing a groan. "It's you, love. You turn me on just by breathing, and now you're sitting on my lap with no panties on. Do you know how much control it takes for me not to fill that pretty mouth of yours with my cock just to shut you up?"

Calla can't hide the desire that seeps its way onto her expression. Her mouth parts, and her eyes glaze with a want—a need.

"Ace." Her voice is barely a whisper, and she clears her throat.

"Yes, love?"

I don't hesitate when I set my hands on her waist and pull her closer against me. There's no more power left in me when she's in my lap like this, and no matter how much time I spend with her or the amount of times we claim each other, I'll never get tired of *this*.

She regains her voice, and with it comes the demand that turns into a frenzy. "So many words..." she tempts me.

"Oh really?" I trail my hands up, lifting the thin, flimsy material of her cami.

My thumbs make a path over her soft skin and sweep the sides of her full breasts. All the while, I keep my eyes solely on her face, watching how her expression alters with each motion.

She rocks her hips back and forth on my thighs, and a low groan stems from the back of my throat. While I know how to drive her crazy by touching her in the right places, she knows how to do the same to me.

When I reach her nipples, I pinch them—not hard enough to cause pain, but enough to elicit the pleasure deriving from nipple stimulation.

Calla responds exactly the way I expect her to, by tilting her head farther back and allowing me access to her body to do as I please, because she too knows I'll provide her with anything she needs and more.

She moves her grip from my shoulders to my sweatpants, clutching the material between her fingers. "These need to go. Now."

I chuckle. "When will you realize we have all the time in the world. There's no need to rush." But even my words don't sound genuine to me.

I'd like to believe we have a long time together, and in a

perfect world we would, but a perfect world doesn't exist—especially not for me.

Calla's gaze meets mine, and unspoken words flare through.

Liar, she says.

I lower my head and claim her mouth with mine. *Just pretend*, I seem to say, striving to take her worries away even if it's just for the moment. Her lips taste like a drug—addictive, powerful and full of ammunition to wreak havoc.

She grips me with her soft hand, causing me to buck my hips into her, and she strokes me from base to tip. All the while, her gaze doesn't leave mine, watching as my teeth clench and my eyes glaze over with rapt desire.

Her expression turns brazen, and she slides down from me and drops to her knees. And fuck me—that's a sight to behold.

My fucking fiancée on her knees for me.

She strokes me, her hand not entirely able to wrap around my shaft. Then she leans down and swirls her tongue around the tip, licking up the beaded precum and moaning as she does it.

I jerk forward, buck my hips into her as a rousing wave of pleasure courses in my veins. She continues to tease me, looking up at me through her dark, long lashes while her tongue does some fucking magical shit on my dick.

I grasp her jaw in my hand. "Open your mouth." My voice comes out raspy.

She does as she's told. She wets her lips and then wraps them around the tip of my cock while her hands move around my base.

A rumble leaves the depth of my chest as her warm mouth encloses me.

Fuck. Me.

I clench my fists tightly. "That's it, love," I coax her as she takes me inch by inch, getting accustomed to the size of me in her mouth. Her eyes begin to water as I hit the back of her throat, but she doesn't stop, doesn't even fucking gag. Instead, she hums enthusiastically as her silken tongue kneads me like a good girl.

Calla continues to look at me through her lashes with those big hazel eyes of hers that hold so much fucking power over me. She begins sucking faster, her cheeks hollowing, her nails digging into my thighs.

No, no, no.

If she doesn't stop, I'm going to blow my load straight in her pretty fucking mouth.

I push her gently off my dick and clasp her jaw, forcing her attention on me. "I need to be inside you."

She understands, perhaps has that same desire. She stands and sits back on my lap. Her need is clear on her face as she positions herself over my cock so only the tip is brushing against her wetness, and a low groan leaves me.

She rubs me against her clit, and with each stroke, her head goes farther and farther back. Her eyes close, and she chases her relief.

I'm not having any of it.

I need to be entirely buried inside her. The anticipation drives me insane. My mouth is on her chest, my lips wrapped around her nipples—sucking, swirling as I feel the precum bead off me and meld with her own arousal.

"God, yes. That feels so…good," she rasps, grinding herself on me.

"You know what will feel better?"

"Hmm?"

I fist myself and position it under her entrance. I wrap my other hand around her nape and bring her head back to me so I can see the way she looks at me when I enter her without hesitation.

Without remorse.

She clenches around me. It's fucking heaven. Calla's gaze is like a possessive caress against my skin. Each time I claim her, she does it right back.

A small whimper falls from her lips, and it vibrates straight into my veins, into the blood pumping through me.

"Ace," she hums.

"You know how much I love hearing you say my name."

I hold her by the hips as I drive myself into her.

Over and over.

Until the conversation we had earlier is a distant memory, and nothing matters except for the crashing of our skin together. The breaths she takes clash with my own.

Rain pounds on the roof, almost masking the sound of everything else around us. Nothing else matters in this moment except for us connecting in the only way we know how.

10

Obsessive Guilt

Calla

Sweaty and spent, we lie in the hotel bed on our backs. Ace's arm draped on my bare stomach. My heart still pumps erratically, the adrenaline and endorphins whirling in my blood stream as though they crave more.

"You know there are people who don't enjoy sex," I remark, still catching my breath.

Ace lifts his head, props it up on his hand. He raises an eyebrow, and a mischievous glint sparkles in his eyes. "Are you trying to tell me that was shit?"

I laugh. "No, definitely not saying that." I meet his gaze with a teasing smile. "I'm just surprised at the concept that there are people out there who don't get pleasure from something so intensely intimate."

"Not everyone has what we have," he says.

"And what do we have?"

His lips brush the underside of my jaw. "The stars on our side."

"Doesn't feel like it lately," I admit, push him back and lay my head on his chest.

I feel him sigh beneath me. "I know, love."

A few moments pass between us before I say, "I like the way your heart beats."

He chuckles, it's kind of this sad sound that tears a small hole in my chest. "It's yours. Every beat of my heart belongs to you, love."

My stomach does this little flip, and color rises to my cheeks as I bury my head in the crook of his neck. "I wish we could stop time."

Ace tightens his hold on me, silently conveying he feels the same way.

"Are you sure you want to come with me today?" I ask.

A part of me hopes he's changed his mind. It would be much easier to go to the place where my mom was buried on my own. I won't have to pretend that I don't feel anything. It's not that I can't be myself around Ace—he's one of the very few people who truly knows me for me—but I'm nervous how he'll react to seeing me there.

I'm nervous how *I* will react.

"Of course. I wish I could say I want to do this entirely for you, but I also need to do this for me." He bears himself vulnerable. "I don't think I'll ever forgive myself for what I did. But I need to learn to come to terms with it, to accept it. It's the only way to move forward."

After his admission, there's no way I can tell him I don't want him to accompany me today. If he thinks it will help him heal, help him forgive himself for the past, even if it's just a little bit, then it's not the time for me to be selfish.

"Of course. I understand," I tell him, grateful he's chosen to explain, to let me in without me nagging him to.

He rises from the bed and tugs me up with him. "Come take a shower with me."

With each step my boots squelch in the mud, the rain relentlessly pelts at us from every direction. The black umbrella I hold in one hand fails to give us enough cover. In my other hand, I tightly grasp a bouquet of daisies. My mother's favorite.

She'd purchase a bunch from the markets each Sunday.

I haven't been here since the funeral. I don't believe in visiting a patch of dirt and acting like there's someone here. I know other people find comfort in this, but it freaks me out more than anything.

I don't know. Maybe that's just me. I'm wired differently in these aspects. I'd rather believe my mom is all around me, always watching over me, instead of buried in one spot, six feet under.

I wish I could say I remember that day clearly, the day her body was laid to rest, but I don't, and sometimes I think that's a blessing in disguise.

Bits and pieces flow through my mind. Some details are vivid, like the burgundy color of the casket or the way the sun cast its rays on it and caused me to see my own tormented reflection. I recall my dad by my side struggling to hold back tears as they lowered the casket into the ground. I don't remember what my mother wore or who even picked her outfit.

Was it my father? Did he stand in her side of the wardrobe and debate what to put her in or was it a quick decision like plucking a flower from a field?

I did a good job of blocking out the days, weeks, months following my mother's death, and even after years of therapy, I'm still unable to get those memories back. To be honest, I'm not even sure if I want them back. I'm certain I was on autopilot mode.

The storm doesn't seem to be easing up. Perhaps it's another omen. The universe seems to be providing me with many of those lately.

How will the events that occurred in the last couple of days change everything? Change Ace? Change everything we've become? I fear Ace will begin to pull away again—it seems like he's already doing so—and I'm not sure if I can deal with that again.

This relationship will only work if we grow as a couple. We can't remain stagnant.

"I did this," he says, his voice filled with self-recrimination. "It should be me in there." He points his finger accusingly at the ground. "Not her."

I don't respond, because maybe he's right, and nothing can be done about it. No amount of remorse can undo the past. I've learned to live with the fact that she's gone forever, and that I'm in love with the man who blames himself for it.

It seems like Ace hasn't. Or he hasn't learned to live with the mental consequences of the actions that brought him here in the first place.

He told me he took a few therapy sessions during the time we were apart—when I was in Switzerland, and he was in New York. They helped him become more open with me, but he still carries a significant amount of guilt.

His pale eyes and the solemn look he gives me make it clear. I often wonder whether his obsession with me is due to the events of the past. If our circumstances were different, and we met some other way, would we have felt the pull toward each other?

Even though Ace assures me his love for me is genuine, regardless of our past, I can't help but question if it's somehow rooted in an obsessive guilt he carried over the years.

After all, love and obsession aren't so different. On the contrary, they are almost one and the same. Both consume and possess. They trigger chaos and elicit an unexplainable need that only abates in the presence of that person. They are equally addictive and unexplainably compulsive.

The hardest part for me is differentiating between them in Ace's actions.

Mentally, he's been through more than an average person experiences in a lifetime. How much can one person bear before it all becomes overwhelming? Will we make it out the other side together? Or is that impossible for two people who have faced the worst of life together?

Is there a time where it'll become certain we have to walk away from one another, and when and *if* that time comes, will it be clear to us? Will it end up being the abyss of our existence?

I gently place the flowers near the charcoal-colored tombstone and stare at it for a while, hoping to feel something. Perhaps even *needing* to feel something to make me believe I'm not insane.

What do other people feel when they visit their loved ones who've passed? Is it a sense of closeness? Do they stand or fall to their knees and feel like they are somehow more connected to them?

I glance at Ace. He has his eyes closed, and raindrops trickle off his dark lashes and stream down his cheeks. One hand rests on his chest, while the other touches the tombstone.

This moment feels sacred, as if I shouldn't be here—and yes, I know that sounds bizarre considering this is *my* mother's grave. But this is a moment where the consequences of the perpetrator's actions are glaring them in the face, and there's nothing they can do to make it right. All Ace can do is pay his respects and spend the rest of his life trying to do good deeds to outweigh this one bad one.

Looking down, I force myself to garner at least some sort of emotion.

Nothing.

I don't feel a thing.

I admit that if an outsider could see the battle in my head, I'd probably seem crazy. But I can't help the way I feel and how my brain is wired.

As we drive in the direction of the airport, thoughts of suggesting couple's therapy weigh on my mind. I promised myself I wouldn't walk on eggshells around Ace anymore. The only way to move forward is to address issues when they arise. We've experienced the consequences of letting them accumulate for days, even weeks. We become a ticking time bomb, a grenade with a pulled pin ready to explode.

I stare at the passing buildings, lost in thought. Finally, I gather the courage to speak. "I'd like us to see a therapist together." I fidget with the straps of my black faux leather bag.

There's a brief pause before Ace asks, "Like couple's therapy?"

"Something like that. I just feel like it would benefit us, especially with everything we've been through and continue to go through."

It might even bring us closer together.

He clears his throat. The resignation in his face vividly shines, and he doesn't attempt to hide it. Although his expression is neutral, I've come to learn all the signs that indicate what kind of mood Ace is in. Maybe that's what happens when you know someone better than you know yourself.

The way his breathing slows and deepens. The way his gaze fixes straight ahead and not directly at me. The way I almost *hear* the wheels in his head spinning while he's processing his thoughts and the next thing to say.

"Okay," he finally replies, his voice devoid of emotion.

I'm surprised by his direct answer. I thought I'd have to persuade him, to convince him that it will be good for us. I'd already compiled a pros list in my mind and quickly googled statistics of how many relationships are saved or improved by attending therapy—seventy five percent.

"I was thinking maybe with Addilyn, since we're heading back to New York, and she knows our situation better than anyone?" I suggest.

"Make an appointment. I'll be there."

Why does it sound like an agreement but a dismissal all in one?

Either way, it seems like we're both offering what we can in this moment, and I'll accept it. No matter how seemingly small the gesture.

I just hope he follows through with his promise.

11

Life As We Know It

Calla

Driving in the bustling streets of New York once again brings back a lot of core memories. It's mayhem compared to the serenity in Switzerland—and even Idaho. But that's why I moved here straight after college.

I needed change. I needed to step out of my comfort zone, and that meant exchanging the quiet for chaos. I needed to get far away from the place that brought nothing but hurtful memories.

That worked for a while. Until in a city of more than eight million people, I ran into Ace.

Some would call it luck, but *fate* is a word I've come to use when it involves the events that led me to Ace.

Even when I was doing my best to avoid him.

Now, I'm lost on what to do. My career, everything I've

worked for what seems like my entire life, is miles away from here. From the person that needs my support right now more than ever. Although Ace would never ask me directly, at least not after everything, I know he's counting on me to stay.

I only have a couple more months left on my contract in Switzerland, but am I willing to risk that time when I don't know what will happen with Ace? When two months could mean everything? Will regret linger in the back of my mind?

On the other hand, I've already given up so much for him. Is it fair to keep sacrificing my life, my career, for him?

This job could set me up for life if I play my cards right. The opportunities and benefits that come with working for *The Times* are enormous. I'd be an absolute idiot if I threw it all away.

My gaze drops to the ring on my finger, and guilt eats me.

I don't regret saying yes, at least I don't think I do. It was unexpected but not completely out of line considering both of us know what we want.

The timing wasn't perfect, but will it ever be?

Ace could've gotten down on one knee and proposed when we were still in Switzerland, and I would have said yes. We'd still be in the exact same situation now. The problem is that I *can't* continue to put my life and my career on hold for someone else.

I also can't just pretend that my nightmare isn't coming to life. I can't return to Switzerland and carry on like everything is normal when it isn't.

What have I got myself into?

I wish there was a handbook on how to deal with fucked-up situations the world throws at me, but unfortunately, there isn't, and I have to take it one day at a time.

Denzel, Ace's driver, pulls up at Ace's apartment building. I peer up at it through the window, and a bolt of déjà vu passes through me. My mind heaves me back to almost a year ago, to the day when I packed my bags and was on my way to stay with Ace for two weeks.

If only I'd known what the future held for me.

Ace opens my door, and I snap out of it. I take his hand and step out of the car.

"Someone will bring our bags up. Here's a key." He places a keycard in my palm.

"You're not coming in?" I ask, slightly confused.

He shakes his head. "I'm going to go into the office."

I nod slowly, taking it in. He doesn't *need* to go into his office. He can do everything his company requires remotely. So perhaps he needs some time alone.

"Okay," I say.

Two days have passed since we arrived back in New York. Ace and I briefly caught up with his mom and sister at a café yesterday before they had to run to Ellie's dancing lesson. It's clear that his mom is taking the upcoming trial hard. Dark craters, matching Ace's, dwelled under her eyes.

We refrained from talking about the trial for Ellie's sake,

but the atmosphere was different. On the border of grim and worrisome.

Apart from that, I've spent the majority of the time cooped up inside.

I've offered Ace—or rather I *insisted*—that I head to the store and grab groceries since Ace's fridge didn't have anything, and I needed something to occupy my time. I spent hours walking the aisles of the supermarket, finding it surprisingly therapeutic. When I was finished, my shopping cart was overflowing. I may have gone overboard. Denzel helped me lug it all into the car and then into the apartment.

This penthouse—Ace's penthouse—brings back many memories even though I've spent less than a month here overall. Ace hasn't changed a thing about it. All the furniture is in the same spot, and there isn't a speck of dust anywhere, indicating that he still maintains a regular cleaner.

Why didn't he lease out the apartment while he was in Switzerland? It would have provided him with another source of income. Of course, he doesn't need it, but he's always been smart with his money. It seems like a waste to let such an expensive property stand here gaining dust.

Living with Ace has become the new normal, and perhaps it always has been. When we first met, we lived only a floor from each other. When we reconnected four years later, we spent the bulk of our time together, acting like we were a married couple.

Perhaps that's where we went wrong.

I feel like we skipped the majority of the dating stage

since our relationship turned serious quickly. It's only now we've decided to take a small step back.

Now that I'm back at the penthouse, Ace isn't here.

He's either at Blackwell Enterprise headquarters or training. He recently began working on a new clothing line for his business. It's still early stages but he's already began marketing it on social media, and the response the brand is getting from the public is phenomenal.

I flip my laptop open, using this time wisely and dive into work.

Besides working for *The Times*, I've also been busy with my own work; freelancing and posting articles on my personal website in my spare time. I've covered a range of topics and continue to gain an audience from all over the world.

It seems that people are interested in the topics I cover—from feminism and women's rights to euthanasia. I dive into arguments that are controversial, which is what I think makes them so interesting.

I've started social media accounts on Twitter, Facebook and Instagram to further expand my readership and brand. Even though my dream has been to work for *The Times* for as long as I can remember, I can't help but allow my mind to wander to bigger opportunities.

What would it be like to start my own company?

I would need to come up with a business plan and funding. I'd also need to recruit and manage a team of talented journalists and handle all the administrative and logistical aspects of running a business.

That thought seems daunting.

I don't know anything about running a business, but perhaps I could take a few pointers from Ace. He seems to be doing a fantastic job at managing multiple businesses at once.

Either way, that idea will have to take a back seat for the time being. At least until we get through this frenzied chapter of our lives.

12

Digging Through Your Mind

Calla

My therapist, Addilyn, is usually booked out for weeks in advance. She doesn't take on new clients since her books are full with her current ones. However, when I called to make an emergency appointment, her secretary informed me she had a cancellation.

So two days later, Ace and I sit on the updated plush black sofa facing Addilyn's desk, made of rich, dark wood and clutter free. The walls are a soft, neutral color, and the room bustles with natural light from a large window overlooking a garden. On one wall, a bookshelf overflows with volumes on mental health and psychology.

I cross my legs and then uncross them.

And then cross them again.

I rest my clammy hands on my knees. The flared jeans

I pulled on before we left now feel too hot, the material too constricting. I never thought Ace and I would be in therapy together, yet I'm glad he agreed to do this for me.

Our relationship has been a roller coaster from the minute we crossed paths, and it's only a matter of time before we fall back to where we don't want to be.

For the past couple of days, we've barely seen each other. I know he's been busy with work, but I can't help thinking it's him putting distance between us, and not because he means to, but because he's accustomed to doing so when things get tough.

He refuses to talk to me about how he feels about the impending arraignment. I don't know where his head is at. Nik hinted that Ace may plead guilty.

Whenever I try to talk about it, he always changes the subject or finds a way out of it. He either has an important phone call to make or a meeting he's running late to. Eventually, I stopped trying to bring it up. I'm beginning to wonder whether Ace has any idea what he's going to do or how he'll plead. I want him to make his own choice. He's the one who has to live with it.

Distance is his way of coping, even though in the past, it proved to be stupid and drove us apart. I can't go through that again. *We* won't survive it.

Together, we can overcome anything, but when one of us pushes the other away, it's a recipe for disaster.

Have I done the right thing by asking Ace to attend therapy with me? Doubt flares and forms an ominous haze.

This will be good for us, I try to convince myself. *We have to try something.*

It's better than the alternative. Better than going back to our old ways.

The snap of Addilyn closing the black folder on her desk jolts me from my thoughts. I reposition myself on the sofa, unable to find comfort in the generic room.

Addilyn hasn't changed a bit. She still has ink-black hair and a bony figure. It brings a sense of déjà vu from the last time I was here. Although I've been away for the last year, I continued to have my weekly therapy sessions remotely. I kind of hated it. It didn't feel the same as face-to-face. I could hide my emotions better, and Addilyn wouldn't pick up on them.

Therapy hasn't always been on my to-do list. Following my mother's death, my father tried to get me to talk to someone, but back then, I discarded it too soon. I decided it wasn't for me. Upon moving to New York, I knew it would be beneficial to talk to someone to overcome much of my suffering and trauma—so I gave it another go. When I opened myself up and *accepted* help, it was like some weight was lifted off my chest with each session.

"So what brings the both of you here today?" Her eyes flicker from Ace to me.

She's the only person that knows *everything* about us. The number of times I sat in this room and relayed the events of that night to her are countless. And every time I did, she wrote pages upon pages of notes. At least, I think they were notes, unless she was doodling or writing totally irrelevant things. I wouldn't even know.

It's strange to think that while she knows my life inside and out, I don't know a single thing about her except for her occupation.

Does she have a family? A husband and kids? Pets? Or does she live alone? What does she do in her free time? Does her job end when she leaves those doors or do the problems she hears on an everyday basis haunt her?

When neither Ace nor I speak, she prompts, "Calla, why don't you start?"

I knew I would have to open up during this session, and usually that's not a problem...when I'm by myself. But for some reason, this time, with Ace by my side, my stomach twists with nerves.

There's a part of me that's always holding back with him. Will it always be this way?

I take a long breath before speaking in an attempt to adjust to the atmosphere I've forced us into. "I feel like Ace is slowly starting to push me away again. When we're doing good, he's open and honest with me. I can see he's trying. But when things go wrong, he shuts down. Pulls away. Confines himself to the pit of his mind, which I think we can all agree isn't always a safe space."

I don't look at Ace, although I see him shift on the sofa and the muscles of his legs tighten. His entire body becomes taut in the span of seconds, like he didn't expect me to say any of that.

I was afraid to tell him this myself. Anxious of starting an argument. And me not speaking up is a clear sign that we're falling back into the same unhealthy pattern.

"Okay, good." Addilyn turns to Ace. "Do you hear what Calla is saying? How do you feel about that?"

Ace flinches at the question like he can't stand it. I have to admit that when I first began coming here, Addilyn's questions made me want to run my fingernails against a chalkboard. But now I understand it's the only way to make people open up and talk.

My eyes hover on the modern clock above Addilyn's desk. It's silent, but I imagine the sound it would make with each stretching second.

Thirty seconds pass before Ace answers. "I understand how Calla feels, but I can't help keeping things to myself while I process them. It's what I've done my entire life, and it's not going to change overnight."

Addilyn nods. "Of course not. But Calla hasn't asked for this overnight. This is a process, one that should be improving over time and not just when there are no issues between you. Do you think you can let her in now? Tell her how you've been feeling the last couple of days."

Ace sucks in a harrowed breath, letting the both of us know he'd rather be anywhere but here.

Noted.

"I don't know how I feel."

"Try," Addilyn says.

More silence passes, and then Ace surprises me by

speaking his mind. "I'm not sure how to feel," he rephrases. "There's a part of me that's relieved."

"Why relieved?"

"Do you know how much guilt I carry on a day-to-day basis? How that affects everything I do?" His voice emerges hoarse and exhausted.

Addilyn nods in acknowledgement. "You think this will take the guilt away?"

"Fuck no," Ace says without missing a beat. "I know it won't, but I think paying for what I did will be a start."

I don't exactly agree with that. At least, I don't think I do.

"You said only a part of you feels relieved. What does the other part feel?"

"Frustrated. Angry," Ace answers.

"And why is that?"

"Because I should've confessed a long time ago. I was a coward back then, and now I have too much to lose. I know the right thing to do is to plead guilty to all the charges, but what would that mean for us?" He looks at me as he says this. He's not searching for answers. The question is merely hypothetical.

What would that mean for us? What if Ace gets convicted, what then?

"Worst-case scenario. Fifteen years."

Nik's words echo inside my head. Am I meant to just put my life on pause? My throat is on fire, and tears threaten to surface when I think about it.

"And how do you feel about that, Calla?" Addilyn

prompts, trying to get us to talk to each other instead of doing what we do best—ignoring all our problems until it gets too much.

"I feel like the past continues to haunt us when we're trying to move forward. I'm not sure if it's a sign."

"A sign?" Addilyn questions.

"A sign that…" I pause, afraid to voice my thoughts after all we've been through. "A sign that we're just not meant to be."

Ace fists clench together, his knuckles blanching.

Uh-oh.

He's so pissed.

"Perhaps it is," Addilyn begins. "But perhaps you're actively searching for those signs."

Actively searching for signs? The signs are jumping at me from every direction. It's not like I can ignore them when they are right in front of me, glaring me in the face.

"No," I argue. "That's not true."

How can she suggest that knowing what we've been through to get where we are?

"Isn't it? Think about it. Why are you viewing it as a sign then? You can view it as a challenge, an obstacle, something to overcome. Instead, you're choosing to see it as a sign your relationship is doomed."

Ace continues to look at me as Addilyn speaks, waiting for my reaction or a reply.

I bite my lip in frustration. It's *not* like that. It's not like I want there to be issues. I'm not the one creating issues for our relationship, but when they present themselves in such glaring light, it becomes hard to ignore them.

"I-I…" I stammer, trying to find the right words, afraid whatever I say in this moment, Ace will take them the wrong way. He always does.

"I want this to work." At least I'm certain of that.

"But?" Addilyn prods like she can read my mind, like she knows there's a "but" I'm burying inside.

I hate it.

"But there's something in the back of my mind that's afraid Ace's feelings for me aren't real."

"Aren't *real*?" Ace turns to me abruptly. "Aren't *real*?" he repeats like he can't believe I said those words. His expression twists into shock—eyes widening, mouth opening and then shutting, forming a tight line. "What the fuck, Calla?"

"I didn't mean it like that," I quickly say.

"Enlighten me on how you think my feelings aren't real after everything we've been through." His tone is cold, and a recognizable flash of hurt sparks in his voice. A glint of it shines in his eyes, but he clears his throat as if trying to get rid of it. He slips his mask on so quickly that I have to question whether I truly saw it or whether it was just my imagination.

I close my eyes for a brief moment, searching for a way I can explain what I meant without hurting Ace. "I know you think you love me, and maybe you do. But I can't help but think your feelings for me are connected to the accident and come from a place of guilt."

"Who the fuck cares where my feelings come from?

Shouldn't it just matter that I love you?"

"I think what Calla is trying to say is that she's worried your feelings are more of a—" There's a pause while Addilyn twists a pen between her fingers, pursing her lips as she thinks of the right word, "—a must, a need. Instead of being something that developed organically, they developed due to guilt."

Ace stares blankly at Addilyn like she's speaking a completely different language.

He's definitely pissed.

A few more moments pass in silence.

"I'm afraid that's time. My next client is waiting."

Is she freaking joking? This session feels like it created more problems between Ace and I instead of solving them.

"For now, I'd like for the two of you to explore more of your emotional connection instead of the physical—" Addilyn begins.

Ace's eyes widen, and he interrupts her. "You mean no sex?"

"Amongst other things."

"Yeah, this isn't going to work," he says.

Addilyn looks between us. "This relationship borders on the physical aspect. How many times have you resorted to sex instead of talking about the issues you both are experiencing? If you are here, whatever you're doing is clearly not working."

Ace stares at her dumbfounded, like he's examining some exotic animal or an alien from another planet. Then he scoffs as though he's waiting for her to tell him this is a joke. When

Addilyn doesn't say anything, he leans forward in his seat.

"Sex is the one of the only things working for us, and you're saying to refrain from it?"

"For the time being, yes. Until you work through your communication issues by actually talking and not resorting to sex."

"We *have* been talking," Ace argues. "More than ever before." He looks at me for confirmation. "Like now. I've expressed my *feelings*," he spits the word like he's appalled by it. "And Calla has expressed how my feelings are a figment of my imagination, so that's fucking great, isn't it?"

Shit.

He's so *so* pissed.

I agree he's been more open with me recently, more than ever before. But there's still a barrier between us, maybe there always will be. So much happens inside both of our heads and *if* and when we do let it out, there's always an explosion.

Before I have the chance to voice my thoughts, Addilyn says to Ace, "You're frustrated. It's good to let your emotions out, to speak about them. This relationship won't grow unless you both learn how to communicate with each other, and since you're here, I would wager you want to make it work."

Ace leans back against the sofa, exhaling a frustrated breath. His expression—dark eyebrows knotted together, lips in a thin line and jaw tight—indicates that he's got a lot to say.

"How long do you suggest this...*experiment* last for?" Ace bites out.

"For as long as necessary. I don't like to give my patients

timeframes, so how about we start with until our next session, and then we'll revisit."

Ace doesn't acknowledge her words, but it's clear he's heard them.

We walk out of Addilyn's office in deafening silence.

13

Challenging Boundaries

Calla

I'm glad for the New York traffic buzzing around us. It gives me time to gather my thoughts. It's obvious Ace didn't take too well to therapy, and I'm unsure if he will be eager to return for another session considering he already had an opinion on shrinks before this. I doubt that opinion was changed today. On the contrary, I think it solidified that therapy "isn't for him". I can only hope he'll give this a hundred percent.

Conveniently, Ace's phone rings as soon as Denzel picks us up. His manager is on the other line. We go the entire drive without exchanging words. It's not till we arrive at the penthouse and I count to ten that I finally break the silence. "About what I said in therapy—"

"Forget about it." Ace shuts down, not wanting to talk

about it. He's running away from the conversation once again when that's exactly what Addilyn told us *not* to do.

But I let it go, at least that part of it. Maybe because I'm not sure how to entirely explain what I meant without it getting heated between us—and not *heated* heated. But heated as in volatile, and I hate arguing with Ace. It's like walking through a minefield.

"I think we should try it. You know, what Addilyn suggested in therapy," I say instead.

Ace laughs in response, opens the fridge and grabs a bottle of water.

"I'm serious."

He throws me an incredulous look, both dark brows raised. "You are? I'm a little off my dates lately, but I don't think it's April 1st just yet."

I press my lips together and swallow. "We agreed to go to therapy together, so I think we should be open to trying whatever Addilyn recommends. Otherwise, what's the point?"

He takes a step closer, and I can't help myself, I take a step back. His posture spills authority, and the way his muscles ripple along his chest is both a blessing and a curse.

He's been training for his fight for months on end, and it shows. He's a predator by nature.

Another step from him, and I follow suit, shuffling my feet in the opposite direction until my back collides with something cold and hard. I can't retreat any farther, and the pure influence of Ace knocks the air out of me.

"So let me get this straight. You think we can refrain from

sex until our next appointment, even though there's nothing more I want to do right now than fuck some sense into you and make sure you know how *real* my feelings are for you."

A shiver races all the way up my back. I nod in confirmation. "That's the point, Ace. We can't just resort to sex every single time." *Even though it doesn't sound too bad right now.*

"Why the fuck not? It works for us." He grabs my hips, pulling me into him.

God, help me.

He's hard. Already. It digs into me, and I do everything in my willpower to place my hands on his chest and push him back even though I want to do exactly the opposite.

"Ace." I shake my head. "Don't."

He scoffs, his molten eyes sparkling with a small victory. "You think you could tell me to stop each time I want to touch you. Each time I want to bend you over the furniture. Each time I want to spread your legs and taste your sweet little pussy. Each time I want to take you from behind in the hot tub while your clit rubs against the jets."

My mouth and lips feel dry, and I swallow. Again. His words remind me of our time in Switzerland, which seems like a lifetime ago now. Each night, after I wrapped up with my work, and Ace finished with his, we would make dinner together in the vast kitchen overlooking the frozen lake.

We picked a recipe from the vintage cookbook I bought from a secondhand bookstore. There were hundreds of recipes, so we never had anything more than once unless it became one of our favorites. Then I poured us a glass of red and got the ingredients ready. We cooked with the music oozing from the speaker. Ace chopped the vegetables, and I threw it all together. Hoping for the best.

There were intimate touches here and there. When I was at the sink, he would reach both steady hands around me just to get a sponge. His warm body pressed into my back, and my heart galloped. And then he'd pull back, leaving me wanting more. I was a shit cook prior to this. Probably still not the best, but now I trust myself to make a meal and not burn the kitchen down. We ate by the crackling fireplace while talking about nothing and everything all at once.

Then, like a ritual, we disposed our clothes on the timber flooring leading up to the porch and slid the patio door open, allowing the cool breeze to caress our bodies. Even though it was freezing, the thought of just us surrounded by miles of nature was enough to warm my insides up. And even then, something urged me to take these moments like they would be my last—to relish them, because the world is full of surprises.

We'd get in the bubbly water of the hot tub, the water so hot that the steam curved around us and shielded us from the biting chill of the freezing air.

We were surrounded by a lake that was frozen over and trees blanketed by a thick layer of snow. I sipped the wine from a glass while we chatted and laughed. Our words were carried away on the steam, rising from the water while the snow continued to fall.

The moments spent in the hot tub were our most intimate yet. Nothing beats seclusion with the person that makes you feel like you're high on life.

Now, Ace's lips twist at the corners into a grin, like he knows the memories are filtering through my mind. After all, the months in Switzerland were the best ones yet.

He's not going to make this easy for me, because he thinks this step is unnecessary in our relationship. He made it clear our sex life is the only thing that works, and why bother fixing something that's not broken?

But I think it's the only way we can move forward and explore a deeper connection, be more open with each other emotionally instead of burying things inside and resorting to sex—the exact thing we've both done for the past few years with our past hookups and each other.

Perhaps then I can figure out whether Ace's feelings for me are genuine, as crazy as that sounds.

"Yes." The word comes out ragged and forced. "I will tell you to stop." Although I'm not so sure I can resist him every single time, but I'll do my damn best to try.

"Are you trying to convince yourself or me, because I know for a fact you won't last more than a week, love."

"Is that a challenge?" I tempt him.

His eyes flare. The incessant blue in them reminds me of the hottest part of a flame.

"Calla." His voice drops to a dangerously low borderline whisper. "Don't start something you have no intention of finishing. Before you know it, you'll be begging me to fuck you."

14

Sperm Donor

Ace

For the first time in a long time, I go to bed with fucking blue balls. And the thing I want to do more than relieve my *situation*, is to strangle that damn therapist. Not only is she the catalyst of *this*, but I also can't stop thinking about what Calla said in her office, how my feelings for her aren't real.

Was she fucking joking or just trying to piss me off? Because if it's the latter, she succeeded.

How can she say *that* after I constantly show her she's my damn world? Guilt may consume me for obvious reasons, but it has nothing to do with my feelings for her.

We've been in bed for an hour now, but I can't drift into sleep. I lay on my back, staring at the fucking ceiling.

Just as I feel myself about to drift off, Calla nuzzles her

perfect little ass into my side. I glance at her. She's fast asleep. Her soft, deep breaths fill the vast room. Even in her sleep, she makes it her mission to drive me fucking insane.

I turn on my side facing her and drape my arm over her waist.

When the sun rises and streams into my apartment, we eat breakfast like two civilized human beings. No touches, no kissing, only coffee with raspberry croissants. There's a part of me, a very small fucking part of me that thinks we might be able to do this. Then Calla brushes a little spread of raspberry on her lip with her thumb and places the tip of it in her mouth. Sucks it.

I'm distracted.

I'm not usually like this. Yes, I like sex. Is there any fucking guy who doesn't? And sex with Calla is on another level. However, it's not usually the only thought on my mind.

But now? It consumes me. It's true when they say you want something one hundred times more when you've been told you can't have it.

"I have training," I grumble, rising and pushing the chair harder than I should.

Training has always been a way to keep my demons at bay. It's what catapulted me into the sport from the beginning. I found that once I'm in the zone, every self-destructing thought entombs itself deeply where I can't reach it.

And for the last seven years, that hasn't changed.

Nothing else has made me feel that way, and I'm dreading the day when my sporting career draws to an end.

I don't see Nik come in, and it isn't until he's standing in front of me dressed in his work gear—a light-blue shirt and dark-gray slacks with a briefcase in his right hand—that I acknowledge him, but I don't stop my routine.

Left punch, right kick, two jabs.

The familiar rhythm of my training routine pulses through my body, granting me a momentary escape from the outside world. As I throw another left punch, the tension in my muscles melts away. My body instinctively shifts, launching a powerful right kick. Two jabs follow, quick and precise.

I'm not wearing any gloves. My knuckles are bare and swollen red. I'll get an earful if and when my trainer sees the damage I'm causing. But neither of those factors make me think twice.

The boxing bag has taken away most of my tension. I've been at it for the last hour. Training for the fight. Or that's what I keep telling myself. In fact, if I'm being honest with myself, a different force drives me this morning. My frustration is definitely at an all-time high, even a cold morning shower did little to help.

If last night was anything to go by, I'd wager I'll be having many mornings like this for the foreseeable future. I have little to no desire to return for another therapy session following yesterday, but I know Calla will want me to give this a decent go, so I'll do it. Even if it's just for her. Just to show Calla the lengths I'm willing to go for her.

"You seem tense," Nik says.

I scoff. "Wonder what gives that away."

"I did some digging on our father..."

The mention of our father piques my interest. I pause, finally taking a much-needed break. Although the adrenaline doesn't cease. It pulses in my blood stream for hours following a training session and days following a match.

"The last time I saw him, he was asking me for favors. Something about getting his license back. I assume you had something to do with him losing it in the first place." A hint of a smile crosses his face.

"Yeah, I made sure he lost his license to practice law a while ago." I grab a towel and wipe the sweat off my face. "Surprised he can't get it back, knowing the connections he has."

Even though my father has connections around this country, there's not much that money can't buy. And I have a lot of it to offer.

Nik nods. "I figured that was you. But considering the amount of shit he's done, he could've lost it by himself. It seems like he's getting off too easy."

My father is a piece of shit. I knew that from the moment he walked out on my family. I should've figured it out sooner—when he took *business trips* so often he was barely home. No amount of remorse will make me change my mind, though I doubt he feels a lot of regret for anything he's done. The amount of people he screwed over just because he was bribed is insane, and he deserves to face the consequences of his actions.

So do I.

So how can I judge him for his crimes when mine are a hundred times worse?

"I know what you're thinking," Nik states.

I snicker. "Really?"

"You're thinking whatever he's done can't be worse than what you've done. And let me tell you something, little brother, you're probably right." I didn't expect that. It's like he read my mind, thought for thought. "But the difference between our father and you, is that he doesn't care how his actions impact anyone or how many lives he ruins for his own benefit. The only person he cares about is himself, and unless someone stops him, he'll continue to do as he pleases without any repercussions."

He's done that his entire life. I'm not sure how bringing a lawsuit against him will change that. And I doubt he'll be punished for his crimes. Years of being a lawyer built him connections with the right people. Politicians, judges, high-ranked businessmen who are just as corrupt as him and willing to do anything it takes to circumnavigate the law.

Nik places his briefcase on the counter with a thud and clicks it open to reveal files and files of paperwork. They don't seem to be organized in any particular order, but Nik pulls out the third one from the top.

He flips open the file and lists all the reasons why our pathetic excuse for a father should be prosecuted. "Ten years ago, he took a bribe from a politician and represented him knowing that the six sexual assault charges brought against him by *minors* were legit. He tampered with evidence, and the politician got off without any consequences."

My gut twists at the thought, but that's probably not even the worst, so I allow Nik to continue listing all the vile things our father's done in his entire life. How he used the degree that was meant to bring justice and uphold the law, to his advantage.

As much as some believe that my father is the main reason I dislike lawyers—especially those who spend most of their career in a court room—it's not the case. Long ago, I learnt that appearing in court is a totally different game. It's a game of deception, of twisting stories to fit the narrative. If you tug at the right heart strings in the jury, juggle the events to suit your needs, you can just about get away with anything.

"So what's the plan?" I interrupt Nik. "Try and put him behind bars? You don't need me to tell you that people like him don't stay there for long."

He'll manage to twist his way out of there like a dirty fucking snake.

"You think I don't know that?"

I know he knows. He of all people is well aware of it. So why bother wasting time and resources putting that man behind bars when he'd be out in probably less time than it takes us to get him in there.

"You're wondering why bother…"

"You have to stop doing that," I say, referring to him reading my damn mind. "It's fucking weird."

He ignores my remark. "I can't just sit back and do nothing. I have to at least attempt to do everything in my power. That way I'll know I tried instead of letting him get away with all the shit he's done."

"I have a few ways to sort out the problem."

"No. You're in the middle of a trial. You'd be a fucking idiot to put a toe out of place right now. There'll be eyes on you everywhere."

"I wouldn't have to lift a finger." I have connections, people to do it for me if I offer the right price. Though to be honest, I hate people doing my dirty work.

Nik glares at me.

"Fine." I hold my open palms up. "We'll do it your way."

Nik doesn't smile. He's not doing this for himself. He's not doing this because of his ego or whatever other people might do it for. He wants to do it because he believes in the system. To a degree.

Ironic, because he helped me and continues to no matter what fucked-up situation I land myself in. He says I'm family. So it's different.

Even though Nik doesn't talk about his past much, especially his relationship with our father, I believe somewhere along the line, our father damaged all his kids. Blood to him is like dirty fucking water. He wouldn't even wash his hands in it.

I'm reluctant to ask Nik why now? Why did he wake up today or whatever day this thought popped into his head and decide today's the day he tries to get the man to pay for all the shit he's done. But I don't ask.

Some things are better left unsaid.

If Nik is anything like me, he won't want to talk about what our father's put him through.

Fair enough. Understandable. I am more than thrilled to help him.

15

Betty

Calla

One of the things I've been looking forward to since returning here is seeing Betty, my old neighbor. While I lived in my old apartment, I helped her with her groceries, and she became an important figure in my life. I've made sure to keep in touch with her while I was away in Switzerland.

In the beginning, we talked on the phone. I kept her in the loop about my job, Ace, and updated her on how beautiful Switzerland is. I was hesitant talking about myself at first, but Betty assured me she loves listening since she doesn't have many friends or any family left.

Since I was dying to see Oreo, my cat, I suggested we Facetime. It took a few tries to succeed, and even then, at times I saw more of Betty's forehead or ear, sometimes even a closeup of her teeth.

It turns out Oreo is living his best life and probably hasn't realized I'm not there. Betty is also reveling in his company. He keeps her on her toes, that's for sure.

I knock on the apartment door a couple of times. The last time I spoke to Betty was almost two weeks ago. She has no idea I'm back, and I hope I don't give the poor woman a heart attack from the surprise.

The door swings open, and when Betty sees me, her face instantly crinkles with joy. I haven't seen her in almost a year, and the screen lies. I didn't notice a change in her over Facetime, but now that I'm seeing her in person, I realize just how much she's aged.

There's no defining thing I can pinpoint that's different about her—maybe it's her eyes—but whatever it is, it reminds me how quickly time goes. Even though it felt like time without Ace was going slowly, looking back on it now, the months I was in Switzerland flew by.

"Calla, dear?" She adjusts her wide-rimmed glasses on her nose as if she can't believe I'm here.

"Hi, Betty." I grin.

"Aren't you supposed to be in Switzerland?" she asks, like I'm an imposter.

I chuckle. "I'm visiting for a little while," I say, unsure of how long I'll be staying. It's something I can't stop thinking about.

"Ah, you should've told me. I would've cooked up a storm."

"You don't have to." I wave her off. "I brought some

groceries for you, just the essentials and a few goodies."

"Oh, that's nice of you, but you shouldn't have. Denzel has been great. I have everything I need without having to leave my apartment. I still haven't figured out if that's a blessing or a curse."

Ah, I didn't realize Denzel was still taking the task seriously. Has Ace been paying him this entire time to do this?

I'm mad at myself for not asking Ace. We've been in our own bubble, locked away from the rest of the world for the last couple of months. In my naïve mind, I hoped and wished with all my being it would stay like that forever.

Betty stands aside to let me in, and a shadow lurks behind her legs.

Oreo.

I look at him, and he nuzzles his head against Betty's legs and lifts his furry head, his eyes seem to be saying *traitor.*

"How has he been?" I squat and drop the bag of groceries beside me. I extend my arm and keep it still, waiting for Oreo to approach me. He pads forward through Betty's ankles and pauses, examining me. "Have you forgotten me? I wouldn't blame you."

"He's been spoiled rotten. Just the other day, I was making dinner and had to step away from the kitchen for a moment. When I came back, the salmon I was seasoning was gone. Poof." She makes the motion with her hands. "And then I find this rascal licking his paws."

Oreo meows like he knows she's talking about him.

"Yeah, you." Betty shakes her head.

I'm glad the two of them are getting along. It makes me feel less like a shitty person for leaving Oreo behind when I left for Switzerland, though I still feel like a shitty person.

"That's a shame, because I bought you treats." I point to the bag.

He takes another bold step forward, and then another, until the top of his head is rubbing against my hand, granting me permission to pat him. I scratch his head and his chin, and he purrs in satisfaction. With each purr, he moves closer and closer, until he's practically in my lap.

Well, it didn't take long for him to warm up to me. I think we just might have a chance to reconcile.

I pick up the grocery bag and follow Betty into her apartment. Nothing has changed. I'm not sure why I expected it to. The fake pot plant still lives by the entryway. Her place still smells delicious, like sugar and nutmeg. And the hallway runner that reminds me of my dad's place is still here.

I set the bag on the counter and pull out the groceries I bought in a rush—some of them may have been impulse purchases like the chocolate chip cookies.

"Make us some tea, would you, dear?"

I busy myself with the task, finding my way around her kitchen like it's my second home.

"How is that hunky boxer of yours?" she asks while I'm pouring the hot water into the mugs.

I laugh.

So she hasn't seen the news yet. I doubt she watches it much, if at all. She prefers those soapy TV shows. I helped her set up Netflix and all the other streaming applications to keep her busy.

"He's…" What do I say? I pause, clear my throat.

"Oh, no. What's happened?"

I sigh. I should've known my pause would give it away. But I don't have the energy to explain to her everything we're going through right now.

So I just say, "We're having some issues."

She reads the room and doesn't push for more detail. "Every relationship has its complications, but if you still want to be together while going through these problems, it's a good sign."

"You always have words of wisdom."

"How could I not? I'm a hundred years old."

I chuckle, carrying our teas carefully to the coffee table by the sofa. "Not quite, but I'm sure you'll make it."

I return to the kitchen to grab the chocolate chip cookies and arrange them on a plate.

"So do you?" Betty asks when I plop down on the sofa.

"Do I?" I echo, not sure what she's asking.

"Do you want to be with him despite the…complications you two have found yourself in?" She takes a napkin, sets it on her lap, and then grabs a cookie.

Oreo jumps on the sofa next to Betty and nuzzles his head into the side of her leg. She automatically places her wrinkly hand on his furry head and scratches him.

I don't hesitate to answer her question. "Yes." Of course I do.

"Then that's all that matters."

That's all that matters.

I think about that for the remainder of the time I spend with Betty. It's always been like that with us—with me and Ace. I've always wanted to be with him despite everything that's happened. My heart has always craved him, still does. But instead of listening to my heart, I've always listened to my head, since it's more rational. So when it told me I shouldn't be with him, I listened.

Although I've finally figured out my heart will always pull me toward him. We're like magnets. Wherever he goes, I go, even if it's unintentional. There's no escaping it.

16

Alone But Together

Ace

The hot shower water sluices down my body as I grip my cock in my hand. A week has passed since the therapy session. A week since I touched her, fucked her. Claimed her as mine.

An entire week of fucking torture.

Some days, I meet with Nik to discuss the trial. He doesn't sugarcoat it for me. I know what this means for both Calla and me. She could be called to testify against me, but Nik assures me he will do everything he can to prevent that from happening.

I'm kind of glad he still has feelings for her, as fucked up as that is. It means he will be more inclined to protect her no matter the cost.

So after the long days, the only relief I'm able to seek

is the comfort of my own hand. I never thought it would come to this. I never had issues seeking someone to fill these kinds of needs. I've rarely had to resort to taking care of them myself.

But the only person I want—*need*—is hell-bent on making my life difficult.

Isn't she always? But I wouldn't have it any other way with her.

I steady myself, resting my other hand on the glass shower panel. The water cascades down, reaching the maximum heat I can endure. Steam rises and curls around me.

I block all other thoughts out that have taken up residence in my mind, including the trial and how it will affect my life, my relationship with Calla, the negative effect it will have on my career.

Instead, images of Calla flash in my mind. I imagine that instead of my hand around me, it's her rosy lips and full mouth wrapped around my length.

I stroke myself once from base to tip and groan. It feels so good, yet not as good as the real thing. It's imagination, just enough to quell the need, but not entirely satisfying.

Tightening my grip, I do it again.

And again.

Until my teeth clench so hard I think my next dentist visit will be much sooner than previously planned.

The bathroom door slides open. I don't stop stroking myself.

Calla saunters in, and I lift my head to look at her.

Our gazes collide.

Steam permeates the bathroom, fogging the shower screen, but I know she can see exactly what I'm doing, and I don't stop. I let her watch me get myself off to the carnal thoughts of her.

My strokes quicken, and I don't remove my eyes off her. She seems so innocent as she stands there, watching me with her plump lips parted, her chest moving raggedly, like her own breathing has increased tenfold.

The steam is thick, but I know her cheeks would be flushed with need and pulsating desire anyway. I know under that oversized shirt, which is mine, her panties are soaking wet. The thought of it makes me want to fuck a whole ton of sense into her. I revel in the fact that she's just as turned on as I am—like seeing me please myself is something she has dreamed of all her life.

Her hand slowly drops to her body, caressing her side and lower...until she reaches her thigh.

Fuck me.

Is she fucking serious?

She restrains from allowing any physical contact between us, but she won't shy away from both of us getting ourselves off in front of each other.

What the fuck?

She positions her slender body in an immaculate position, offering me the full view. She pulls her white lacy panties to the side, which she knows I fucking love, did she wear them on purpose? To tease me one way or another? Is this some sort of twisted game to her?

Calla slides a finger up until she reaches that sweet spot. Then she starts circling it with her middle finger, all the while maintaining eye contact with me. She leans against the tiled wall and opens her bare thighs wider.

I'm like a fucking puppy, salivating at the sight of her. This is going to kill me. So hypnotized by her, I suddenly realize I've stopped stroking myself.

"Come here." My voice emerges so hoarse.

She shakes her head and mouths, "No."

No?

Fuck. That.

This would turn me the fuck on if I knew I'd get to have my way with her at the end of it. But that's not the case. And instead of turned on, I'm goddamn frustrated. I'm not about to have another case of blue balls.

I swing the shower door open and take two strides toward her. Water runs down my body and onto the floor, creating a small puddle. Without a second thought, I grab her arm and pull her into me. Her body collides with mine like a fucking meteor.

"Ace, don't." She retreats, taking a step back. The white shirt soaked up the water from my chest and now leaves little to the imagination. Seeing her like this—not entirely naked but just enough to make me want to rip all her clothes off—sends me into a frenzy.

Fuck that. I *always* want to rip her clothes off even if she was wearing a garbage bag.

Her rejection feels like I've been punched in the face. "Calla..."

Perhaps she notices the hurt flash across my expression. I need to do a better job of hiding it. It's hard to conceal my emotions around her. She's the only person that can see right through my bullshit.

She steps closer. "If we both love each other, we'll try to do this. What's one more week?"

One more week will be the death of me.

I sigh, take her hand and tug her toward the shower. She opens her mouth to protest, but I quickly stop her. "I won't touch you if you don't want me to, but you're going to fuck yourself with those pretty little fingers of yours, and I want to watch."

Her eyes glaze over, and she swallows. She doesn't resist when I pull her into the shower. The water soaks her instantly. The shirt clings to her body, outlining every curve. She leans her head back under the shower head, letting the stream soak her hair, and she pushes it back with her hands. The droplets on her throat and jaw begin their descent. I clench my teeth.

When she tilts her head forward again, she looks directly at me. Her eyes blaze into me like two fiery comets. She's a fucking goddess, a force to be reckoned with. And goddamn, I'd kill anyone if they tried to mess with her.

She shimmies out of her panties all while keeping eye contact. She dangles them in front of me on her two fingers like she's saying *let's do this,* before tossing them to the corner. The air hums with an electric charge.

I swallow, my Adam's apple bobbing in the process. It takes every single muscle in my body to keep my promise to not touch her unless she tells me to. To not grab her curvy hips and pull them to me. To not turn her around and bend her over. To not slide into her warm pussy and feel the tightness, the heat, the absolute perfection of her.

"You're looking at me like it's the first time you've seen me." She giggles.

She fucking *giggles*, and the sound is angelic. So pure.

"With you, every time feels like the first time."

Her eyes glaze over and then dart between us—like she wants to rid the distance, like she wants us to come together, like she too can't stand the physical barrier. But instead, she does the opposite and takes a step back, and then another. She drops herself against the stone wall seat on the other side. I've never wished I had a smaller shower until now.

"You first."

I chuckle. "I'm surprised."

"Surprised?"

"That you're nervous. It's not the first time you've done this."

Not even the second. And I fucking love her for it.

I grab my girth and stroke. It does nothing for me anymore. Not when Calla is here, and it's not *her* touching me. Though when she slides her hand over her thigh, lifting the soaked material up and skating her fingers over herself, I almost come undone.

Watching her is like watching a fucking sunset.

Mesmerizing.

Mind-blowing.

But at the same time, it's excruciating having her only a couple of feet away and not being able to touch her.

Calla slides her middle finger in and her mouth parts. Her head falls back against the wall. My eyes dart from the column of her throat, the rise and fall of her chest, the peaks of her pink nipples, to the way she slides her slender fingers in and out and circles her clit.

I'm taking everything in. Even though I'm able to make her come in my own ways, I adore learning what she likes—how she explores herself, how she teases herself to reach that peak.

I study her like I'm studying for the biggest test of my life.

"That's it, love."

I fuck my hand harder and harder and imagine I'm in her.

"Come for me," I groan.

Her thighs clamp around her hand, and she squeezes her eyes shut. Her body shudders, yet she still manages to call out my name in the form of a moan.

And that's what fucking undoes me.

Not her naked in front of me. Not her touching herself to the thought of me.

It's her calling my fucking name as she comes.

I explode in my hand. The hot flood pours through my fingers onto the shower floor. My gaze lifts to hers. She has that dazed, post-orgasm look in her eyes that I'm so used to seeing, yet it still does something to me each time. Awakens a part of me that only exists with her.

I take a step toward her. She doesn't move from the seat, waiting for me to make my next move. I'm not looking to get off again—even though this was nothing compared to what I wanted. Needed.

But for now, I just want to be close to her.

I take her hand and pull her up, leading her into the stream of water. I tug at her shirt, silently asking for permission, hoping that she can see my intentions flaring through.

Calla nods and lifts her arms.

Once I remove the shirt, I throw it in the corner where her panties lie and squirt body wash into my hands. Beginning at her shoulders, I massage the soap in. She places her hands on my wrists to stop me, compelling me to look up at her.

"Thank you. For coming to therapy with me. For agreeing to try this."

Although I hate every bit of it, I'd do it a million times over for her. "Anything for you." I continue lathering her with soap, ensuring I pay attention to every inch of her. Her full breasts with her pink nipples cresting. I refuse to skip them just because of the deal. Our contact doesn't always need to be sexual. I know that's what she needs me to show her.

"Why me?" I ask.

She looks at me quizzically, not understanding the context of my question.

"Why do you keep choosing me over and over, going through all this…when you can find someone who isn't just one big fucking issue? Who isn't the cause of so much fucking pain? Who could give you exactly what you need?"

She gives me a look that asks *are we doing this again?* Like I'm a fucking idiot for even asking her that.

"I tried that, remember?"

I grimace at the thought of her *trying* to be with other men, including my brother. I'd rather suffer physically than to ever feel that kind of overwhelming jealousy again. Enough to kill a man. But her happiness means more to me than my own, so if she ever told me she didn't want me anymore and meant it with her entire heart, I would let her go.

I'd also make sure no man would touch her if they valued their life. I guess I'm just a selfish prick.

"I remember." My voice is gruff.

Calla shakes her head slightly. "Don't go jealous on me. You've had your fair share of different women in the last five years," she reminds me.

"They meant nothing." I mean every word. They were just a means to an end.

"Anyway..." Calla digresses. "I see *you*, and I accept you for all that you are. The good, the bad, the ugly. I accept your past, and if you're willing to go to therapy with me, to try make this work, then I'm here. I'm not going to take the easy route because easy doesn't mean fulfilling. I want whatever this is. With *you*. No one else."

Every word is like a pickaxe chipping away at all my barriers, at all the doubts I have, but that's a stupid thing to do, because how the fuck do I expect everything to work out?

"Plus, you've ruined me for any other man."

Good.

Her hands are still on my wrists, and she tugs me forward. Our bodies collide, and her breasts press against me. The heat flows between us, and so do thousands of emotions and ifs and buts. I swallow them, preparing to deal with the demons when I'm alone. Calla already has plenty of her own, and as much as she wants me to reveal mine to her, I can't burden her like that.

Not now.

Not ever.

Instead, I slide my hands up her shoulders, up, until I reach her collarbones. I brush her wet hair back and wrap my hands around her nape, lifting her gaze up to meet mine.

"You have no idea how much I needed to hear you say that," I say.

"I do."

I chuckle and brush my lips against hers. Waiting to see if this is okay. She returns the kiss, her lips soft, wet and prompt against mine.

"I love you," she murmurs against my mouth.

"I'd burn the fucking world for you."

I just hope that's enough.

17

Weighty Decisions

Calla

With only a week remaining until I have to return to Switzerland, the life I've built over the past year calls to me.

The decision doesn't weigh lightly on me. It's all I was able to think about last night while I tossed and turned in bed. After what happened in the shower last night, Ace spent the entire night in his home office, insisting that he had work to do. And this morning, when I pad down the stairs, I find the apartment empty.

After a cool shower to wake me up and three cups of hot coffee, I feel brand new. Ready to start my day.

I'm scheduled to meet Ace at Blackwell headquarters around eleven thirty, and from there, we'll head to meet Nik for lunch to discuss the trial proceedings. It was Ace who asked if I wanted to join him, and I appreciate him keeping me in the loop.

Since we arrived back in New York, I refuse to let Denzel drive me everywhere like Ace insists. I want to feel like a normal citizen. I want to soak the city in and remind myself why I fell in love with it, so I take the subway instead.

It's busy for a mid-morning on a Wednesday, but perhaps it's always been like that, and I've forgotten. Got too accustomed to the quiet life in Switzerland.

Crowds move around as though they are in sync, and I wonder how many times a person crosses paths with another without realizing it. I mean, most of them aren't even watching their surroundings. They act like robots that have been programmed to do the exact same thing every weekday—get up, get ready for work, walk to the subway while burying their head in their iPhone, iPad, Kindle or, on the rare occasion, a paperback. At work, they most likely do their monotonous tasks each day while wishing the time would go by quicker with each passing minute. Whereas I'm here begging time to slow down so I would get a few more moments with Ace if it all goes to shit.

When I'm only a few minutes from Ace's office building, enjoying the clear skies, not so much the fumes from all the vehicles, my phone buzzes in my bag. I stick my hand in, rummaging through the clutter until I find the vibrating brick and pull it out.

"Why do I have to find out from the tabloids that my best friend is engaged?" Mia exclaims right when I press answer, before the phone even reaches my ear.

I sigh, knowing this conversation was a long time coming. "I've been meaning to tell you, but with everything else going on, it just slipped my mind." And that's the truth. I didn't purposefully withhold this from my best friend because I'm scared of being judged.

It's not her reaction that I'm scared of. It's the thought of saying it out loud, even though I know Mia is the last person to judge me for my choices. She's always been supportive, never shying away from expressing her thoughts and opinions. She doesn't beat around the bush or worry about being compassionate toward my feelings. Sometimes it's hard to detach from my emotions and see situations subjectively. Mia helps me with that.

"That sounds like a bunch of excuses. I mean, the first thing you should do when you get engaged is share it with your best friend."

"I'm—" I'm about to apologize, but she continues, cutting me off.

"Unless…the first thing you should mention is that Ace got arrested! I mean, what the hell, Calla? Just because I'm in another country doesn't mean I'm not accessible. I'm only a text or a phone call away."

She's angry, and I get it. She's my best friend, and I'm hers. Apart from each other, we don't have many people we can confide in. My list keeps getting smaller by the second. If she kept something like this from me, I would also be frustrated and even hurt.

"I'm sorry," I say. "It's been chaotic. I still haven't come to terms with it in my head. But you're right, you're the first person I should've told. I'm sorry you had to find out through the media."

At one time, I was able to sort through my thoughts internally before confiding in her or anyone else, now I'm not so sure I can. Everything related to Ace is extremely fast-paced. The media acts like a pact of hyenas, eagerly waiting to pounce on fresh prey. And of course, I'd rather be able to share these things with Mia before she learns about them from the tabloids. They always twist their stories, add satire and something that grabs the reader's attention and compels them to continue reading. A skilled writer can shape the reader's opinion, and the reader will willingly succumb to it.

Mia exhales, and just like that, I know she's forgiven me—her anger dissipated. "So tell me everything like I don't already know it."

I snort. "My dad arrested Ace when we landed in Idaho." Mia gasps like she's hearing the news for the first time. "I called Nik, and he flew to meet me the same day." More gasps from Mia, but I can't tell if it's genuine surprise or if she's still playing the game.

"You called Nik," she repeats.

Okay, that was genuine surprise. "Yeah, he's a lawyer and Ace's brother—"

"Ace's brother who you slept with."

My heel catches in the crevice of the pathway. I stumble and swiftly regain my balance, saving myself from face-planting. I clear my throat before saying, "We're past that."

"Is Ace past that?" Mia asks, unaware of my near pan-cake moment.

I would hope that Ace has moved beyond it, but I know he probably hasn't. I'm not sure if he ever will be completely indifferent to it, and it's reasonable.

"What should I have done? Ace is too proud to have made the call himself, and I *had* to do something to help."

"You could've called a lawyer. Any lawyer, other than his brother," Mia suggests.

"Nik is the best. He knows the situation."

"Okay, Calla."

"What's that supposed to mean?"

"Just that I know you meant well, but the situation is a bit muddy. Maybe next time let Ace be the one to get his brother involved instead of you."

I hate to admit it, but Mia is right. However, if faced with the exact same decision again, I don't think I would do anything differently. Nik's involvement is what got Ace out on bail. While another lawyer might have achieved the same outcome, I can't know for sure.

"Ace proposed. It was very unexpected and came out of nowhere."

"Do you think that might have anything to do with you calling Nik for help? You know men and their egos…"

"God, you sound like my therapist. But I don't think so. It seemed like he's been planning it for a while. It was just bad timing, I guess."

"Bad timing, or the perfect timing since his brother is getting too close to you again?"

He isn't. Nik knows where he stands, and I would never cross that line again. Honestly, I wouldn't have crossed it in the first place if I'd known everything I know now, and Mia is well aware of this. She just enjoys reminding me. "Mia—"

"Fine, fine. I'm just saying what I'm thinking, not holding back."

"And I appreciate that."

"I know you do."

I sigh.

"So should I expect you home next week..." she trails off, waiting for my response.

"I don't know what to do. It seems like I'm always facing difficult decisions. Why can't anything be easy for once?"

She sighs on the other end. "Life is never easy. And if it is, then you're not learning valuable lessons along the way. You're not growing mentally *and* physically."

"Wow. Who are you, and what did you do with my best friend?"

She chuckles. "I just got back from this three-day artist retreat. It was very philosophical. There were motivational speeches, meditation, group yoga followed by nude painting. The whole lot... Anyway, you have to do what's best for *you*."

"Even though what's best for me might hurt someone else?"

"Ace will understand," she assures me. "This is his hurdle to face, and yeah, it would be great if you could stay

145

there to support him, but you built a life here. You have a career here, *and* to top it all off, you also have your own mental battles to face during his trial."

And I know she's right. He will understand, and perhaps that's what makes it even harder to make this decision.

"There's a chance I'll be called to the stand if it goes that far."

"Have you? Been called?"

"Well, not yet..." I say.

"Exactly. We'll revisit this conversation if and when it comes to that."

I sigh. Once again, she's right.

"Anyway, enough about me. Tell me more about the artist retreat." I divert the topic. "Have you given much thought about what's next for you?"

Mia's art career seems to be taking off, and I'm thrilled for her. She's opened up an online shop for her paintings, and there's been talk of her moving back to New York since there are better opportunities for emerging artists here. She even found a small studio that fits her budget. In theory, there's nothing holding her back from pursuing her dreams, but each time I ask when she plans to relocate, her answer remains the same. "When the time is right."

In my opinion, there's only one thing holding her back.

I walk into Blackwell Enterprises, my phone tightly pressed against my ear about to ask her when she plans to move here. I haven't given much thought to where I'll go after my contract in Switzerland is up, but I know I don't want to be far away from my best friend.

Speaking of the one thing, or more specifically, the person holding Mia back.

Wearing a striped shirt tucked into cream-colored slacks, Theo looks professional but still has that trace of style.

"Hey, Theo," I greet him.

His face brightens when he sees me, and he gives me a nod. "Hey, you."

Mia remains silent, but I distinctly sense the shift in energy, even though we're thousands of miles apart and talking over the phone. It's that unspoken connection that occurs when two people are in sync.

There are only two people I've experienced that kind of connection with—Mia and Ace.

I hear her inhale sharply before she chirps in her usual voice, "I have to run. I totally forgot I have this Zoom meeting starting now. I'll call you later."

"Mia—" I begin, wanting to call her out on the bullshit lie, but she has already ended the call.

We haven't discussed Theo much, if at all. I'm hesitant to bring him up given what she's been through in that relationship. Every time I've mentioned him in the past, she changed the subject faster than I could process what she was doing. She hasn't talked to him since she ran away to Switzerland with me, although I know for a fact he's been trying to reach her.

Things will fall into place in their own time, I guess.

18

Bad News

Calla

Speaking with Mia brought clarity to a few things. The first being that I can't sacrifice my career for anyone, not even Ace—my *fiancé*. The weight of that new title feels strange in my mind.

It's not that I'm choosing myself over Ace...or maybe it is. But can't I be selfish for once? I've worked my ass off for the last few years to be in the position I am today, and it seems counterproductive to throw all of it away when I'm almost at the finish line.

Once my one-year contract in Switzerland is complete, I'll have the flexibility to work from anywhere I want. While the job will still require occasional travel, it will also provide me with some leniency.

So here I am, about to tell Ace that even though I'll stand

by his side until the end, I need to return to Switzerland until my contract is finished. It's the least I can do for myself, for my career, for my dream of becoming a successful journalist who makes a difference in this tumultuous world.

However, as I pass by reception and step foot into Ace's office, everything changes. The decision I made just mere minutes ago becomes nothing but a distant hum in my mind.

Before I even seek out Ace, I sense something is wrong. My stomach drops, and a sour feeling expands in my throat.

In all the years I've known Ace, there was only one instance when I walked into a scene similar to this. It happened back in college. I returned to our shared house after visiting my father, and when Ace didn't respond to my pounding on his door, I barged in to find a turbulent mess.

His room was flipped upside down, as if a monster had ravaged through it—the same monster Ace battled within his own mind.

Though not as horrifying as the scene five years ago, this is reminiscent enough to freeze me in place.

Loose papers litter the marble floors, some crumpled, others bearing the imprint of footprints, as if Ace was examining them before succumbing to one of his episodes. His leather office chair lies overturned by the window, and his shattered phone rests on the floor. The vase, filled with fresh flowers that get changed each week, now lies shattered. The water seeps onto the scattered papers.

I don't waste time looking around the rest of the room for damage. Material possessions can be replaced. Instead,

I rush into his personal bathroom, following the sound of running water.

As soon as I fling the door open, our gazes meet in the mirror. Ace's bloodshot eyes reflect anguish, his expression grave, as if the worst has happened. And of course, that's where my mind spirals. What else am I supposed to think?

Did he hear something about his trial? Did he get some insight into the jury? Nik suggested it would be a good idea to apply for a judge-only trial considering Ace's reputation. He said the jury would be more likely to have biased opinions before the evidence is presented.

"Ace, what's wrong?" I step closer to him. "Whatever it is, we can work through it. We can fix it."

He shakes his head. "Ellie—" He struggles to get the remainder of the words out, but I already know what he's about to say.

My world shatters.

That one word, one name, is enough to change everything.

"No." I refuse to believe it. "She's okay, isn't she?"

Among all the scenarios that had plagued my thoughts since entering the bathroom, I hadn't considered this one while preparing for the worst. The shock must be evident on my face. I can't conceal the overwhelming disbelief rapidly consuming me.

My heart pounds in my chest, and a lump forms in my throat. It's impossible to swallow, no matter how hard I try. It seems to grow with each attempt, threatening to suffocate me. But I can't allow myself to reach that point. I need to hold it together, for both of us. Taking a deep breath, I attempt to fill my lungs with as much air as possible, but it's not enough, especially when Ace continues to speak.

"She's sick again," he whispers, his voice on the brink of breaking.

"Wh-what do you mean? How? She just recovered." She just finished her last round of treatment before I left for Switzerland.

"They found abnormal cells at her routine checkup. The doctors think it's from the intensive treatment she's received over the years. There was always a chance of side effects, of her developing other types of cancers from the aggressive treatments..." Ace's voice wavers. "The chances of her developing another type of cancer were slim. Even the doctors are taken back by her situation," he says this like he thinks it's his fault. As if he could have prevented it.

Shaking my head, I counter. "There's *nothing* you could've done to prevent this."

He swallows hard, the weight of guilt pressing down on him. "So why does it feel like it is my fault? I should've been there for her. I shouldn't have left the country. I should've spent more time with her, because now we don't know what's going to happen, whether she'll be able to recover from this."

"There's *nothing* you could've done," I repeat.

Unable to bear the distance between us any longer, I cross the room, stumbling over my own feet and wrapping my arms around him. I'm not sure if I do it for myself or for him. It feels like we both need this, and I feel selfish for being as broken as him.

I should be his support, but with everything going on, I'm not prepared for *this*. This is the worst-case scenario, and I'm afraid of what could happen if he loses Ellie.

If we *both* lose Ellie.

How much can a person endure before they simply can't anymore?

Can't breathe.

Can't handle everything the universe throws at them.

Can't survive.

Just *can't*.

"Ace…" I have no words to lessen the blow of the news he received.

"Calla. I need you right now more than ever. I need you to make this day bearable, because I don't know what the point is anymore," he says, his voice desperate.

I look into Ace's eyes and see the battle raging inside. It brings me pain to see him holding on to the last thread of hope, not knowing what will come out of things.

His body collapses against mine. At first, I do my best to hold the both of us up, but he's extremely heavy, and after a few seconds, my body gives in. Ace notices my struggle, and he directs his weight off me, but it's like his legs can't physically hold him up any longer. His knees hit the bathroom floor. The thud in the awfully silent room is like thunder.

I flinch from the impact.

I've only seen him on his knees once before, and that was when I found out the truth about the car accident.

It hurts to see him like this, so broken, so beyond hope and full of guilt for something he couldn't have prevented. But he thinks it's his karma for what he's done, and I can't imagine what a toll that's taken on his mental health.

We remain like that for what seems like an eternity. His head cradled at my chest, my arms around him—fingers intertwined in his soft hair. He lifts his head and looks at me with those damn broken eyes. The ones that could stop the world from spinning on its axis. They are filled with a decade of shit that no person should ever have to go through, but it made him the person he is today.

And I understand the unspoken plea in his eyes. People have ways to deal with pain—for some it's alcohol or drugs, for others it's seeking adrenaline. For us it's the physical act that brings two people together and makes them forget about all the horrible events happening around them.

And even though Addilyn warned us that a moment like this would come, and we'd need to confront the issues and not rely on that physical connection, I can't deny him right now.

His eyes hold a clear need, one I haven't seen before. It's desperate, frenzied and anarchic. And for the life of me, I can't resist it.

Not this time.

He needs me. And perhaps I need him just as much too.

19

Beg Me

Calla

Ace lifts his head, looks at me with those blue-green eyes. "Calla," he rasps my name, his breath hitting my chest.

We both know I'm done for. I'll give him anything in this moment if it means he will feel even a tiny bit better. If it means those eyes will contain a little less pain. I can't bear to see him like this.

So I do the only thing I know to do. I cup his cheeks with both of my hands, run my thumb over his soft lips. He plants his hand on my wrist, keeps it there for a little while longer. We just stare into each other's eyes.

The moment intimate and vulnerable.

And then I see the exact moment Ace buries that vulnerability deep within. It's almost like a switch flips, and there's this void in his eyes. No sadness, no anger, no joy. Just nothing except perhaps a glint of desire, and it's directed solely at me.

He does what he does best. Blocking the painful memories out. Burying them in the deepest parts of himself. Looking for something that will numb the pain, if only just for a little while.

His hand leaves my wrist and trails up my neck, to my jaw. His touch awakens every part of me. He tilts my face down so our lips are parallel, and only a breath apart. We remain like that for a few beats, but those few beats are an entire silent conversation between us.

Ace brushes his soft lips against mine. The touch is so faint and tempting, I lean down for more. The second time, it's firmer, more convicting. His warm tongue plunges into my mouth, meeting with mine.

I allow myself to get lost for a second. But then I hear myself saying, "We probably shouldn't." Even though there's nothing more I want at this moment.

Ace pulls back, looks directly in my eyes. "Say the word, Calla, and I won't. I won't kiss you. I won't touch you. I won't make you have that ache in between your thighs that I know you love."

"You're being unfair," I complain. This man knows me in and out, knows what words to say to make me cave. Even though I should tell him to stop, I don't want to.

I crave a hit of him like he's a damn drug.

Addictive.

Tempting.

His crooked smile is both cheeky and irresistible. He knows he's got me this time. "Life is unfair. Sometimes we have to seize the moment and enjoy the *ride*." He slides his hand down my waist, pulling me closer.

"Ace…"

"Yes, love?"

My gaze darts to his wooden desk and the floor-to-ceiling window overlooking the entire city, and I can't help where my mind goes. From the first time I walked into this office and saw him behind it, dressed in work wear and all muscle, it's been in the back of my mind. Of course, at the time I blocked those thoughts out because… Well, because I'm stubborn.

Ace notices where my mind is at, where my eyes are still lingering, and he seizes the opportunity. "You want me to fuck you while you watch the entire city below? How long have you fantasized about it?"

I gulp. Still not used to Ace's way with words. Each time he says something crude, it makes me feel a million things. All of them are filthy. My legs weaken at the thought of him bending me over that desk or pressing me against the window. And as much as I don't want us to always resort to sex in these situations, perhaps it's the way we'll always be. It's like trying to change our neurons. It's not entirely impossible, but if you manage to do it, you'll also change as a person.

So I let go. I stop fighting it. I allow this intimacy between us to numb the ache in my heart. To freeze my wandering thoughts. If only just for a moment.

"Since I walked into your office almost a year ago," I admit.

His eyes charge with electricity, indicating he's basking in my answer. "Why didn't you say so, love?"

He's up on his feet in an instant, pulling me up with him and leading us for his desk. In a fluid motion, he clears his desk, adding to the mess on the floor. My heart rate accelerates as he turns to me, his hands finding my waist and pulling my hips to his.

His shaft grows against me, straining his jeans. It seems like it's always ready to go. "Are you always hard?" I push myself into him to prove my point.

Ace chuckles. "Ninety nine percent of the time when I'm around you."

I move my hips slightly up and down, teasing him and loving how he feels on me through the stiff material. My hands fly to his belt and undo the buckle.

Ace perches my ass up on his desk, picks up his office chair and rights it as if nothing happened. He sits in it, deliberately positioning himself between my legs and rolling up his sleeves, revealing his toned, veiny forearms.

Excitement surges to the apex of my thighs, the uncomfortable pressure building there with each one of Ace's moves.

With his gold watch gleaming on his wrist and the intricate ink designs on his hands and arms, he exudes an unmistakable aura of authority and dominance. A powerful man who seems to want only me.

"What... What are you doing?" I ask, breathless while my stomach does these little somersaults.

"What does it look like?" Ace sets each of his hands on my thighs and pulls them apart, revealing the dusty-blue G-string with little diamantes. "I haven't had lunch yet."

Oh my. This man, *my* man, is unapologetically filthy.

I'm a sucker for lingerie, my taste for it has grown in the last year. It's beautiful and makes me feel like a million bucks. The only downside—it's expensive as shit. But when someone as sensual as Ace stares at me with this much desire, it makes every dollar spent worth it.

"Fucking hell, Calla." Ace sucks in a breath. "And you wonder why I always have a hard-on around you. Are you trying to fucking kill me with these?" He runs his thumb down my slit, and the material of the G-string dips into my folds.

"Something like that," I manage to say while he keeps moving his thumb in an up-and-down motion meticulously slow.

He pulls back, dips his middle finger in his perfect mouth—*God, help me*—moves my panties to the side and slowly slides the finger inside of me.

A moan escapes my mouth while Ace's eyes are on me. He has a satisfied expression on his face like he's getting his own pleasure by watching me react to him.

In an instant, that expression turns devilish, and I know exactly what's coming. "Don't rip—" I go to warn him, but the material of my underwear tears under his touch.

"You know me better than to ask that of me." His smirk is both condescending and cocky. "I like to unwrap my presents." With both of his hands on my thighs, he wraps his fingers around my flesh and jerks me forward.

A gasp leaves my throat as my ass floats on the edge of the desk. He leans down, trailing his incredible mouth over one of my thighs, taking his goddamn time. He sucks on the inner part of it, and I gasp, arching my back.

I grab his head and guide it on my aching core. I hear the rumbling of Ace's chuckle, *feel* the vibrations of it against my inner thighs pulsating all the way to the tender spot requiring all his attention.

"So fucking impatient," he murmurs but obliges me. He dips his head and drags his tongue up my slit, gathering all my wetness.

If I could see the scene from a different perspective—me on the wooden desk with my thighs spread, Ace lounging in his leather chair all businesslike with his head buried in between my thighs—I think I would come undone on the spot. Just from witnessing how freaking erotic the image is.

When he wraps his entire mouth around my clit and sucks with pure determination, I grab his hair tightly and cry out. "Yes, just like that."

He worships me with the tongue I'll never get enough of, while his fingers plunge inside of me, curling, hitting that upper wall with such precision that my eyes roll in the back of my head. All thoughts evade me, the good and the bad. All I can think about is how I'm so close to coming on his face.

Ace groans when I squeeze my thighs around his head. "So fucking wet."

I feel every single bump and groove of his tongue gliding over the needy bundle of nerves. I continue to tangle my fingers through his hair, guiding him—not that he needs it—exactly where I want him. I grind my hips in his face shamelessly while his mouth makes out with my pussy. Circling his tongue in a beautiful rhythm with just enough pressure to make me die completely satisfied, he also manages to praise me.

"Fuck yeah, this is so fucking hot," he groans against me. The deep rumbling of his voice, and the way he wraps his mouth around me, continuing to suck and twirl his tongue in an unholy manner sends me over the edge.

I throw my head back and squeeze my thighs tightly around his head when the euphoria takes over, consuming me like a wild, raging fire. I'm writhing and panting his name the way I know he loves.

"That's it, love. Come on my face. Just like that." Ace finally stops licking, but he continues to fuck me with his fingers slowly, cupping my breast with the other hand, letting my high take over. Once I come back down, he places the palm of his hand on my clit with some pressure, and my world explodes.

I'm coming again.

Hard.

Where the fuck did he learn that trick?

When it finally dissipates, I return my gaze to him. He

has this content look on his face like he's won the lottery. I place my hand on his cheek, which is glistening with my arousal, and I wonder how the hell I got this lucky.

"I'm nowhere near done with you, love," he says as he rises from the chair. His jeans strain against the massive hard-on he's sporting.

"I would hope not. Otherwise, I'd probably have to file a complaint with HR for unsatisfactory service," I retort, breathless, unable to resist the urge to tease him.

He raises a dark brow, but a shadow of a smile dances on his lips. "Unsatisfactory? You shouldn't have said that."

"Is that so?" I continue to tease him, getting a thrill out of it.

Ace pulls me up from the desk, keeping me steady with his hand around my waist. His lips ghost mine. "I'm going to fuck you so hard that you'll forget your own name, let alone the meaning of *unsatisfactory*."

With his words, exhilaration surges from my toes to deep within my belly. He slips the straps of my dress off, and it pools around my ankles.

"Place your hands on the window," Ace instructs. I gulp but do as I'm told. He rewards me with, "Such a good girl."

Looking out at the view of the city below me, I stand naked with both of my hands on the window. The thought of someone seeing me, seeing *us*, doesn't shame me. Instead, it thrills me to no end, adding to the intensity of the moment.

I hear the sound of Ace's jeans unzipping and then dropping on the floor. His strong hands grip my hips as he presses himself against me from behind, his mouth grazing along my neck. "You're so beautiful," he murmurs, his voice thick with desire. "So perfect like this." His erection presses hard against my ass and sends a shiver of pleasure down my spine. "You're mine," he states possessively. "All mine."

In this moment, with the cityscape spread out before me and Ace's hands on my body, I feel truly alive.

I push my ass out, and Ace places his large hands on it, digging his fingers into my skin. "Now beg me to fuck you."

"Wh-what?"

"You heard me, Calla." He spreads my thighs, cups my breast in one of his hands from behind, toying with my nipple. He circles my sensitive clit with the other hand. "Beg. For. My. Cock." With each word, he plunges his middle finger inside of me, ensuring that it hits my G-spot.

Moans spill from my lips as I recall the words he said to me following our first therapy session.

"Don't start something you have no intention of finishing. Before you know it, you'll be begging me to fuck you."

This freaking asshole doesn't forget anything, but I refuse to let him win. Yes, I'm stubborn. We both are.

"Ace...please." I try again, grinding my ass on his fingers, but each time I push myself back, he inches away. Toying with me.

"Please what, love? I can do this all day. I know your body better than you do. And this pretty pussy—" he cups it in his hand, "—won't come until I tell it to."

I know he means each word. I'm once again aching for

his touch, aching for that release, aching for him to be inside of me. "Ace, please fuck me."

He chuckles. "I thought you'd never ask."

He drags his shaft up and down my entrance, lubing it up with my own arousal. With his length coated, Ace slowly teases my entrance, eliciting soft moans within my throat. His warm breath hits the back of my neck as he positions himself perfectly and then begins to push inside of me.

"Take all of me. Just like that," he encourages.

The sensation is intense, overwhelming, and I gasp as he drives all of himself into me. As I adjust to the size of him, I feel every inch of him, stretching me in all the right ways. The position we're in, with me bent over, only adds to the depth of the sensation. It feels as if he's reaching places no one else has before. "You're so deep." I breathe, feeling him fill me completely. "It feels incredible."

Ace's grip tightens on my hips as he sets a relentless pace, each thrust bringing us closer to the edge. He pulls out almost completely before driving himself back in. Over and over. Hitting all the right spots with each stroke.

As he continues to move inside me, his fingers find my clit, and he begins to circle it in time, his thrusts sending sparks of pleasure coursing through my body.

"Yes. Harder," I moan.

He obliges, not only with his strokes but also with his fingers, and the cavernous feeling in my belly comes alive, intensifying. Building.

The only sound in the room is the sound of our skin

clashing together in a sinful rhythm. It's like the entire world has faded away, leaving the two of us lost in a haze of longing.

The tension in me snaps. A wave of pleasure washes over me. It's so intense that I can't help but cry out as I come around him. My walls clench, every muscle in my body tightens and releases with waves of pleasure.

I can barely hear Ace's grunts as my own climax hurls him over the edge, his length pulsing inside of me.

When the physical bliss fades, the reality sets in again. And all the shitty feelings we were trying to bury come rushing in.

20

In Sickness & In Health

Calla

A ce parks in the driveway. The load of our shared silence sags heavily in the air. Soft music from the car stereo seeps out, the familiar tunes of the Arctic Monkeys satiate the space between us.

When Ace cuts the engine, we both sit in the car for a moment longer. I brace myself for the worst, even though I only saw Ellie a few days ago. She looked fine, healthy...didn't she? She couldn't possibly deteriorate in the span of days...

Deteriorate. That word is vile when used about the human body, but how else can I describe what cancer does to someone so important in your life? It eats away at the vital parts of a person. It's a parasite.

Ace exits the car, heads over to my side and opens the door for me. His mask slides on effortlessly, as though he's been practicing since he heard the news. I'm not as good at hiding my emotions like Ace is. Even though I try to put a brave face on for Ellie and Reese, I'm sure they can easily see through it. It almost feels like a lie to pretend that everything is okay. But Ace knows his sister and his mom better than anyone else, and if he thinks this is the right way to approach it, I'll follow his lead.

Reese, Ace's mom, works in the garden. A white shirt beneath denim overalls clings to her, and she turns at the sound of our footsteps. Strands of hair come loose from her ponytail. Tired eyes flicker over us, and a small smile paints on her mouth.

"You're gardening," Ace observes, more of a statement than a question.

"The weeds are taking over the beds." Her words carry an undercurrent of something deeper than just concern for the plants.

Perhaps she needs a moment alone to process the news she's received. Or maybe she's exhausted after putting on a smile and a brave face for Ellie. Whatever it is, she has every right to have some moments to herself.

Ace stares at her and then nods in acknowledgment.

"Go on in. I'll finish up here and come in soon."

He nods again and then asks. "Are you okay?"

That's a bit of a stupid question. How can Reese be okay? She watched her daughter go through treatments, not once but twice, unsure if she would make it. And now she's about to repeat the process all over again.

Ace must realize this, and his eyebrows furrow together. He shakes his head slightly.

"Sure," Reese replies, her tone implying she's far from it.

We walk into the house, and I'm taken aback by how much has changed. Yet at the same time, nothing has. Physically, the house remains the same. Perhaps the only difference is the bouquet of flowers on the hallway table. The atmosphere has shifted though.

The last time I was here, it felt warm and smelled of freshly baked cookies. Now, I shiver as we walk through the sweeping hallway. I'm not sure if it's the colder weather or the reality of Ellie's sickness staring me straight in the face. As much as I try to come to terms with it, I can't.

Why?

Why her? Is this truly karma for what Ace has done? But it can't be. The world can't be that cruel to punish a little girl for her brother's mistakes. No matter how terrible they are.

Ellie's on the sofa, perched in front of the flat screen TV, cocooned in a cozy blanket. Her bright eyes peek out from the pillow stack she's built.

"Hey." Ace is the first one to speak.

Ellie's head spins toward his voice, and her eyes instantly light up. I'm forever in awe of the bond between them. Despite their significant age gap, it has never been a barrier.

"Hi! I didn't know you were coming today," Ellie says, her voice full of genuine astonishment.

Ace shrugs casually, offering her a small smile. "Surprise. How are you feeling?"

"Fine." Ellie brushes the question off. "Hi, Calla."

What does "fine" feel like for her? I bet it's different from an average person's fine. What does it feel like to have your own body relentlessly attacking itself, even after you believe the battle is won?

"Hey," I greet her, attempting to infuse my voice with artificial optimism. Deep down, I know it emerges hollow. I can't help but feel guilty for putting on a show. I have a nagging suspicion that Ellie can see right through it.

"What are you watching?" Ace asks her.

Forest Gump. I recognize the movie before Ellie answers.

"*Forest Gump.*" Ellie holds up the remote and twirls it in her hand. "Number three on the list of one hundred must-watch movies before you die."

Ace's brows shoot up, obviously not expecting that answer. "Morbid," he mutters under his breath, shaking his head. Then in a louder voice, he asks, "And what was number one?"

"*The Shawshank Redemption.*" Ellie's eyes wander back to the screen when the main character sits on the bench and delivers one of the best lines in the movie about life being like a box of chocolates.

As those words hang in the air, I can't help but find them relatable.

"Good movie, but *The Lion King* should've made number one," Ace remarks playfully and winks.

"I'm not five anymore," Ellie retorts matter-of-factly, rolling her eyes in response to Ace's comment.

"Wow." Ace raises his hands in surrender, a mock expression of surprise on his face. "Didn't think there was an age limit on Disney movies. Did you, Calla?"

"Disney movies are the best," I chime in.

"I'm trying to explore other genres," Ellie says. "There are a few lists that I've saved. Must-read books before you die, 101 things to do before you die."

A faint crease builds in Ace's forehead at her words. She's not saying it outright, but it's clear she's somehow come to terms with her prognosis and is possibly expecting the worst.

"Well, you have a long time before that happens," Ace says in his most convincing tone, like he genuinely believes it himself.

For the remainder of the day, we make a small dent in Ellie's to-watch movie pile. Reese comes in near the end of *The Silence of the Lambs*—a sinister movie for a kid, but Ellie didn't seem to bat an eyelid throughout the entire film.

Freshly showered and dressed in a cozy striped cashmere sweater and black leggings, Reese joins us on the sofa, cradling a steaming mug of coffee. Ace and Ellie are engrossed in the climactic scene of the movie, where Hannibal Lecter escapes from prison. I've already seen this movie and know how it ends, so instead I watch Reese.

A bittersweet smile graces her lips as she brings the "best mother in the world" mug to her lips once more. Her eyes remain fixed on her two children together, talking, smiling, laughing at something Ace said that I missed. It's these little moments that become big memories. They usually go unphotographed, so I quickly pick up my phone and snap a photo, but not even a photo can do it justice.

Reese's eyes slide to me, and for a brief moment, there's this current that passes through us. Like somehow, we know this exact point in time is special.

Just then, Nik emerges from the hallway, his imposing figure jamming the room, his eyes scanning the four of us. In one hand, he holds a rectangular box.

"Sorry, I knocked a few times, but no one answered. I saw Ace's car in the driveway and heard the TV, so I figured you didn't hear me knock."

Reese waves her hand. "Don't worry about it. You're welcome here anytime. You're family." She barely gets the words out before Ellie leaps off the sofa and races for him.

"Nikky, you're here!" Ellie squeals, wrapping her arms around his torso.

Nik gently pats her back, a slight furrow forming on his brow. "What did I say about that nickname?" he chides.

"You said if I ever called you that again, you wouldn't bring me donuts. But..." She takes the box from him, a mischievous glint in her eyes. "You brought donuts, so..." She peeks inside the box. "My favorite, too."

Nik shakes his head, a smile playing on his lips. "There's always next time."

"Oh, does Nikky not like his nickname?" Ace teases from the sofa, chuckling.

Ace had told me he'd introduced Nik to his family. He'd mentioned they all got along, but this is the first time I'm witnessing it for myself, and I'm looking forward to seeing more of it.

"Shut up," Nik grumbles, though his tone is laced with amusement.

"Okay, if you two are going to start a fight, maybe do it outside. The last time you broke the glass on my coffee table." Reese rises from the sofa and retrieves the empty mug from what I assume is the new coffee table.

I raise my brows in surprise. "They broke it?" That would've been a sight to see, two grown men going for it in the middle of the room—though I hope it was play fighting and not an actual fight.

"It was Ace," Nik says at the same time Ace says, "It was Nik."

Ellie and Reese both roll their eyes, and then Reese disappears into the kitchen while Nik makes himself comfortable on the sofa. Ellie opens the box of donuts, and Ace reaches for one, but she slaps his hand away.

"Wow, is that how it is?" Ace feigns hurt.

"Don't you have the biggest fight of your career coming up? Weren't you the one who told us to make sure we keep all the junk away from you?"

"Hmm. Nope, don't remember."

"Well, I do."

"You can't just eat that in front of me. It's cruel."

"I can, and I will."

Ace shakes his head like he can't believe it.

I mean, Ellie does have a point. Ace's fight is in a couple of weeks, and he's been on top of his diet and training. It would be a shame for him to fall off the wagon now, though I think he's joking about the donuts. He has more self-control than most.

Ellie pushes the box in my direction. "Do you want some?" she offers.

"I drove forty minutes to get them. They're the best you'll ever taste," Nik says.

"In that case... Sorry, Ace." I shrug apologetically as I take one from the box Ellie still holds out for me.

I bite into it, and I'm in heaven. The soft and pillowy texture gives way to a burst of sweetness from the sugary glaze. "Wow." I cover my mouth as I chew. "This is so good."

"I know," Ellie replies and offers the box to Nik.

I leave the three of them to bond and make my way to the kitchen where I find Reese peeling potatoes.

"What can I do?" I ask her.

She lifts her head at my voice, a small smile painting her mouth. "Here, if you can take over this, that would be great."

"Of course." I pick up a potato and start peeling.

As we prepare dinner together—a roast with potatoes, carrots and pumpkin—we listen to the laughter emanating from the living room.

"How was it when Ace first told you about Nik?" I ask Reese, hoping I'm not stepping out of line. After all, I'm sort of asking her how she felt about her ex-husband cheating on her all those years ago.

Surely she knew about all the women, or at least suspected, like Ace did.

She exhales.

"Sorry," I say. "It's not any of my business. I shouldn't…" I begin to stammer my apologies. What was I thinking, asking her that?

But she surprises me by replying, "To say I was shocked wouldn't suffice. Though I think a part of me knew there was a possibility of it. I just never thought the result of one of his affairs would end up on my doorstep dressed in a suit."

I can't imagine what it felt like when Ace brought Nik here to introduce him to his family. I hope he warned them beforehand and didn't just show up on the front door with his brother.

"How did Ellie react?"

"She took it quite well. Better than me, I suppose. Although it might have something to do with Nik's age. It was easier to explain to her that she had another brother. It would've been more difficult if Nik was younger than Ace," Reese says. "But I need to give her more credit. She's acts a lot older than her age. She probably knows what we're all trying to hide from her."

We finish up with dinner, and then everyone gathers around the dining table. We've all ignored the elephant in the room till now.

"So when does the treatment start?" Ace asks. "I want to be there." Even after everything, there's hope in his voice, a tiny spark of optimism flickering.

Ellie and Reese exchange a look containing so much. Ellie drops her gaze back to her plate and picks at the food.

It's like she's afraid to glance at Ace when her mom delivers the next few words, afraid of how Ace will react to them.

"Ellie isn't doing the treatment."

My head darts to Ace, watching his reaction.

He sets his cutlery down, grabs a napkin and wipes his mouth. He's biding his time, processing the information before reacting to it. Eventually, his piercing eyes find Reese's. "Why the hell not?" His voice overflows with acute confusion and accusation.

Nik doesn't say anything. Though instead of carrying the potato to his mouth, he sets the fork back down and focuses on the conversation.

"We decided it's not the right path for Ellie anymore." Reese comes across calm, but I spot her right hand unsteady. She quickly tries to hide it by placing it on her lap underneath the table. She's not scared of Ace, but she's scared of how this decision will affect her family. She's scared how Ace will take the news, and what will result from it.

She's worried not only about Ellie, but how Ace and maybe even Nik will cope with that decision.

"*Who* decided that?" Ace bites out, his jaw working a million miles an hour.

Nik clears his throat. Ace either doesn't hear him or pretends not to. I watch as Nik fights with the decision of whether to say something or whether to remain silent and watch how this plays out. Usually, he has no issues with calling his brother out, but in this setting, he might think it's not his place.

"The doctors say there's little chance she'll recover from this. Treatment might do more harm than good..." Reese begins, but Ace doesn't let her finish.

He clenches his jaw and shakes his head like he can't believe what he's hearing. Like he's trying to understand what Reese is saying but his brain can't compute it.

"More harm than good? Ellie is *dying*—" he spits the word like it's acid in his mouth. Reese physically flinches, but Ellie doesn't. "What's more harmful than that? *Who* decided not to do treatment?" Ace asks again.

Nik sits up straighter, his shoulders taut. He might not be used to this—the family arguments—and may be unsure of how to act. I'm in the same situation. I'm used to arguing with Ace. I can hold my ground with him and tell him when he's in the wrong, but this is different.

Do I have any right to say anything?

Do I want to?

If I look at the situation impassively, I can understand both perspectives. Ellie's life quality has decreased over time. Her life has been consumed by treatments—attending appointments, enduring the side effects, missing out on typical childhood activities. All of this, only to be given false hope and then be told she has to go through it again. And now once more. We *all* can see what she's going through, but it's one thing to see someone suffering and another to experience it firsthand.

"Ace—" Reese begins.

"I did, okay?" Ellie says, her voice desperate to stop

the tension building. Ace's eyes navigate to Ellie. "I can't do this anymore. All I've done these last few years is go to treatments, be pricked and probed like I'm a human pincushion, and each time, the outcome of the treatments gets less certain. I don't want to go through this again and be told it didn't work and there's nothing else they can do for me." Ellie speaks and acts older than her age. Gone is the little girl I met five years ago.

"What? So you'd rather give up and *die*?" Ace's question pierces the air, causing both of their faces to reflect the pain they feel.

"Ace," Reese hisses.

"What, Mom? You don't like me telling the truth? You all want to pretend that's not the case? That's what is going to happen if she doesn't do the treatment. She's going to die," Ace says. Although he isn't exactly yelling, his tone is equal parts accusatory and impulsive.

"It's not your decision," Reese calmly responds, attempting to maintain her composure.

"So you're going to let a ten-year-old dig her own grave?"

"Ace!" I say, finally unable to sit back and watch him be spiteful just to get what he wants. Because that's what he's doing, isn't it? Trying to say anything to get Ellie to change her mind. To make Reese force Ellie into treatment.

He shoots me a look. "Whose side are you on?"

Whose side I'm on? Is he for real?

"I'm on no one's side, Ace."

"Sure fucking seems like it."

"The doctors say there's little chance that the treatment will even work. It could be all for nothing," Reese says.

Ace considers this, shaking his head in the process. He's looking at all of us like we've gone mad.

"I'm coming to the next doctor's appointment. I want to hear it for myself."

And that settles it. The remainder of dinner passes in awkward silence. Everyone's lost their appetite, so it's just the sound of forks scraping against plates, pushing the food around aimlessly.

Ace doesn't say another word—not when we leave, not on the drive back despite my attempts to talk to him, not until we're parked in the basement of his apartment building.

"Fuck!" Ace slams his palm against the steering wheel. And like that's not enough, he proceeds to do it three more times.

I don't flinch, I don't blink, I don't react at all. I've grown accustomed to his rare outbursts. They used to be much more frequent than this. I wait in case there's more, but when his broad shoulders sag, and his body sinks further into the leather seat, I know he has nothing left to give.

I place a hand over his, gently caressing his knuckles with my thumb. "You can't make her go through treatment again."

"I know." He sighs like he's already come to terms with it. He turns his hand up, lacing our fingers together.

Does he regret his outburst at dinner? I've never seen him behave like that around Ellie and Reese. Was that a first or have there been other instances?

"What will happen if she does the treatment because of

you and it fails? She might spend whatever time she has left resenting you."

He gives my hand a light squeeze. "I'd rather her resent me and fight for her life than to just give up."

"I don't think she sees not doing the treatment as 'giving up'," I tell him. "She sees it as her chance to do everything she hasn't yet. She has a bucket list, and she's not going to tick anything off it confined to a hospital bed or going to doctor's appointments every second day. You've seen her go through treatment before. You've seen what it does to a person. How can you expect her to do that again when she doesn't want to?"

"You're on her side," he simply states, disappointment wavering in his voice.

He's acting like we're all against him. Like it's Ace versus everyone else. This isn't about him, and he doesn't understand that. All he can think about is not losing his little sister.

"There are no sides. Don't you see that, Ace? We're all in this together. We need to support Ellie no matter what."

"She's just a *child*. She doesn't know what she wants."

"Why is it so hard for you to accept that it's her decision?"

"Because if this all goes to shit—my trial, her prognosis... She'll be dead when I get out of prison."

My head swirls with the words he's thrown at me.

Dead.

Prison.

21

Therapy

Calla

I thought the second couples therapy session would be less nerve-racking than the first, but I was wrong. Standing near the entrance of the brick building, waiting for Ace, my mind races through countless scenarios. Some are hopeful, while others are not so much.

We have plenty to talk about. I have a feeling that both of us have been avoiding certain topics until this session, which is not what Addilyn wanted us to do.

There's also the...sexual encounter...we had in the shower. I'm sure it falls into the section of what Addilyn told us *not* to do. Although we did end up talking after, so I guess something worked. But that doesn't even matter, since we resorted to sex in his office after he received the worst news possible.

I know some people might not understand, but that's

just how it is between us. That physical connection numbs the hurt for a little while. And sometimes, we need a few moments when it feels like we're not falling apart anymore.

It's half past seven. Our appointment time is ticking. We only have half an hour, which isn't nearly enough time to discuss everything we haven't spoken about since the last session with Addilyn.

I shift from foot to foot and check the time on my phone for the third time.

We agreed to meet here since Ace had training right before this session. But seconds turn to minutes, and he still isn't here.

A surge of disappointment hits me. It seems like I'm being stood up by the most important person in my life. I try to convince myself he's just running late, yet something tells me that's not the case, and today will be just me.

An uncomfortable feeling of being watched gushes through me. My neck prickles, and a shudder jolts up my back. I take a moment to glance in both directions, trying not to appear too conspicuous as I act like I'm waiting for someone, but nothing out of the ordinary catches my eye.

People buzz about the streets, some strolling, some determined to get to their destination quickly. In the distance, the towering skyscrapers illuminate the city, casting a warm glow. Everything seems the same, but the feeling of unease persists. It unnerves me.

Am I just being paranoid?

Paranoia or not, I shoot a text to Ace asking him how

far away he is and whether I should go in or wait for him out front.

Ace: Can't make it today, sorry, love. I'll see you tonight.

No explanation. No phone call to let me know what's holding him up. His training sessions are usually flexible, and he's able to leave whenever he needs to. Even though I had a feeling this would happen, that he wouldn't come or eventually bail, it still hurts.

It feels like he's giving up on us, but that's probably not how he sees it.

On top of that, I'm angry at myself for being mad at him, considering everything's he's going through. It's understandable why he wouldn't want to participate in this. Our relationship and communication issues probably seem like minor hurdles to him amidst everything else.

And they are, but if we continue like this, it could easily create distance between us. We could find ourselves trapped in the same cycle we desperately tried to escape from.

I can't help but think that therapy is what he needs, not just for our relationship, but for himself as well. He's going through a major mental battle, and he's only letting me see the smallest part of it. It's not that I believe I can help him, but I want to be there for him. I want to be the person he can confide in against all odds.

But I also understand in respecting his decision. If he says therapy isn't for him, I shouldn't try and force it upon him. If I begin to press my opinions on him, it will break us.

Entirely.

I sigh and pull open the door to step inside Addilyn's building. The receptionist, a tall brunette with a blunt haircut, informs me Addilyn is ready to see me, and my feet carry me down the hallway and into her office.

Addilyn waits for me in her usual spot behind her desk. When I walk in, she briefly looks up at me and says, "Hello, Calla. Take a seat."

Though she doesn't say anything right at this minute, her gaze flickers behind me as if she's expecting Ace to be here too. When she understands he isn't with me, her eyes return to me.

The thing about Addilyn is that she never makes me feel judged, no matter what I disclose to her. She must have the best poker face in the world, because despite all the shit I've told her, she's only squinted at me a handful of times.

"Ace didn't come," she says in a flat tone that could imply a number of things.

Did you really think he would come to therapy with you?

Didn't you know after all this time that he would disappoint you?

At least she waited for me to take a seat before jumping in. I shake my head. "No."

Obviously not.

Addilyn gives me *that* look—the one that says *we've been at this for years. Tell me how you feel about the situation without me having to ask you.*

She's right. And as much as her questions annoy me sometimes, it's what I'm here for. "I'm not mad. I can't be. We only just found out his little sister is sick again, and he's not dealing with it well."

"Is that why he didn't come today? Because he's spending time with her?"

"I'm not sure. He didn't say."

Addilyn nods. "Okay. And has anything changed since the last time I saw you in terms of what I suggested?"

I really hoped Ace would be here with me so I didn't have to shamefully admit that we couldn't maintain a purely emotional relationship. There was still some level of intimacy between us, both in the shower, and then the other day. We've had two instances in the past two weeks, which I consider a good start for us.

"Intimacy helped us communicate."

Her eyes pierce into me, but as usual, she shows no emotion, leaving me clueless to her thoughts. I'd do anything to be able to get into her head and see how she views me.

Does she see me as this pathetic woman who longs for a man who caused her so much pain?

Does she see me as weak?

"So you didn't implement the changes to your relationship that I suggested?" she prompts.

"We tried," I say. "And it somewhat worked. We found a way to…satisfy…ourselves without the contact of the other person." Color rises to my cheeks. "But then we found out about Ellie…"

She nods, seemingly grasping the situation. I doubt she truly understands, so I refrain from saying more.

"Do you think now that his sister is going through this

again, he will begin to shut you out?"

"He'll shut everyone out. That's what he does best when so much is going through his head. It's his way of dealing with it. He'd rather be a burden to himself than anyone else."

"And how does it make you feel when he fails to open up to you after all you've experienced together?"

We seem to be going around in circles with no resolution in sight. But I have to be patient and give him time. I admit, I sound like a broken record, but how can I expect Ace to focus on our relationship when there's so much turmoil surrounding it?

I shrug in response to Addilyn's question. "It's his way of dealing with it," I repeat.

She continues to look at me. I didn't answer her question about my feelings, and truthfully, I'm unsure how I feel. "I don't know how I feel about it. Disappointed? But that's not the right word. More like frustrated, but I've learned to come to terms with it, I guess. That's just who Ace is as a person, and I know he's doing his best to let me in."

"Why do you think it's so hard for him to do that?"

"I think he has abandonment issues, starting from his father leaving when he was young and then..."

"And then?" Addilyn prompts me to go on, but I don't.

I shouldn't feel the way I do. I shouldn't feel guilty for leaving Ace after he revealed the most life-changing secret, but a part of me does.

And that's on me.

"Do you think you leaving him during college also contributed to Ace developing those abandonment issues?"

"How could it not?"

"Hmm."

Hmm.

Is that all she can say after such a confession?

"Let's shift the focus to you since Ace isn't here. You mentioned visiting your mother's grave. How did that go?"

I suck in a breath.

Here we go.

By the time I finish with therapy, I step outside into the refreshing night air. That familiar chill, the same as earlier, creeps up my spine, giving me the sensation of being watched. Once again, I glance around, concluding that I'm losing my mind. Adjusting the strap of my black handbag on my shoulder, I take a step forward.

Should I take the subway or get a taxi?

A car pulls up in front of me, and my heart rate spikes. Due to the anxiety rushing to my throat, it takes twice as long to recognize it, but when I do, a wave of relief washes over me.

Denzel.

Despite telling Ace I can manage on my own, I'm secretly grateful he arranged for Denzel to give me a ride. I swiftly climb into the back seat, shutting the door behind me, stealing one last glance at my surroundings.

And that's when I spot it—a shadow lurking near the

side of the building, blending seamlessly with the darkness.

"Everything alright?" Denzel asks.

I jump at the sound of his voice, and when I turn to look back at where I saw the shadowy figure, it has vanished.

What is wrong with me?

"Calla?" Denzel calls out, concerned.

I shake off my unease. "Yeah. Yeah, everything is fine."

Denzel continues to look at me through the rearview mirror for a moment longer, disbelief veiling his deep-set eyes. He chooses not to press further. Instead, he gives a slight nod and focuses on the road, shifting the car into drive.

When I return to the apartment, I find Ace already there, his phone pressed to his ear.

"I'll talk to you later." He ends the call when he notices me.

"You didn't come to therapy," I mention without accusing him, without questioning why he wasn't there. I want to give him the chance to explain himself without prying it out of him.

"Sorry," he replies. "I don't think I can do it at the moment. Not with the trial and Ellie. And the fight coming up."

I nod. "I understand."

He looks at me with an apology swirling in eyes. He comes closer and cups my cheeks in his large hands. "I'm sorry. And I promise once everything settles down, I'll come to therapy as much as you need me to."

"Okay."

"I mean it, Calla."

"I'm not mad," I say.

"You're not? I know how much it means to you."

"It's not what's important right now. There are bigger things at play."

Ace nods and takes a step back.

I swallow. I can see how Ace shuts down in front of me, and I hate it. I hate how easily he slides that mask over his face, trying to hide his emotions from me. Even though he doesn't fully succeed, I hate that he tries at all.

Talk to me.

Tell me how you feel.

We're meant to be a team.

I'm here for you.

Please don't push me away.

It's only the gist of what I want to say, but when I open my mouth, words evade me, and the night slips away.

22

Crystal Clear

Calla

After Ace told me about Ellie, there was no more wondering or asking myself what I should do. The answer is crystal clear. It became clear the moment I was presented with the heartbreaking tragedy.

I made my decision to stay in New York. Yes, my job is important to me, but being with the people I love is more important. Time is uncertain, especially for Ellie, and I couldn't bear the thought of leaving and something happening while I was away. I have to be here for her. For Ace and Reese. They need support now more than ever. They are facing the biggest challenge yet.

So my choice isn't really a choice. I need to be here for the people I love.

They are my family.

I sent an email to my boss, explaining the current situation, from Ace's trial to what's happening with Ellie. I'm praying the company understands. They don't have to accept my excuses. After all, there's a contract, and I'm not upholding my end of it. They could easily reply, stating I've breached the terms and terminate my employment. But I hope we can reach some sort of understanding or arrangement.

Ace's trial looms with each day, but we haven't discussed it since learning about Ellie. We spend every spare second with her, trying to tick off things from her bucket list. Some things were easy to tick off, others not so much due to Ace's confinement to New York.

Apart from the time we spend with Ellie, I rarely see Ace until I'm already nestled in the sheets, my eyes growing heavy. It's then he slips into bed beside me, smelling like his aftershave, burying his head in my hair and softly murmuring, "I love you."

Sometimes, when I'm still awake, I roll over to face him and reply, "I love you, too."

Lately, his eyes have appeared distant, somewhere a million light-years away. The only way to connect with him is to place my palm on his cheek, graze my fingers over the stubble there, and bring my mouth to his.

It's only when we get a taste of each other the world around us crumbles away. It's the only time when our defenses fall, and so does reality. In that moment, we're just two people who need to cling to each other. To cling to hope for the uncertain future.

Our movements are feverish. He wants to forget, if only for a few moments. I want to be burned, branded by him. To remember how it feels when his mouth touches my neck, his hands caress my curves. How he smiles when I gently bite his lip. His smile is everything and more when I haven't seen it in weeks.

His mouth, even though balmy, feels cool against the inside of my scorching thigh. I cling to his hair, which is longer, ragged at the top. His outgrown stubble intensifies the pleasure in between my thighs. His tongue teases me, and I throw my head back onto the pillow, chanting his name like it could be a damn prayer.

I want to remember all of this. Every single millisecond, because there might come a day when memories will be all I have. So I become in touch with all my senses as our bodies tangle in the sheets, fusing as one.

During the days when Ace is at work, training or keeping his distance from me, I busy myself as much as I can. I visit Reese and Ellie often, sometimes I run into Ace, and when I do, he always claims he's just about to leave.

Other days, I find myself on Betty's doorstep, desperate for guidance and human connection. I have Mia, but talking through a screen isn't the same. I wish she were here with me.

I'm at Reese's when I get a ping on my phone, alerting me that an email has come through. We just returned from lunch from an all you can eat dessert buffet. I feel ten pounds heavier, and I basically roll into the living room alongside Ellie and Reese.

"I don't want dinner." Ellie collapses on the sofa, her hands behind her head. She seems so normal today, it's hard to believe she's unwell.

Reese and I chuckle.

I glance at my phone screen, there's an email taking up most of the screen from *The Times*. My heart gallops. This is it.

I slide my finger over the screen, and the lengthy email opens. At first, I skim over it, not bothering to read the details, searching for the most important answer. *Am I fired?*

My heart sinks when I find the answer. It's not written in black and white, they concealed it in between the lines—perhaps not to seem insensitive to my situation. Yet it's clearly there.

"*It is with regret we inform you that we currently have no positions to offer you in New York. If you wish to return to Switzerland at a later date, please do reach out to our recruitment department.*"

But when will I return to Switzerland? Will it be weeks? Months?

The email basically says I'll have to reapply, and there's no guarantee I'll get a job again with *The Times*.

So that's it.

My fiancé is on trial for causing the accident that took my mom's life.

My father hates me.
Ellie is sick again.
And I lost my dream job.

23

Bucket List

Ace

The trial date has been set for exactly one month from today.

It will be the day that will alter everything. I struggle to imagine a future beyond the trial. I don't let my mind wander that far. Instead, I occupy my thoughts with other matters.

There's less than two weeks left till the biggest fight of my life, and it's not at the forefront of my mind like it should be. I've dedicated an entire year to training for this moment, and under different circumstances, I would be buzzing with excitement. But it has become yet another responsibility consuming time that could otherwise be spent with Ellie.

I should be focusing on getting in as much training as I can, but I don't care about any of it. None of it matters in the grand scheme of things.

"I don't agree with this," I say for what feels like the millionth fucking time, tightening my hands around the leather of the steering wheel. My knuckles blanch, but I can't stop.

"Don't agree with going to the museum or laser tag after?" Calla asks. "Actually, I'm astounded that Ellie hasn't done either of those things." She tries to make light of the situation, but it doesn't work.

"You know what I mean. Ticking items off the bucket list with her that she only made because she doesn't want to do the treatment and would rather die. It feels like I'm taking part in signing her fucking death sentence."

The leather creaks underneath my hands.

"You don't need to agree with it. You just have to accept that it's her decision." Calla places her hand on mine, comforting me.

We're once again sitting in the car in the driveway of my mom's house. I can't believe everyone talked me into this. I can't believe we're chasing fucking fairies instead of trying to convince Ellie to do the fucking treatment.

"How are you so okay with this?" I grit my teeth.

Her eyes flash with hurt, and she shakes her head. That was a stupid question.

Fuck.

My head's all over the place lately, thoughts scattered. I can't lose Ellie.

"I'm not okay with this, Ace. But there's nothing we can do or even say without taking this decision away from her.

And in a world where she doesn't have much control as it is, it will break her. She's made up her mind. She knows the consequences."

"Does she? There's a reason why the legal decision-making age is eighteen." My voice emerges harsher than I mean it to. My anger isn't directed at her, but I'm taking it out on anyone that gets in my way.

"Don't do that." Calla shakes her head.

"What?"

"Don't undermine her. You know she has the capacity to make this decision for herself."

"Does she?" I ask again, trying to keep my cool. "We all know the true consequence of her decision, but does she? She knows she will die, but it feels like she doesn't know the true meaning of that word. There will be no growing up, no falling in love with some jackass who will probably break her heart that I'll have to beat up because that's what big brothers do. No prom or graduation, no going off to college, or for her first job interview. No starting a family of her own."

How can she so easily palm her future off? I don't understand how our mom is letting her do that without a fight.

I'm so fucking mad. Mad at the both of them. I'm angry at Ellie for not continuing to fight, and I'm angry at our mom for allowing this to happen.

I don't know what it's like for Ellie, and I won't pretend that I do. But she has a lot to fight for. Her entire future is ahead of her. What's a decade when you could have at least seven times that?

I would do anything to trade positions with her. To bear all of it for her.

No one knows what it's like to be on the verge of losing one of the most important people in your life until it's actually happening.

Nik arrives ten minutes after us. I didn't realize he was invited.

A family reunion.

Fucking great.

What more could I fucking want?

Ellie skips into the hallway with a big smile on her face. It wipes my frown right off seeing her happy. It also brings an extra pang to my chest knowing our time is limited if she doesn't do any treatment. Unless there's a miracle.

And we all know how I feel about miracles. They don't exist. At least not in my world.

"Ready to go?" I ask all of them.

"Oh, cheer up," Ellie says. "I'll go easy on you in laser tag."

"You better," Nik chimes in. "We all know how much of a crybaby he is when he doesn't win."

I death stare him for a few seconds.

"What? Did you forget the time we kicked your ass in Mario Kart?" he reminds me. "You stormed outside like a two-year-old with your tail in between your legs." He chuckles.

"I got a fucking phone call." I shake my head.

"Hey, language," Mom warns.

I roll my eyes. Ellie has heard it all before. She's witnessed far worse. She's picked a death sentence, goddamn it. But I keep my thoughts to myself. I don't want to ruin this day, and my opinion doesn't make a difference here apparently.

They made that pretty fucking clear.

We shuffle out the door and pile into my car. It's a bit stuffy, or it might just be me. I crack open my window to allow the fresh air to filter through and turn up the music.

Our first stop is the museum, an impressive structure, sleek and modern, standing tall before us. I've managed to book out the entire place for a few hours, so it's just us. We have a guide, a young guy with a nose ring. He seems like he knows what he's talking about. Or he could be just making shit up on the spot, who knows? He speaks at the rapid pace of a race car, and I can barely keep up.

Eventually, I stop listening.

All I know is that Ellie seems happy. Her eyes light up with excitement and curiosity.

And that's all that matters.

So the rest of us trudge along, taking it all in, but mostly watching her, because as much as everyone likes to believe that miracles exist, sometimes they come too late.

Probably an hour passes with none of us speaking much. We're too absorbed by the wide collection of contemporary artworks—paintings, sculptures, multimedia installations and performance pieces.

We enter a large, darkened room with the sound of falling

water echoing throughout. The droplets of water plunge from the ceiling, illuminated by the warm blaze of the lights above.

It's like we're standing in the rain, but the water seems to fall around each of us, creating a curtain of silver beads. No matter where I move or stand, the rain seems to be avoiding me, creating a dry circle around my body.

Ellie skips from side to side, flailing her arms in awe while watching the rain react to her movements.

Calla shoulders me. "You look amazed."

"It's pretty fucking cool, isn't it? I can see why Ellie wanted to come here."

We both look at Ellie, and Calla takes my hand, lacing her fingers with mine. My mom remains by Nik's side, and they seem to be having a conversation about something. It hits me in this moment this room is bursting with all the people I care about the most. As I watch Ellie skip around in the rain, her laughter echoing through the room, I feel appreciative of this moment.

Laser tag is where the real fun shit begins. The lights glow and flash around us, and the air pumps with the upbeat music and the whirring of machinery.

"I'm going to kick your fucking ass," I say to Nik.

He snickers and raises a cocky eyebrow. "Bring it, little brother."

My mom shakes her head, but a small smile emerges on

her face. Ellie jumps up and down with excitement, eager to begin the game. "Come on, guys! Let's get started!"

Usually there are teams, but since there are only four of us, we decide to do free for all. We take our positions behind the obstacles, and when the countdown hits zero, I waste no time and sprint into action.

My eyes lock on Nik darting across the arena, and I take aim, firing a shot that narrowly misses him. When I turn, Ellie trails right behind me. She fires and darts away before I can respawn.

I'm on the hunt for Nik. Or really anyone that I can shoot to gain more points, because there's no way I'm going to let Nik win this. He won't shut the fuck up about it for decades to come.

I round a corner and come to an abrupt halt. Calla leans against a fake boulder, peering above it on her tiptoes. Long, dark hair covers most of her back, and her tanned legs look so fucking good in that black skirt. I take a step forward, like there's some force pulling me, and all I can do is succumb to it.

I reach out, wrapping my hands around her waist, and she lets out a surprised shriek.

"Shh, love," I whisper in her ear, my lips grazing her earlobe.

As she recognizes my voice—and my hands on her—her body relaxes into me. I turn her so she faces me. Our eyes lock. Every time we're together, it's like the first time all over again. Her long hair is slightly messy, her eyes bright with elation. I can't resist the urge to lean in and kiss her, and as my lips touch hers, the world dissolves.

She places her hands on my chest, and it's so easy to get carried away with her. I pull away before it happens.

Ellie skips around the corner, and her eyes light up when she spots us. She points her gun at my chest first and fires. Then she does the same to Calla.

"I don't know why you and Nik think that either of you will win. He tripped over and rolled his ankle. You seem to be distracted, and Mom thinks she's got a faulty gun, so that leaves it up to me," she says confidently.

"He rolled his ankle?" I chuckle.

"Yup," she says, popping the P sound. "He's hobbling around like a wounded soldier, but he'll survive. Makes him the easier target though."

We laugh.

For a second, I forget about everything awaiting us outside of this room. For the first time in what seems like a fucking eternity, I feel my age.

And then it all happens at once, like a horror movie playing out right before my eyes.

Ellie coughs. Within a few moments, her eyes go wide, and she clutches her chest. She gasps for air, and I'm at her side within a second. "Ellie, what is it?"

She tries to answer me, but she struggles. Her hands grasp my biceps, her nails scraping against me like she's trying to ground herself, trying to get her lungs to work. And when I glance in her eyes, there's undeniable terror.

I scoop her into my arms and race for the exit while bellowing for help.

24

The Fight

Calla

One of my favorite pastimes has become watching Ace fight. I didn't use to like it. I used to detest it, even though I couldn't peel my eyes away from the action. It entranced but terrified me at the same time. The thought of someone I love getting hurt raised the hairs on my arms, made my heart gallop at a million miles per hour and brought my anxiety to an all-time high.

Over time, I've learned to accept it. It's Ace's job, after all, he's a professional fighter, and it's something he's passionate about. Although I often wonder whether a big part of his reasoning to fight comes from his need for control and dominance. Both in and out of his career.

The stage lights strobe, and loud cheering erupts. Thousands upon thousands of people occupy the stadium. It's a full house. The tickets were sold out in less than ten minutes. It's not surprising considering this is the biggest fight of the year.

Excitement and adrenaline charge the atmosphere. My stomach is full of nerves, I can't sit still and bounce my leg up and down.

Reese, Ellie and I occupy the best seats at the front where only VIP, family and personnel are allowed.

I glance at the time. The fight is scheduled to start any minute. Nik should be here, but he's running late. He was out of town for a meeting with a client, and his flight was delayed. Ace won't mind, I think. He understands his brother and that work comes first for him.

Ace had insisted that the last thing Ellie should be doing is heading to a crowded arena with her declining health, but no one had argued with her when she'd held her ground and demanded she come.

"It's on my bucket list," she'd claimed.

"To what? Pass out in the stadium?" Ace had been making these comments more and more often, especially after the incident at laser tag. Ellie had ended up in the hospital for a night, but there wasn't much they could do for her. Her body was attacking itself, and all the exertion and running around had been too much for her to handle.

Ace is hurt by Ellie's decision, and as much as he tries, he can't understand it or come to terms with it. He's still hoping that she'll change her mind on the treatment. Does he realize each day that passes, the treatment success rate declines? Her symptoms are worsening and progressing rapidly in front of our eyes.

He was there, we all were, when he sought a second—and third—opinion. The doctors said there was an option for treatment, however, the chances of success were in the single digits. The best-case scenario was she'd get a few extra months, but even then, the treatments would take a massive toll on her.

"But there's a chance she could live with treatment? There's a chance she can survive this?" Ace had asked, hope glinting in his eyes.

The answer was miracles do exist.

I think Ace has been clinging to that this entire time.

Ellie had squinted her eyes at his response and frowned. "I want to watch my big brother kick some ass."

That made him laugh.

A part of me agrees with Ellie on this one. She's been battling with illness on and off for years. No one knows exactly how much time she has left or whether she'll be able to continue doing everything she loves as the days pass. She could wake up tomorrow and be completely bedridden, so it's only fair we give her every opportunity while we can.

Now, the crowd roars. Their shouting deafens me and rings through the entire stadium. My eyes dart to the corner where I know Ace strides through the entrance surrounded by his team.

The black jacket hugs his body, displaying every muscle underneath that he worked so hard for. His pace, posture and demeanor emanate power.

He's incredible. I'm in awe of everything he does. His

determination to succeed at everything he sets his mind to is inspiring to many, including myself. He steps through the door into the octagon, and the crowd cheers even louder.

Ace's trainer joins us, but he doesn't sit just yet.

He paces.

His expression and body language betray his nerves. I haven't seen him *this* on edge previously. Granted, I've only attended a handful of fights, and they were pretty much a "sure thing", at least that's what Ace said.

But this is Ace's biggest match. If he takes the win, it would do wonders for his sponsorships and brand deals. It could take the public eye off his trial. Or maybe it will do the opposite and bring him more attention than he wants.

Either way, I have every bit of faith that Ace will win, and we'll deal with the rest once it comes.

Together.

I clench my hands, waiting for the fight to begin. My purse vibrates, and I fish out my phone to find the screen lighting up with my dad's contact picture. It's one that we took on Christmas Eve when he came to visit me in Switzerland. A Santa's hat perches on top of his head, and he's crookedly grinning at the camera while holding a mug of eggnog in his hand. I'm in the background with Mia. She's kissing my cheek, and I have the biggest smile on my face.

Melancholy sets it. I can't deny that I love my dad, and I miss him. We haven't spoken in weeks, not since he had Ace arrested at the airport.

Why is he calling now? To make amends? Or is something wrong? I should answer it, but I can't do it here. I barely hear myself think with the boisterous crowd and the music blasting from the speakers.

"I'll be right back," I tell Reese and Ellie, motioning to my phone.

Reese gives me an inquisitive look with a small glint of worry behind her eyes. In the time I've known her, she's became somewhat of a mother figure to me.

I weave through the crowd muttering "sorry" over and over while getting a few shoves along the way. I grit my teeth in annoyance.

I head out through the back, flashing multiple security guards my exclusive lanyard, and get let through. I finally step into the crisp air and press my dad's contact, returning his call.

The nape of my neck burns with heat, and a sickening twist of worry tightens my gut, signaling that something is wrong. The roar of the crowd cheering rises and dissipates in waves. Even from here, it's so loud that I have trouble thinking clearly.

"Hello?" I say into the phone when the ringing stops and it seems like someone picks up the phone. "Dad? Can you hear me?"

No answer.

"Dad?"

Splitting pain shoots across the back of my head, my eyes roll back for a split second, and the next thing I know, someone's lifting me and lugging me across the sprawling parking lot. Rough, sturdy hands clamp down on me, their grip growing tighter when I twist against my captor. Their fingers dip deeper into my flesh, threatening to leave behind brutal bruises.

I struggle to open my eyes, trying to identify my attacker, but a flurry of black dots dance across my vision from the violent blow. All I'm able to decipher is the vast height difference between us and the unmistakable smell of bourbon mixed with smokey cigar.

I reach for my purse that's slung around my chest, and the pepper spray I always carry in there for emergencies. I've never had to use it before, but as the daughter of a former sheriff, I've never gone without it.

Curling my hand around the bottle, I get ready to pull it out and use it at the first chance I get.

"I wouldn't do that if I was you," a gruff voice murmurs into my ear, leading a million spiders to crawl up my spine.

At the same time, a cool, hard object presses against the center of my shoulder blades.

A gun?

My aching muscles tense, and my throat constricts. When I try to swallow, it feels like sandpaper. It takes a few seconds for me to consider my options.

I don't have many, if any at all.

I can try my luck and hope that one: the pepper spray is still in date and works—do they have an expiry date?—and two: that I'm able to efficiently disarm my attacker and dash inside to seek help. That puts me at risk of getting shot.

I release the grip on the pepper spray and reluctantly heave my shaking hand out of my purse, deciding against the risk.

"Wise choice," the voice mutters.

It sounds awfully familiar. I've heard it before. But with the terrifying situation before me, I can't think properly. My mind is thrown into survival mode, and nothing else matters except for what will happen to me. What does this person want from me? And where's my dad?

Without warning, the attacker flings me into the back seat of a van, and my head strikes something hard. A thumping pain shoots through my entire body, but I'm not willing to go down without a fight.

My fear turns into panic. I kick my legs as hard as I can muster and feel them colliding with something, *someone*.

"Ow! You bitch." I take that as a sign to continue.

My head feels hazy, and something runs down my face. I rub it off with the back of my hand and glance down to see crimson blood.

I struggle to keep my eyes open, and the shadow leaning above me becomes more distant, more blurred as each second passes until eddying blackness encompasses me completely.

25

Adrenaline

Ace

I've trained as hard as I could for this moment, even with all the obstacles hurled at me. When the opportunity to step out of the boxing ring and straight into the octagon presented itself, I took it without much thought.

My therapist at the time had hinted I was too comfortable in my habits, that I needed to challenge myself both mentally and physically. I agreed since at the time I had everything I could ask for, and the only thing I needed was to work on myself. Become a better version of myself for Calla.

In the past year, I chose to step out of that comfort zone, not realizing that by the end, I'd be drained by everything. As the upcoming fight nears, I would be too preoccupied with the trial and Ellie to even care what the outcome will be.

Over the last few years, my mom and Ellie have been

my biggest support system. Even now, when the last thing they should be doing is attending a match with thousands of people, they still insisted on coming tonight.

Of course, I couldn't argue, because even though all of us are aware of Ellie's situation and the slim chances of her recovery without treatment—and even with treatment—we've been advised to make whatever is left of her life as normal as possible. It could be a couple of weeks or a couple of months, no one really knows.

Each day, I try to think of ways to get Ellie to do the treatment. I thought the trip to the hospital after laser tag would put the situation into perspective for both my mom and her. But it may have done the opposite. Ellie's mind is set on doing as many things as she can before she's not able to anymore, and my mom is determined on making that happen.

Ellie's fate is in the hands of the universe. And we all know how cruel that motherfucker is.

The pre-fight ritual passes in a blur, and before I know it, my team leads me out into the octagon. One of them is my trainer. Cheers erupt in the background. The crowd rises on their feet, trying to get a look at me striding out.

I've been acquainted with my opponent over the last year through meetings, weigh-ins and conferences. He's a few years older and has years upon years of experience on me, but as far as our physical differences stretch, it's an even playing field.

Same weight, even height, equal muscle mass.

Intuitively, I bounce from one foot to the other, keeping my heart rate up.

I turn my head to look at Calla one last time before the bell rings and the fight begins, and I spot someone lurking in the shadows. I barely see them, but something forces me to look twice. Even from this distance, I'd recognize that figure anywhere.

He's ditched the bald look for a short buzz cut and shaved his mustache from the last time I saw him.

Logan.

I knew he'd come after me eventually, and I'd been expecting it. Every single breathing moment.

Except for *this* one.

After all, he claims that I ruined his life. I refused to allow him to fight in my former clubs. I set up the arrest of his girlfriend. In his eyes, I got the dream career, the money, the fame, the girl. What he doesn't realize is those things come with a hefty cost.

I'm frozen in the middle of the octagon, my vision tunneled on Logan. He glares right back at me. And then the fucker smirks like he knows something I don't.

He holds a phone in one hand and his head swerves. His menacing eyes land on the empty seat where Calla was not even two fucking seconds ago.

What the fuck? Where is she?

At the beginning of the fight, the first few seconds are vital. In most cases, they determine who has the upper hand, the strength and the power to win. It's when I usually search for tell signs and weak points, analyze how my opponent carries themselves—whether they are confident or just faking it.

This time, I missed that opportunity.

In less than five seconds, my opponent detected my distraction and used that to his advantage. Before I realize what's coming, I'm slumped on the ground, and my face throbs with hot pain.

My opponent is on top of me, his powerful legs on either side of my body, his face teeming with premature excitement.

I admit, being trapped in this position isn't an advantage for me. Most of my life, I've been accustomed to the rules of boxing where you're only allowed to use your fists.

The octagon is more brutal and unrelenting.

I have two options. One, allow the man who's currently landing punches to my ribs victory. Or two, snap out of it and fight.

There's no telling how long this fight could last. If it was my usual ring, I would be more confident about finishing my opponent in less than five minutes, although even that seems too long.

The only thing I can think of right now is Logan and Calla. There's no telling why he's here or what he'll do. I can only assume it's to seek revenge for what I did to him and Cassidy. It can't be just to taunt me, to see me fail.

Logan is unhinged, but he's not stupid.

So I do the only rational thing to protect *her*. I don't fight back.

I allow my opponent to cannon fist after fist into my body and face. I take the brunt of each intense knee jab to my ribs. After what seems like a lifetime of surrender, I feel myself blackout for a second.

When I open my eyes, the referee stands over me, and I know the fight is over. I jump to my feet unsteadily and glance around the crowd. There are people everywhere—some cheering, others disappointed because they had placed bets on me.

I don't give a shit about any of it now.

My name echoes behind me as I race toward the back where I last saw Logan, but my strides are long, and I shoulder past anyone who gets in my way. Stars shoot behind my eyes, but I keep going.

Even though my sights are set on the back door, I feel hundreds of eyes piercing me. Wondering what the hell happened in the octagon.

Some would be flamed with anger since they paid big bucks to watch this fight, only for it to end in less than two minutes. Not to mention the bets that have been placed prior.

I'm sure I'll hear about it from my manager when he gets hold of me, but for now, none of it matters.

Only Calla.

Adrenaline, more than I felt before the fight or perhaps before *any* fight, pumps through my veins and directly into my heart. Charging me.

I once said if he ever touched her, I'd kill him.

That promise still stands.

And for every second she suffers, he will endure agony.

26

The Confession

Calla

Excruciating pain thumps in my head, originating from my temple and molding a tight band around my forehead. I force my eyes open, though that's the last thing I feel like doing right now.

Pain sluices behind my eyelids.

Everything hurts.

At first, there's nothing but darkness, so I rely on other senses. A musty odor assaults my nostrils. The space chills me, and the ground beneath me is concrete hard.

I shiver, but I'm not sure whether it's from the cold or the reality of situation slamming into me.

I've been taken.

Kidnapped?

What's going to happen to me? What do they want?

My hands are tied together behind my back. The ropes burrow uncomfortably into my wrists. I attempt to tug on them, but they remain firm. I slowly wiggle my hands, and the rope eats away at my flesh, but I'm hoping that eventually it'll become loose enough for me to slip out of the restraints.

Something warm and sticky trickles down my right cheek, and I recall seeing red before I passed out.

It takes a while for my eyesight to adjust, and when it does, the first thing I notice is the shadow above me in the form of a human shape.

I didn't get a good look at who attacked me in the parking lot, but from the size and shape of the person, and their voice, I assumed it was a male.

A light flickers to the right for a split second. I flutter my eyelids closed and open. That's all it takes for me to identify my kidnapper as the man who has haunted my nightmares for the past five years.

I can't pinpoint why I have such a peculiar feeling about him. Maybe it's because, to my understanding, he played a significant part in Ace's actions *that night*. I know that sounds like I'm trying to blame anyone else but Ace for the accident, but I'm not.

Or perhaps I am.

Or maybe it's because instead of feeling any remorse for his actions, Logan doesn't feel anything at all. He doesn't have a care in the world.

The last I heard, he was in jail, but only an idiot would be naïve enough to think a building and prison bars would keep him locked away for long. People like Logan have connections. I suppose it's not too difficult to bribe or blackmail someone corrupt in the system.

Ace and I have spoken briefly about him. Each truth and revelation raised the hair on my arms. Logan has been a part of the illegal clubs run by Ace, and during one of his first fights, he killed someone. Even though Ace didn't go into the gory details, my imagination ran wild—thinking of the brutal scene that must've been. When Ace got offered a chance to sell Cassidy and Logan out for his own benefit, he took it. But he also knew the consequences that could potentially stem from it.

And perhaps *this* is the consequence.

I don't think either of us were expecting this. At least *I* hadn't been, and if Ace was, he didn't share his thoughts with me. A pang prospers in my chest.

Is this another thing he kept from me?

"Where's my dad? What did you do to him?" I force my hoarse voice to ask.

"Relax. Your father is fine." Logan waves the question off like it should be the least of my worries.

"What do you mean? Where is he?" I ask, hoping to gain some answers.

"He's fine."

"Why are you doing this?" My voice surfaces sturdier than I expected considering the circumstances. "What do you want with me?"

I'm tied up like a dog, and I'm not sure how long I've

been out for. It couldn't have been long...could it? Am I still in New York?

"Why? Let's see..." Logan scoffs. His thin lips curl over into something that could only resemble a wicked smile. "Ace was my best friend until *you*," he spits the last word at me like it's poison eating away at his flesh.

"Until me?" I don't understand how I caused their fallout. From what I know, Ace and Logan ceased their friendship long before I met Ace in college.

Is it because of the accident? But how is that my fault?

I don't have to wait long before Logan dives into an explanation.

"Until that car accident. We were inseparable, always doing everything together, from getting kicked out of class to crashing parties together in school. We were like two peas in a pod." His jet-black eyes grow distant as he recalls the memories from a decade ago. He shakes his head. "You should've died like your mother. I should've made sure of it."

I flinch in response to his awful words. The hatred flares off him, and I cower back as much as I can muster despite being restricted by the restraints, afraid of what the next couple of minutes, hours, or days will hold.

Each time he looks at me, it seems like there's this emptiness he falls into. A void filled entirely with another reality. It's like he's looking at me and imagining what it would be like if I didn't exist, and the thought of it brings him pleasure, because he gets this horrid curl of the lip.

It shakes me to my core.

My back collides with the wall, and I'm unable to move any farther away. I continue to work my hands out of the ropes.

Will I walk out of here alive?

The more time I spend with Logan, the more I determine that he's mentally sick, and there's no predicting what he'll do next.

The crazed look in his eye roams over me from head to toe. I swallow the bile rising in my throat. "I shouldn't have slowed down. I should've made sure you were dead like your mother," he mutters under his breath, just loud enough for me to hear. He paces the room, rubbing his head. Every now and then, he checks his phone as if waiting for something.

Is he being led by someone else?

Cassidy?

But she's still in jail, isn't she?

I haven't heard much about them since I left for Switzerland, and once Ace came back in my life on New Years, it was the last thing on my mind. Perhaps it should've been higher on the list.

If Logan is out, there's a good chance Cassidy is too, and they both seek revenge. Logan may be trying to finish the job he couldn't at the time of the accident, but Cassidy probably wants revenge for the time she's spent in prison because of Ace, and I may be the leverage.

You should've died like your mother. I should've made sure of it. I shouldn't have slowed down.

I.

218

Shouldn't.

Have.

Slowed.

Down.

The words play in my head once again. So many thoughts and feelings brew inside me that it takes a while for me to register what Logan said minutes ago.

"*You* shouldn't have slowed down?" I question, the words finally sinking in.

It can't be what I'm thinking, what my mind is formulating.

Logan's eyes dart to me, and he pauses pacing the room. His expression turns taut. He doesn't provide a reply, and even among the shadows dancing in the room, I *see* the wheels spinning endlessly in his mind. Like he said something he shouldn't have.

No...

That can't be right.

No...

He shakes his head, like he's removing all the thoughts penetrating his mind. Perhaps that's when he decides that me knowing isn't going to be an issue, and maybe that should terrify me more than reaching the conclusion that I have.

Loud clapping penetrates the room, and I flinch in response.

"Finally. You've figured it out," Logan applauds. "Took you a while. But we got there in the end. Only had to wait seven years." He chuckles darkly.

"It was you…"

He takes a small bow in front of me, proud of himself like a madman.

"But-but you made him…" I shake my head, trying to form actual words. I'm stunned by the admission. I sway from side to side, my body weak like a deer that just came out of its mother's womb and thrown into the dark, scary world. "You made Ace believe it was him all along?"

Logan shrugs. "It was easy. He was so fucked up on alcohol and other shit, and he did drive, until we swapped, and I took the keys from him. My father would kill me if someone crashed his Chevy. And then you came around the corner, there was no controlling the car on the icy road, no matter how much more sober I was and how much driving experience I had."

The admission is everything I didn't expect and more.

So much more.

I thought I knew the truth all this time, but perhaps I didn't…

"How could you do that to him and say he was your best friend? Did you see the struggle he faced every day from it? How it ruined him mentally and emotionally? And the consequences he's facing now for it?"

"You don't understand," he says between gritted teeth, like he has to explain the concept to a small child.

He squats directly in front of me, our faces parallel. "If he knew it was me driving, he would've gone to the police. He would've told them the truth and allowed me to deal

220

with the consequences. I couldn't let him do that. I couldn't let him ruin my life like that..."

"So you ruined his life."

His fists clench together. He shoots up, and I squeeze my eyes shut, anticipating a blow, but it doesn't come.

"He was all his mom and sister had. All it took was me reminding him they were relying on him, and I knew he wouldn't turn himself in. He couldn't do that to them after his father just left." His eyes cut back to me. "And don't try blame all this on me either. If you hadn't gone running your mouth to your daddy dearest, this wouldn't have happened. You and Ace would be living it up on a tropical island. This is *your* fault."

I don't know how to comprehend what Logan just told me. It's like everything I've known since I met Ace—since he revealed the secret that brought us together and tore us apart—has been a lie.

The trauma he's carried—endured—was all for nothing.

The blame I projected on him was aimed at the wrong person this entire time.

The weight of Logan's admission slams into me without mercy, forcing me to imagine how different everything could've been if I'd found this out years ago.

The what-ifs pile in like a snowball rolling off a hill and collecting more weight with each trundle.

What if I'd met Ace under different circumstances?

What if instead of telling me he was the cause of the accident, he told me it was Logan?

What if I hadn't left him that day, five years ago?

What if I hadn't told my dad that Ace was the driver?

What *if* I'd told my dad it was Logan, and we both could've gotten justice?

The dim room turns shaky and even darker than it was seconds ago.

The *what-ifs* cram my mind at a greater speed than I can process them.

I feel myself losing control, letting go of the reality in front of me, which is extremely dangerous in the situation I'm in.

"What do you want with me?" I manage to ask.

"Well, we had a plan, but things never go according to plan. You out of all people should know that."

The ropes on my wrists begin to loosen, but not enough for me to escape them. I need to keep Logan talking without him growing suspicious.

"So what now?" My voice is taunting—trying to get his attention away from my hands. I find a sharp edge on the wall behind me, and I flank my wrists against it desperately.

"Well, I'm sure Cassidy won't mind if I take care of you myself. And now that you know the truth, I can't possibly let you go. That would be incredibly fucking stupid given the circumstances. So you see, that doesn't leave me with many options…"

He takes a step closer, and I halt any movement. Remaining still.

My heart beats erratically. At any point, he could figure out that I'm trying to claw my way out of these ropes, and he'll react in any number of ways. None, I imagine, would be good.

My wrists burn in pain, but my mind is in survival mode.

His head twists around the room. He's searching for something. I use his distraction to good use, finally loosening the rope enough to slip my hands out.

Dark eyes land back on me.

It's now or never.

I spring to my unsteady feet and manage to balance myself. Grabbing the nearest thing next to me, which ends up being a sturdy milk crate, I swing, driving all my body weight and force into it.

He doesn't see it coming.

A loud groan echoes followed by swearing when it collides with the upper part of his body. The force of the impact reverberates through me. I don't pause to see what damage I've caused.

There's no time.

I turn on my heel to run, but Logan's iron grip clamps on my arm, his fingers dig into my flesh. It's painful enough to leave marks, and I hate that. I hate that when and *if* this is all over, I'll still possess his marks on me, reminding me he's the one who took everything away from me and made me believe in lies.

A deep rumble emerges from his chest, pouring out of his mouth like a menacing growl.

I hit his chest solidly with the crate, but it must've nicked his face as well. His lip bleeds, and raw scratches mark his cheek. He continues to laugh, shaking his head with a twisted display of sadistic amusement. "I'll give you points for trying, but did you really think that was going to work?" His eyes trail over me like I'm a piece of dirty gum on the bottom of his shoe. "You thought you could overpower me?"

I clench my jaw, bracing myself for what comes next, but his raised hand strikes without mercy. I stumble backward, and as much as I try to hold myself up, to not give the sadistic asshole the satisfaction, my legs can't hold me.

I hit the ground.

27

Endless Abyss

Ace

*S*he's safe.

She's safe.

She's fucking safe.

I continue repeating those words in my head until they are the only thing I'm chanting in my mind like a fucking mantra. I still glance at her every two seconds and stroke my hand over her to fully believe it.

"Where is *he*?" I seethe.

The moment I discovered Logan took Calla, I've been deliberating all the ways I'll make him pay. The thought of her being anything but safe drove me crazy with worry.

Vile thoughts of what he may have done to her crossed my mind and left me reeling with anger. Luckily, I set up a tracker in Calla's phone—thanks to Josh, Theo's brother.

Perhaps a part of me had been expecting something like this or I'm rightfully paranoid.

If she'd known she would've had a lot to say about it. I wasn't willing to budge on it though. Not in a million fucking years. Her protection, her safety, is my number one priority. Especially since this is happening to her because of *me*.

Each incident that brings sadness or puts her in danger makes me wonder why she chooses to be with me.

Why I choose to stay with her despite knowing what's at stake. Maybe it's not our choice, like breathing isn't our choice, but a mechanism to keep us alive.

"There doesn't seem to be anyone here. If Logan or someone was here, they made a damn quick escape once they knew we arrived," Denzel says.

Coward.

I'm not sure if Logan orchestrated this on his own or had company.

Either way, he's playing a game. Toying with me. Using the most important people in my life to provoke a reaction. Little does he know I don't take well to threats.

Actually, I don't take threats at all, and Logan will find out what it means to gamble with Calla's life.

"Fuck," I roar, punching the stone wall.

Once.

Twice.

Until my knuckles are raw and bleeding.

It's all my fault. Everything is my fucking fault. All the damn time.

I return to the car where Calla lays in the back seat cocooned in a blanket. I lean over, careful not to put pressure on any part of her. Her long hair sprawls on the seat, and some strands glue to her forehead by the dried blood from the gash on her forehead. I can see without proper examination that it requires stitches.

Her lips, stained with blood, are parted, and a bruise forms on her jawline.

I brush the loose strands back and dust my lips over her temple. I squeeze my eyes shut, and all the terrible things that could've happened to her, if I didn't find her in time, flood in like a tsunami.

She stirs, and when I draw back, our eyes clash. Instant relief engulfs her expression, and her eyes glow with warmth. The fusion of brown mixed with green forms a stark contrast against the remaining whiteness.

My attention darts to the purple-red marks on her delicate wrists where she'd been bound. Anger rages inside of me, spilling over the edges into an endless abyss.

In addition to the blatant marks on her wrists, the deep gash on her forehead and the massive bruise on her jawline, other scratches and bruises mark her skin. The more I scrutinize her injuries, the more I have to stop myself from going to search for Logan myself. But I can't do that. Not at the moment.

Calla needs me right now.

"My dad... Where is he? Is he okay?" Calla murmurs weakly. It's the first thing she's said since collapsing into my arms.

"Your dad?" I repeat, confused. What does her father have to do with any of this?

"He-he's the one who called me. I went outside to answer the phone."

I allow the information to sink in for a moment. Logan must have known it was the only way to get her alone. I'm ninety-nine percent sure her father is fine. Logan could've tapped into his phone and made the phone call that way. But I'll have to double-check as soon as possible.

"Your dad is okay. Nothing happened to him," I reassure her even though I don't know for sure. It's no use worrying her in her condition. She needs rest.

A sigh of relief escapes her.

"I'm so sorry." I can't quite seem to spit the words out, but she understands me.

Her relief twists into confusion, her brows scrunching together in that adorable way. She lifts her head. "What are you sorry for? This isn't your fault," she croaks and coughs to clear her voice.

It hurts me to see her like this. I hate myself for failing to protect her.

"Maybe not directly, but Logan went after you because of me."

The guilt accompanying that statement is far worse than I expected. The admission of the words when spoken out loud is much stronger. I'll carry the blame for this to my grave.

I should've been on alert when it came to Logan. I knew

he was released from prison, but I didn't think he would try something at my fight in front of so many people. Yet he knew what he was doing and managed to get her alone. It wasn't a spur-of-the-moment action. He orchestrated this.

"Ace..." She shakes her head. "It's not your—"

"It is," I interrupt, not wanting to have this conversation. She'll try to convince me that it isn't. That there's nothing I could've done to avoid this. Nothing I could've done to protect her. But there were things I could've done that would've avoided this exact situation.

I should've never let my guard down. I should've hired security to follow Calla everywhere even though she wouldn't have been happy with it. I should've never taken my eyes off her.

Should've. Should've. Should've.

But I didn't.

I clench my hands, forming tight fists. The veins on my hands protrude. The deep-blue lines pulse with the rest of the anger and frustration that's finding residence inside my body.

Now there'll be no *should haves*.

I'll do *everything* not to allow this to happen again. No matter what it fucking takes. I'll burn the world for her. Move the planets for her. Rearrange the stars so no forces are able to cause her any harm.

There'll be at least two security guards accompanying Calla anywhere she goes. Another two will be stationed outside my apartment for further security measures. My building has one of the top security setups in place, but the problem with that is people are easily bought or influenced.

Pay them the right price or offer them a deal they can't say no to, and they'll forget the meaning of loyalty within seconds.

There are only a handful of people I trust, and even those I'm wary of.

Calla's eyes narrow, and her unwillingness to accept that her being in this situation is my fault shines through them.

"You need to rest. We'll talk about it later," I say.

We won't.

There's nothing to talk about.

I'll live the rest of my life knowing my actions put her in danger, and I'll strive to make it up to her as best as I can even though nothing will ever make up for the fact she could've been killed by someone I should've taken care of already.

"Ace." She parts her lips like she wants to say more, but nothing emerges. She's trying to force her eyes to stay open though her body fights it.

"I'm right here. Rest."

I slide into the seat next to her, and she dips her head on me.

Despite everything that happened in the last few hours, my body relaxes to her steady breaths. My fists unclench, my knuckles still covered in blood, and my rigid shoulders sink into the leather of the seat.

I finally calm down enough to wrap my arms around Calla, and she scoots closer to me.

28

It Changes Nothing

Calla

As I open my eyes, I immediately scan the room. My heart thumps even though everything around me tells me I'm safe now.

Familiarness of the room interspersed with the smell of vanilla and cedarwood helps my body relax into the white sheets. I nuzzle my head further into Ace's pillow, nestling my nose in the remnants of him.

To my right, the dark-gray blinds remain drawn closed, but a subtle flicker of light seeps through the edges, teasingly dancing with the gentle breeze stirring them.

How long have I slept for?

I don't remember how or when I ended up in Ace's bedroom, but I figure he must've carried me from the car. I don't recall much after Logan grabbed me and threw me onto the ground. I must've hit my head or completely zoned out.

In an instant, he was on top of me, gun pressed to my temple. Words spilled from his lips, but I didn't register much of what he was saying. I guess that happens when faced with imminent death.

He'd leaned down, his face too close to mine. His breath, warm yet unwelcome, lingered like an intruder on my doorstep. "I'm not this type of person, but I might as well try the thing Ace has been obsessed with for years." And with those sinister words, his hand slithered under my skirt.

I snapped out of the stupor I was in.

It's funny how I was ready to accept death if it meant dying with dignity, but as soon as that line was crossed, I was ready to fight again.

The events blur, but I can't stop wondering how Ace knew where to find me so fast. I couldn't have been in Logan's lair for more than a couple of hours.

Memories of Logan's revelations swamp my consciousness, and instantly, my thoughts run at a million miles per hour. My head throbs, whether it be from the gash on my head donning a bandage over it now, or from everything that's unfolded in the last twenty-four hours.

I climb out of bed, my head spinning with each movement. Grasping the bedside table for support, I steady myself until I no longer feel the urge to collapse. Then I slowly navigate my way to the bathroom, aware of every ache and twinge in my body.

Standing in front of the sink with my hands gripping the

stone countertop, I bring myself to steal a glance in the mirror.

I'm a complete mess.

My hair, which has almost become my natural choco-late-brown color over the last few months since I stopped dyeing it, is a tangled haystack on top of my head. Some strands stubbornly cling to my forehead where the stark white bandage serves as a reminder of the injuries.

I run my fingers over it, wincing in the process. I remember the blood gushing down my face, but I don't recall who bandaged me up, though I assume it was Ace.

Distorted, bloodshot eyes with dark craters underneath stare back at me. If I weren't looking in the mirror, I wouldn't recognize the person standing before me.

I brush my hair and teeth, splashing cool water over my face while avoiding the blood-stained bandage. Before making my way downstairs, I slip a white tee over my pant-ies, concealing the bruises peppering my abdomen and ribs.

As I open the bedroom door, and pad down the hallway, a piercing shriek escapes my lips. Standing there is a man I've never seen. Clad in a black polo shirt and dark jeans, his presence screams danger. His arms are solid, and his hands are crossed at his front. Everything from his tattoos to his serious expression rings alarm bells in my head.

"Um, who are you?" I manage to stammer, desperately trying to pull down the white tee to hide my ass and flipping my hair forward so it would cover the fact that I'm not wearing a bra.

This is not an ideal situation to be in.

I thought it would only be Ace and me here. I wasn't expecting company lurking right outside the room. If I had, I would've taken a moment to at least throw on a pair of pants.

"Leo," he utters, as if his name explains everything.

It doesn't.

"Security," he adds. He doesn't spare me a glance, and I wonder if he's been warned not to look at me. It seems like something Ace would do. Where is he, anyway?

With cautious steps, I descend the stairs, my hand tightly gripping the handrail. I can't ignore the overwhelming exhaustion in my legs. It will take more than a few hours of sleep to recover physically, and a lot of therapy to recover mentally—if that's even possible.

More therapy.

Does Addilyn have a more fucked-up patient than me?

I highly doubt it.

Recovery is the last thing plaguing my mind right now, and I can't even rest if I try.

I need to tell Ace what I know.

It will change *everything*.

Ace works in the kitchen, his back turned to me as he cooks something that smells heavenly. My mouth is dry, I haven't eaten in what seems like decades but probably hasn't been more than a day.

He doesn't hear me pad behind him until my arm brushes against his bare back where a purple, angry bruise stretches across his side. The suddenness causes his body to stiffen and twist with urgency. His eyes blaze with danger until they settle on me, and then they soften.

We are usually super aware of each other—in tune.

He would normally sense when I'm the same room as him, but he seems on edge. Even while he's looking at me now with concern and undeniable guilt, he's also a million miles from me. He hasn't been himself, not since he found out about the trial...then it got worse when he found out about Ellie...and now? Now I don't know where he is.

Come back to me.

Dark bruises decorate his face, including a nude-colored butterfly stitch on his cheekbone. What happened at his fight?

"What's with muscles?" I nod my head at the stairs where Leo descends, maintaining a professional distance but never averting his watchful gaze.

It's unsettling.

"What are you doing? You should be in bed." Ace abruptly abandons the spatula on the counter and closes the gap between us until our chests meet. His eyes rake over me, his jaw working as they graze past my nipples, faintly concealed beneath the inadequate white tee, down to my bare legs.

I feel his stare low in my belly.

"I swear to fucking God, Calla," he seethes, the intensity in his voice unmistakable. "You better not have walked out of your room dressed like that. If you did, Leo better be fucking dead, or he's about to be. No one gets to see you like this. Only me."

The heat in my chest intensifies, stirred by Ace's possessive nature. It's extremely sexy.

Leo remains still, a silent observer to our heated exchange.

"Don't make this a big deal," I say. "I didn't know he was down the hallway, outside the room. You should've told me. And I'm fine." Before the last word leaves my lips, Ace scoops me up in his arms, holding me in a bridal-style carry as he transports me toward his sofa.

"Ace," I try again. "Really, I'm okay." I attempt to flail my legs to prove my point, hoping he'll set me back on the ground, but he doesn't buy it.

He gently places me on the sofa, ensuring my back is supported by two cushions and my legs stretched out in front of me. His touch is so gentle, like I'm fragile chinaware. Then he pulls back ever so slightly, his overgrown stubble brushing against my cheek.

"Don't lie to me." Ace's voice, low yet firm, sends a shiver straight between my legs.

"I'm not," I argue. "Lying," I clarify.

I'm probably far from fine. Considering the bloody bandage on my forehead, I probably sustained more than minor injuries. None of that seems to matter right now.

"I know you better than anyone else, and I can tell when

you're lying," Ace says. "You have a gash on your head that needs stitches. I have a doctor on his way here to take care of that and take a look at everything else."

For the first time since I came downstairs, Ace directs his gaze at Leo with pure fire. Understanding the unspoken orders, Leo nods and quietly exits the room, granting us the privacy we need.

Ace waits a few beats before setting his gaze on me. His eyes rake over me again, his Adam's apple bobs up and down. He briefly looks away, working his jaw. "Did *Logan* do anything else?" he finally asks, spitting his name like it's the most disgusting thing he's ever had to say.

"Anything else?" I echo.

"Did he…" His words trail off, but the meaning is crystal clear.

"No," I quickly say, shaking my head. "No," I repeat, almost as if I'm trying to reassure the both of us this could've turned out a lot worse than it did.

Ace must see something in my eyes, my expression, or he quite literally reads my damn mind.

"Calla," he warns. "Tell me the truth. He's dead either way."

He's dead either way.

Ace's words are chilling, like stepping outside the warmth of your home and into a blanket of snow, but then you realize you knew that winter was coming all along, and it suddenly doesn't feel so cold anymore.

"He tried," I confess, my voice barely a whisper.

Ace squeezes his eyes shut, and I count the beats of silence that pass.

One.

The veins in his neck pulse, and he sets his jaw so tightly that I can tell it must be painful.

Two.

The sofa behind me strains under his grip, the material protesting.

Three.

I want to know what he's thinking. I want to assure him again that none of this is his fault. But I know him too well to believe my words will make a difference. He'll still blame himself for it, and my words will do nothing but fuel an argument between us.

Four.

His eyebrows furrow deeply, and I raise my hand, gently smoothing my thumb over one of the creases. He remains motionless, but his breathing quickens, though it could just be my own.

Five.

His eyes fly open, gaze fixing on me like a volcano on the brink of eruption. Never have I ever seen him so furious. There's such raw rage rumbling within him. It's as if the world is coming to an end, and in this moment, I'm scared that it just might be for him.

"Tell me exactly what he did," he demands, his voice commanding and resolute. There's no room for argument, so I recount what I remember. Each breath, each word, each hesitation fuels the inferno within Ace, as if I'm pouring gasoline onto an uncontrollable blaze.

A deep rumble emanates from his chest, and I instinctively place my hand there, though I don't know what I'm hoping to achieve. To calm him? He's too consumed by his own thoughts. He won't stop until he finds Logan. He won't stop until he makes him pay, and he hasn't even heard the rest of what I need to tell him.

I swallow, steeling myself. "There was something that Logan said when we were in that basement." Is that where we were? I don't remember exactly. It's all so foggy. My surroundings masked by the knowledge I've gained.

There's a part of me that would do it a million times over. I would put myself in that situation again and again if it meant I would finally learn the truth.

Ace pulls back abruptly, his eyes transforming into daggers at the mention of Logan's name. "What was that?"

"It wasn't you who was driving that night." A heavy weight the size of a mountain lifts off my chest.

His expression turns blank, devoid of any reaction. He doesn't utter a word in response.

Did he hear me?

"You didn't cause the accident," I repeat, hoping for some sign of understanding or relief.

Nothing.

I take a breath and share what Logan revealed, not sparing any detail, no matter how grueling it may seem. I keep looking at him as I speak, waiting for his expression to change or indicate that he understands what I'm saying.

But his expression remains an empty void, an abyss I can't penetrate.

He shakes his head, practically shakes me off him and stands. "It changes nothing," Ace states.

Confusion settles deep in the pit of my stomach. I'd expected a range of reactions—shock, confusion, anger. I'd even expected him to be relieved about it. Wasn't the accident the root of all our problems?

What I hadn't expected was the complete absence of a reaction—no response at all.

"What do you mean it changes nothing? How can you say that?" I ask, dumbfounded. I cross my legs in front of me on the sofa.

"How can you believe what Logan told you? You saw what he's like—impulsive, unstable. He'll do anything, say anything to get to you." Ace takes a step for the kitchen and then backtracks. "And you believed him." He shakes his head, his eyes drilling into me.

"There's no reason for him to lie. He wasn't even planning on telling me until I figured it out, and then I don't think it mattered that I knew because he wasn't planning on letting me walk out of there alive."

Ace winces at my words, and for the second time today, the mass of reality crashes down on me.

I almost died.

Death.

It seems so distant until you're staring it right in the face.

"So what do you want me to do with this information?" Ace asks.

I'm speechless. When Logan revealed the truth, I thought it would change everything we've believed for nearly a decade. I'd hoped Ace could use it to his advantage in the trial. After all, Logan's admission placed Ace in an alternative position to what we previously thought.

"Use it. Tell Nik. I'm sure he can use it to get the case thrown out, or use it as new evidence and you can plead not guilty. This changes everything for us."

Before I even finish speaking, Ace is already shaking his head.

"You don't understand. It's my word against his. How could I possibly stand on trial and say it wasn't me who caused the accident when I don't one hundred percent believe it myself?"

I don't have time to process what he's saying, let alone reply, but he continues, firing words at me that I'm in no state to handle.

"And what if everything he said to you was a lie because he's mentally unstable, Calla? What then? You've always hoped I'm not the monster I say I am, and you've always tried to find reasons to support that. So when he gave you what you've always wished for, you believed him. But what if he's wrong?" Ace fires. "What if he's just fucking with us?"

Hot and cold pours into me. I'm shivering, but at the same time, I feel so hot it's insane. My body and mind don't know how to process anything at this point.

Even though I don't want to admit it, in a way, Ace is right.

I've constantly made excuses for him. I've always tried to make myself think that I can mentally build a barrier between the person who's responsible for my mother's death from the person I love.

And to some extent, it has worked.

In hindsight, he's not an awful person. People shouldn't be defined solely by their past actions. But in the back of my mind, I've always hoped that reality would shift, presenting a different outcome.

Perhaps the universe saw the battle we've faced and finally offered us this redemption.

I can't find the words to respond, silently proving Ace's point. His expression remains unchanged, but the disappointment in his eyes tells me he wanted me to deny it.

"You should go back to Switzerland until all of this is over." His jaw tightens, and his gaze bores into me.

Though he hasn't physically touched me, it feels like a painful blow after everything we've been through. All the promises we made to each other.

How can he ask this of me?

"What?" I ask, bewildered by his request. I didn't mention that I've basically already lost my job. I could return and live with Mia, and I have enough savings to survive a couple of months, but what then?

"I can't protect you here. Not with everything else going on—the trial, Ellie…"

It's all too much for him. There's only a certain amount of responsibility a person can take, and Ace reached his limit a while ago.

"You don't need to protect me. I don't *need* your protection."

He gives me a look that says otherwise. It reiterates his you-almost-died statement.

"I don't need your protection," I repeat. "I need your honesty. If I knew Logan and Cassidy were out for revenge and you thought they could come after me, you should've told me. I would've been more careful."

He scoffs, but I press on.

"I can't leave. Not you, not Ellie. Not right now when no one knows how long she has left." Ace flinches. "I already spoke to my work, and they understand my situation. They've approved my personal leave."

Somewhat true. He doesn't need to worry about me. He already has enough on his plate. I'll handle my own issues.

Ace strains his jaw and runs a hand through his disheveled hair.

How long have I been unconscious? Has Ace rested at all? I doubt it. He's probably been relentlessly hunting Logan since he brought me home. Maybe not physically, but he has his people to handle it.

"You don't want me here?" I try to hide how much his request hurt me.

"You should go back to Switzerland."

He takes a few steps toward me, putting himself directly

in front of me. "Calla, look at me," he urges.

I lift my head to meet his insistent gaze.

"I *always* want you here. Close to me. By my side. Fuck, I'd mold you into me if I could. But I don't know how to keep you safe right now. With everything going on, and now this…"

"Ace…"

"It kills me to know something like this happened when I was right there."

"But what makes you so sure that I won't be in danger in Switzerland? I'm sure he's keeping tabs on me, both Cassidy and him are. It won't be hard for them to track me down in Switzerland, perhaps even easier since you'll be out of the way." I say, pointing out the flaw in his suggestion.

Ace's mind churns before my eyes. I can see the wheels turning, the gears shifting. He realizes I'm right.

"You're right," he admits, clearly frustrated by the fact. Before I'm able to gloat, he continues, "So this is what's going to happen… I'll hire more security. There'll always be one near the elevators. There will also be two security guards following you at all times. No matter where you go. Café, work, mall, Blackwell headquarters, the fucking moon. As soon as you step out of this building, they will be there."

I open my mouth to protest, but Ace crosses his arms, his bulging biceps display his determination. One raised eyebrow silently conveys that this is non-negotiable, and he won't back down if I try to argue.

Did he suggest Switzerland knowing I would refuse, just

244

so he could implement this plan without resistance?

Does he know that I've essentially lost my job?

Once my mind goes there, there's no turning back.

The rational part of my brain tells me it's exactly what he did. He spent so much time and effort rebuilding our relationship, and we're finally in *somewhat* of a better place. Why would he suggest that I leave again unless he knew I would object, allowing him to propose this alternative?

It feels like he tricked me instead of being honest.

I shouldn't be surprised. It's always like this with him.

What next? A freaking tracker in my phone?

"Calla, it's non-negotiable," he says, perhaps seeing that I'm trying to think of a way to get out of this.

"Fine," I force the words out to satisfy him. But inside, a combination of frustration and resignation meet me.

29

Rage

Ace

For the next few days, I refuse to leave Calla's side. I'm at her beck and call, whatever she needs, despite her insisting it's unnecessary. Of course she insists, but she has a concussion for fuck's sake.

There are no signs of Logan, it's like he's vanished into thin air. I have my men extensively covering every inch of this city and beyond…and nothing. But I know he's out there, aware of my pursuit and biding his time. I'm waiting for him to fuck up and reveal his whereabouts. He can't hide forever.

Mia unexpectedly showed up at my apartment this morning. It's probably my fault. I called her when I was in "find Calla mode" to ask her if she'd heard from Calla. That was before I remembered about the tracker in her phone. When she told me she hadn't, I may have mentioned that

Calla was in danger and then ended the call, too consumed with finding my fiancée to explain the situation properly.

Since Calla's best friend showed up on my doorstep at four in the morning—does that woman have a sense of fucking time?—I decide to leave them to it. I go do the only thing that will take my mind off things. Something that will take at least some of the rage from me since at the minute I'm in this circle of fury.

I can't stop the images pouring into my fucking head of what could've happened to Calla. I feel like I might snap at any point. I don't know how I haven't already.

When I step foot into the club after days of not showing up and ignoring calls from my manager, letting the news headlines rip me to bits, he pounces on me the first chance he gets.

He storms up to me, rips my headphones off and shakes his head in disbelief. "Do you realize what you've done?" he exclaims. "This was your biggest fight of the year. You've been training for it like a madman. And you gave the win to your opponent without a struggle."

And I'd do it all over again without hesitation if I were placed in the same situation.

The safety of the people I love is my number one priority, not some fight that would bring me a title in a different sporting category. In the midst of everything going on, that seems insignificant.

Jeremy's words fade into the background as my mind becomes consumed with what Calla revealed about Logan's confession. I've tried to suppress those thoughts in the past few days, but now they flood my mind persistently. After all, the magnitude of it is astronomical.

Calla is right. It could change everything.

If it's true.

But can I trust it? Can I trust what Logan is saying? I have little to no recollection of the night of the accident. My memory is hazy at best. All I remember is how adamant Logan was about not involving the police when I was willing to turn myself in immediately.

I was so damn out of it, consumed by teenage emotions and anger for my father, desperately seeking an escape from my own mind. Alcohol seemed like a tempting distraction from it all at the time. Stupid fucking decision.

Even if what Logan had said is true, it still doesn't erase the past or undo the damage that has been done. The coward couldn't face me directly, and now it falls to me to track him down and take care of him before he hurts anyone else.

There'll be no remorse. No reliance on the authorities. The next time I come face-to-face with him, I'll revel in the satisfaction of watching the life drain from his eyes. I won't even blink, let alone question him about what the fuck happened that night.

I don't want him to spin me stories or feed me lies.

The gratification of imagining Logan dead should sound alarm bells in my head.

It doesn't.

Perhaps that's a clear sign that I'm no better than him.

"Blackwell!" Jeremy's voice booms, snapping me out of

my thoughts. "Are you fucking listening? This isn't something you can brush off. It was the biggest opportunity of your career, and you blew it."

I unleash a powerful punch onto the boxing bag, channeling my frustration and anger.

"Look, I know you're going through some shit right now with the trial and your sister, but I know you, and I know when you're in the ring, it's all or nothing. That wasn't you losing because you weren't good enough, that was you giving up."

I neither confirm nor deny his accusation. I don't even spare him a glance. "Set another date," I demand.

Jeremy gapes at me like I've just asked him for one of his kidneys instead of a rematch. "It's not that simple. Why would Mathers agree to it? He knocked you out within minutes, and now you expect him to grant you a rematch? He's not stupid."

I scoff at his response. Jeremy, of all people, should know how this works. He has decades of experience, and he's renowned as one of the best in the business. That's precisely why I chose him as my trainer and manager.

I halt my assault on the boxing bag and pivot to face him directly, a determined look in my eyes. "And he's not a coward either. If he's confident his victory wasn't a fluke, then he'll have no problem agreeing to another fight. Even if he lacks the confidence... Well, we can always release a statement in the media to force his hand."

"That's not how it works."

Of course it's fucking not. I'm sure he'll manage though. I snatch my headphones from him and insert them into my ears. "Make it work," I state firmly, cranking up the volume to drown out any further objections.

I have bigger concerns than a rematch. Such as finding Logan before he fucks up my life even more.

30

Best Friend

Calla

I groan as another wave of nausea washes over me. I lean over the toilet bowl, retching and emptying last night's dinner.

"I'm so sorry." Mia's at my side, brushing my hair back. "I swear that sushi place had good reviews."

Mia surprised me at Ace's apartment yesterday morning. Bright and early. She stood at the door, hands on hips, shooting daggers at Ace when he answered.

"What are you doing here?" My eyes had widened. I shouldn't have been surprised by Mia's sudden and unannounced appearance. This wasn't the first time she's done this, and it probably won't be the last.

"What am I doing here? Are you fucking shitting me?" she asked with her hands firmly planted on her small hips.

Ace had let out a chuckle, oblivious to the danger he was in by provoking Mia when she was mad.

Her Bambi eyes turned sharply on him. "You know, this *is* your fault. You can't just call me, get me worried sick about my best friend and then not answer your phone for the next couple of days. You owe me a thousand dollars. Flights aren't cheap." She huffed.

"Consider it sorted," Ace replied and backed away from the front door.

"And your *men*," she spat the word, her irritation aimed at Ace's ridiculous security. "They need to keep their hands to themselves. Like what do they think I have hiding in my jean pockets? A fucking machine gun?"

She was on a roll. A force to be reckoned with, and whoever tried would be damned.

Ace's lips curled into a smirk. "Well, I can't take any chances, can I?"

I chuckled. I couldn't help myself. Mia wasn't impressed. As her gaze shifted to me, Ace seized the opportunity to slip away, leaving us to each other.

Mia huffed again, her shoulders relaxing as she practically barreled into my arms. "What the fuck is going on?"

It took me half a day to relay the events to her. I didn't leave anything out, and when I was finished, she insisted we needed a girl's night, complete with dinner and drinks. Of course, we were accompanied by a squad of security—four men.

All of them on high alert.

All of them armed to the teeth.

It felt like I was a prisoner, constantly under surveillance. They tried to blend in, but four men who resembled jacked-up versions of James Bond weren't exactly inconspicuous.

Mia tried to make light of the situation. She flirted with Leo, the one who witnessed me in only a white tee and nothing else. Yet he barely gave her the time of day. Either he was instructed not to talk to us, or he wasn't into women.

The night ended with our bellies full and heads spinning from the cocktails.

So now here I am. Head buried in the toilet bowl.

No, it's not a hangover. I know what one feels like, and this is definitely not that. I didn't drink *that* much.

"This is so not fair," I mutter, my voice strained between bouts of vomiting. "Why aren't you sick?"

"I do feel queasy," she admits. "But I must have a stronger stomach. Do you need anything? Water? Some applesauce or toast? It might help to have something in your stomach," she asks.

"Why? So I can empty it again?"

She looks at me apologetically. "Sorry. The reviews were good, I swear."

By nighttime, I feel a million times better. I've showered—probably close to half a dozen times—and washed my hair, and now I'm dressed in a red silk nightgown with delicate lace at the bust opening.

I reassure myself I didn't wear it for Ace. I'm not even sure if he'll be home tonight, but a small part of me hopes he will be.

Ever since the incident with Logan, Ace has become even more distant. He spent a couple of days by my side physically, but mentally he was elsewhere.

I'm worried about Ace. I know he's consumed by thoughts of getting revenge, but how far is he willing to go to find him?

I sink into the sofa with my laptop, preparing to start researching the next article for my website and turn the TV on for background noise. And maybe to give Leo something to watch, since he's been stationed near the front door for hours now. Surely he's bored out of his mind. I know I would be.

Meanwhile, Mia is upstairs getting ready for some gallery opening that she's attending tonight. I offered to come since I have no plans, but she waved me off, saying it'll be boring for me, and she didn't want me puking all over the place.

Fair enough.

At the time, there was this weird vibe in the atmosphere...almost as if she was brushing me off because she didn't want me to come? I dismissed the feeling without giving it any more thought. But now, as she descends the stairs in strappy-heeled sandals and a form-fitting blue dress that accentuates her slender figure, I can't help but wonder if there's more to her reluctance.

I raise my brows. "Do you have a date?" I right myself and glance over her outfit.

Is this a bit much for a gallery opening? I wouldn't know. I haven't exactly been to one myself, but when she told me about it, she made it seem like it was this casual thing she just wanted to pop into.

It doesn't seem so casual now.

"A date?" she asks in a voice that clearly begs me to drop the subject.

I'm definitely not going to drop it though.

"Yes, a date. You know, a person whom one may go to such events with." I smile innocently.

"I know what a *date* is," she remarks, stuffing her phone into what appears to be my clutch. I don't mind. We always share clothes and accessories without any fuss.

"Well, do you have one?" I press, unable to contain my curiosity.

"Hmm, nope." She pops the *P* in a dismissive manner.

I pinch my eyebrows together and stand from the sofa. I approach her like one would approach a skittish animal.

"What aren't you telling me? You know I'll get it out of you one way or another. Easy or hard way."

I inch into the kitchen, gradually closing the distance between us and the front door. My intention is clear. I won't let her run off without telling me what—or rather who—is waiting for her tonight.

She squints at me, fully aware of my tactics, and lets out an exasperated huff. "Fine. I'll tell you. But you have to promise not to ask any questions about it. At least not until *after* I come back. I'm already running late."

I glare at her. "That's not fair."

"Life isn't fair," she retorts.

That, I know.

"Fine."

She bites her lip nervously, and in that moment, I already know the name that's about to leave her mouth. "Theo. I'm going with Theo."

"I knew it!"

She rolls her eyes. "Now I have to go. He's waiting for me downstairs."

"He's not even going to come to the door? And here I thought he was a gentleman." I fold my arms across my chest.

"I told him not to."

"Oh, that's right. Because you were planning to keep this from your best friend."

"Like you're one to talk. Do you know how many things you've kept from me, and I had to find them out on my own?" she counters.

"Touché," I admit, knowing she has a point.

She walks past me, making her way to the door. Her hands reach up to smooth her hair, and she glides her strawberry-glossed lips together.

"I'll be waiting up," I call after her.

Leo, stationed by the doorway, moves aside to let Mia pass. Someone else might not notice how he quickly slides his eyes over her, clearly checking her out, but I do.

"Don't," Mia says to me as she closes the door after herself.

31

Cinnamon & Oranges

Well after midnight, the door opens, and the scent of cinnamon and oranges floats through the air as Ace steps into the apartment. My nose scrunches at the feminine fragrance, and a pang shoots through me, initiating in my chest and flowing to my stomach. It's so uncomfortable, so consuming that I feel sick again.

"You're still up," Ace remarks when he spots me on the sofa. He gives a nod to Leo, and Leo, following command, exits the apartment.

My back leans against one of the armrests, and my laptop rests on my lap. The screen illuminates my face, casting a white glow, but I haven't been productive for the last couple of hours. Instead, I've found myself drawn to the movie on the massive flat screen before me.

I nod. "Yeah."

"Mia?"

"She went to a gallery opening. Hasn't come back yet."

Ace removes his jacket and casually drapes it over one of the snug armchairs in the living room. "I'm sorry. I would have come home sooner if I'd known you were alone."

"Would you have?" I question, my tone guarded.

His brows tie together. He reads the room—figures I'm mad. I don't even know if I am. This feeling streams with rawness. I shouldn't even be thinking it—that he might have just been with someone else—after everything we've been through, but why else would he smell like a woman's perfume?

I study him, searching to find anything else, silently hoping I don't.

A midnight black long-sleeved shirt molds to his chest. Probably Prada. His closet here is filled with those. He's wearing denim jeans on his lower half and Vans. Casual and effortless, but on Ace, it looks a million bucks.

I hate it.

"Are you mad at me?" He moves to stand right near me, his towering figure causing me to tilt my head back to meet his steady gaze.

I shut the laptop, right myself up on the sofa, wiggling my back further into the armrest, and pull the blanket further onto my lap. "I don't know. Should I be?"

He squints his eyes, as if he's trying to figure out my thoughts. He's cleanly shaven, probably did that this morning before he left.

"Tell me what I've done," he says.

"Where were you?"

"Work. Then I met with Nik. And later, I got notified there were potential sightings of Logan, but it was a dead end."

Right, Logan. I'm still unsure how I feel about Ace hunting him down as though he's a wild animal. But I don't think my reservations are about Ace getting revenge, instead I'm worried about him. Especially knowing how unhinged Logan is.

I try to search Ace's face for signs that he's lying about his night. When you get to know someone the way I know the man in front of me, it should be easy to spot. Though with him, it's different. Sometimes I can read him like an open book, other times, like now, it feels nearly impossible.

"Why do you smell like cinnamon and oranges?" I blurt out the question I probably wouldn't have asked under different circumstances. But I'm both mentally and physically exhausted.

Ace tilts his head at what he probably thinks is a bizarre question at first. It takes a second, maybe a little longer. I notice when the switch flips, and it dawns on him what I'm insinuating.

The asshole smirks, cocks his head again. I grit my teeth in annoyance. Jealousy still courses through me at the mere thought of Ace with someone else.

Leaning over me, he positions both hands on the sofa on either side of me. I graze my eyes over his biceps and the black ink covering them. He's added more tattoos to his body over the past year.

I blink, lift my head up and hold his gaze.

"You think I was with someone else? Another woman?" he asks, his tone laced with incredulity.

I nod and open my mouth to confirm, but nothing comes out.

He snickers, shakes his head in disbelief. He looks at me like I'm stupid for entertaining these thoughts.

"What am I meant to think when I haven't heard anything from you all day, and you return in the middle of the night smelling like another woman?" I retort.

"For fuck's sake, Calla. I can be an asshole sometimes, but I would never do that to you. I would *never* be unfaithful to *you*."

His eyes lock onto mine with an intensity, igniting a spark.

"It doesn't explain why you smell like that," I say, pointedly.

He shakes his head, the smirk still lingering on his face. *What the fuck?*

"Jealousy looks good on you," he rasps, his eyes gliding over me, taking in the sight of the red nightgown peeking out from under the plush blanket. He gulps, then lifts his fist to his mouth and grumbles. "Fuck." His eyes rich with desire.

A fire kindles deep within my belly, my core growing warm in response to his words and intense gaze.

As Ace attempts to place his hand on my jaw, I instinctively pull away, causing a trace of hurt to flash across his features. His smile is wiped away with a mere turn of my head. He releases a breath and rights himself, mirroring my withdrawal.

I hate that he's pulling away too.

Returning to the jacket he'd discarded earlier, he retrieves several white cards from one of the pockets and throws them onto the coffee table in front of me.

"After the meeting with Nik, and before I received the call about Logan, I was at the store. I wanted to get you a gift. I smelt what seems like a fuck load of perfumes, but none matched you. So I created a custom one."

Perfume scent cards.

He wanted to surprise me with a gift, and I've ruined it. I'm an idiot.

"So that's why I smell like fucking cinnamon and lemons—"

"Oranges," I correct with a small smile.

"I can't believe you think I would do that to you."

"Well, what else am I supposed to think, Ace? You've been pushing me away since you got arrested at the airport. It seems like we're more distant now than ever before," I admit.

He gazes back at me, his eyes mellow with sadness. "You're right. I've been pushing you away. I can't let you do this. Your dad is your family... My life is public, and as long as you're with me, yours will be too. It's not a walk in the park when the entire world criticizes your actions, everyone having an opinion. I can't destroy your life even more. You will hate me for it...for the rest of your life."

I'm already shaking my head before he even finishes his

speech. "I don't— I won't." I stand from the sofa, my legs carrying me to him.

"You say that now, but I know you will. And then there's Logan. As long as he's still out there, your life is in danger. Don't you understand? Being with me is like being on a one-way road to hell," he spits.

"Then let me choose whether to burn or not. Don't make that choice for me." I meet his gaze head-on.

There's this push-and-pull dynamic between us all the time. One of us pushes, the other pulls. Then eventually, we switch. It's exhausting, but at the same time thrilling.

It's how we've always been.

It's what we know.

He sighs, recognizing he's not getting anywhere with this conversation.

"You're my family, Ace. I don't care what the world thinks. It's too late for that." I've never been the one to care about stranger's opinions. But now, even my own father despises me. I don't think it can get much worse than this. "And Logan? If we're together or if we're apart, he will still come after me. You know that."

He shakes his head, the weight of responsibility etched on his face. "I've already ruined your life. How could you want to continue this? I'm going to make this clear for you, Calla. I don't want to hold any information back from you anymore, and I don't want you to be blindsided later. I'll take the stand. I'll tell the truth—the entire truth of what I remember that night without omitting anything. It feels like the world is offering me this final redemption, a chance for me to finally make everything right, and I have to take it."

Tears well up in my eyes as his words sink in. I understand what this means for us. If he takes the stand, there's no predicting what will happen. It won't be in our hands anymore.

It will be up to the justice system to decide.

He strides toward me, his presence commanding my attention. He reaches out and touches my cheek, wiping away the unnoticed tear. I wrap my fingers around his wrist, desperate to keep it there, desperate for the connection.

His touch ignites a hunger and stirs emotions that run through my veins.

He leans down and claims my mouth with his. It's raw, unyielding and possessive. It's like he's allowing himself to give in once more, and I'm scared of what that means. I really hope he drops this thing about protecting me from his demons.

I'm a grown woman. I can make that decision for myself. I accept all of his demons—no matter how haunting they are.

I'm completely lost in the kiss, spellbound. It's intoxicating, and I'm drunk from one taste. My hands tangle in his hair, pulling him closer like he isn't already consuming me—inhaling me. It's not enough.

It's *never* enough.

Only when my legs brush against the edge of the kitchen island do I realize he's subtly guided me backward. He lifts me effortlessly, perches my ass on top of it, and pulls away a little like it's the first time he's getting a look at me since he got home.

A damn *good* look.

The way his eyes slowly roam over my body charges me with a sense of empowerment, making my confidence sky-rocket. I'm so glad I chose to wear this nightgown. Though I have no doubt Ace would look at me with the same hunger and intensity even if I were wearing a baggy T-shirt. But for him, red is like a magnet to metal.

He glides his hand over the silky fabric, and its coolness causes goosebumps to rise on my skin. "Did you wear this for me?" His eyes lock onto mine, his words filled with desire.

"No," my response is quick. *Too* quick.

A smirk. "Lies," he murmurs. His hand slips down, sweeping the curve of my waist before settling on the small of my back. My body awakens, and a primal recognition vibrates within me.

My knees weaken no matter how much I try to resist it. I'm powerless to his touch. I bite my lower lip, hiding the smile that's threatening to break free.

Ace leans in closer, his breath hot against my ear. "You know what you do to me when I come home to find you like this." His lips map a path down my neck.

My breathing quickens as he traces my collarbones with his tongue. His head keeps dipping, lower and lower until he reaches the curve of my breasts, and he kisses me there, tenderly flicking his tongue.

"Can we try something?" I look at him with pleading eyes. Both of his hands splay on my thighs.

Logan had bound my hands together, took away my

control. Each time I close my eyes, it's all I can think of. My wrists aren't sore anymore, but they are still marked by Logan. I need Ace to change that, I need Ace to take it away.

I turn my wrists up at him.

He swallows.

Then blinks.

Realization sets in. He knows what I want.

I'm offering myself to him at my most vulnerable, with my guard down and one hundred percent of my trust in him. Something I couldn't give him a year ago, but lots has changed since then.

A slight tilt of his chin is all it takes.

He straightens. His hands reach for his belt, long fingers loosening the buckle with ease, but his gaze is on me the entire time.

He pulls out the belt with one swift movement.

I put my hands further out realizing they are slightly shaking. Either be from the adrenaline or the nerves. Or both.

For me, this has always been something I was unwilling to try. A boundary I was unwilling to cross. But the day I vowed to marry him, I realized I have no boundaries with Ace.

None whatsoever. He can have me anyway in every way he wants to.

He takes my hands in one of his, but he doesn't tie the belt around my wrists just yet. Instead, he brings his lips and holds them there until my hands aren't shaking anymore. The warmth of his breath on my hands is comfort.

He eyes the lingering red marks on my wrists, shakes his

head, becomes distant. "I'm going to kill him," he growls.

I place my hand on his cheek, bringing him back to me. "Ace."

"Are you sure about this? I don't want to hurt you."

"I thought you wanted this."

"Not like *this*," he murmurs, running his thumb over the pulse point on my wrist.

"I need *this*," I tell him. "I need you to take away *his* marks."

His throat bobs as he swallows.

"Please."

He nods, pulls away, meets my eyes once again and loops the belt around my wrists. His touch is gentle and reverent. My hot skin cools against the leather. As he completes the task, he leans in and kisses me deeply, his hands roaming over my sides. The intensity of his touch is overbearing, and I arch my back in response.

"Am I the first to have you this way? Completely unguarded?" His voice is ragged, full of desire. His skilled fingers tail the hem of the nightgown, feathering my inner thighs.

I push myself into him. "Ace..."

"Answer me." He continues to tease me. Each stroke of his fingers against my legs, each breath we share, makes me crave more. The apex between my thighs smolders with need.

"Yes, you're the first," I manage to say.

And the last. The *only* one. I'd never allow myself to be *this* vulnerable with anyone else. He, out of all people, should know that.

As a result of my words, the satisfaction pours out of him like I've turned the faucet on. There's no denying he's wanted this for the longest time. Waited for me to give my all to him. And now that I have, there's no turning back.

I'm in this. Every molecule of me belongs to him. To do with as he pleases.

Does that terrify me?

Completely.

Do I trust him?

With all my heart.

The leather on my wrists is tight—tight enough that I'm unable to slip them out. Tight enough that I feel constricted. Tight enough that my breath hitches in my throat at the thought of giving all the power to Ace. There will be red marks where the leather rubs against my skin. Marks that will replace the unwanted ones.

He finally lets me push myself against him, and I slide my aching self shamelessly into his hand. A low, sexy chuckle stems from the depth of his throat, and then he's obliging me—rubbing me through my panties that I shouldn't have even worn in the first place.

A small whimper leaves me as his fingers make contact with my throbbing center. They slide over the wetness that's already pooled between my thighs. His electric touch sets every nerve ending in my body on fire.

"Do you know how wet you are?" he murmurs, his warm breath tickling my ear. "All for me, huh?"

I nod my head. "Only for you. You know that." His

touch is maddeningly slow, and I try to grind myself on him, desperate for more friction, but I'm restricted by my position on the counter and not being able to use my hands.

"I like hearing you say it."

He knows exactly what he's doing, and he keeps up his torturous pace. Driving me closer and closer to the edge while the tension builds in my body. I'm only moments away from shattering into a million pieces as he circles that tender spot.

"Don't stop." I pant, fluttering my eyes closed.

Suddenly, he stops.

My eyes shoot open, and Ace is smirking.

"Fuck you," I manage to rasp in between pants.

"Oh, love...you will soon." He supports my back with one hand and with the other, he nudges me down on the kitchen counter. The coolness of it hits my back, and I gasp, arching. Ace leans over me, his lips ghosting mine. "Or better yet, I'll be fucking you."

His words jolt lightning strikes down my spine. I'm putty in his hands, and he's using it to his advantage.

He takes my nightgown and slips it off me. "Don't move," he commands. He maneuvers around me, takes my tied-up hands above my head and loops the belt over the sink tap.

I gulp, tugging at my hands, but there's no way they are budging unless I'm strong enough to pull the tap out of the counter as well.

As he positions himself between my legs once again, the anticipation charges the air. With a calculated motion, he discards his shirt, revealing his impressive physique. In the dimly lit room, bathed only by the glow of soft downlights above the sofa and the flickering radiance of the TV, his muscles ripple with each fluid movement. Shadows dance along the contours of his body, highlighting the sculpted lines that I can't look away from.

The absence of a belt compels his jeans to hang low on his hips, teasingly exposing the V-line, leading my gaze to his swelling erection.

I'll never get used to this. I'll never get used to *him*.

With one hand, he grips my hip, holding me in place as he continues to tease me with his mouth. With the other, he strokes me again, his fingers expertly finding all the right spots. I'm moaning, unable to control the sounds dripping from my lips.

"Ace. I need *you* now."

He lets out an amused scoff. "Impatient as always. I'm glad to see that hasn't changed," he comments, and then he finally slips his fingers into my panties, and I almost die from the intense pleasure after being tormented for so long.

I arch my back, trying to push myself closer to him. His middle finger pumps in and out of with ease, and he adds his ring finger while his thumb rubs circles on my clit. "So warm and tight," he croons.

I'm desperate to touch him. To tangle my hands in his hair, tug him closer, feel his chiseled anatomy. Not being able to use my hands is excruciating, but it causes my senses to come to life tenfold.

His erection digs into my thigh, and his mouth finds

mine, swallowing my moans. I feel his lips curve into a smile. He playfully bites my lower lip and pulls away, looking at me or more so, *consuming me* with his eyes alone.

I'm naked except for the red G-string I'm wearing.

"You are the most beautiful woman. And I'm the luckiest man alive to get to call you my fiancée."

Yearning swirls in the bluest parts of his eyes. His words, and the way he looks at me, make my heartbeat race faster. When he leans down and places his mouth around my nipple, I writhe beneath him. He sets one hand on my stomach to keep me still, and his tongue swirls its way to the other nipple, tweaking, sucking, swirling.

"Let me touch you," I plead.

"Not part of the plan, love."

"Fuck the—" His mouth descends to my stomach and down to my core, drowning my words. He kisses me through my panties, his tongue flicking out the tiniest bit, and I'm done for. I'm so worked up, so sensitive down there, that I'm coming from that one kiss.

I say, or more so pant, his name over and over while he watches me come undone on the kitchen counter.

"Incredible," he murmurs, his voice husky.

Then he pulls his pants down, freeing his length. I can barely see it from this angle, but I've seen it enough times to have it branded in my mind. Felt it enough times to know exactly how it will feel when inside me.

My body responds instinctively, a rush of heat spreading through me at the sight of him. At the *thought* of him.

His hands run up my thighs, pushing them apart. A soft moan drips from my lips as he positions himself at my entrance, his eyes locked on mine—like they always are. He utters a set of directions. "Lift your hips for me. Keep your eyes open. Look at me."

He likes to see my face, my eyes, when he enters me. I'm not sure why. Is it a guy thing?

Ace is entirely focused on me. The world could be burning around us, and he wouldn't care. He slowly enters me, and as he fills me, gasps of pleasure fall from me. I'm still sensitive from the orgasm, so the bliss is intensified. I wrap my legs around his waist.

"Do I need to tie these up too?" he teases, massaging my thighs and all the way to my calves.

"You wouldn't dare."

He raises his eyebrows. "Fucking try me, love." He pulls back and thrusts into me slowly. He splays his hand just above my pubic bone.

Ace builds a steady pace, and my body jolts back with each thrust, sliding against the marble counter.

I catch him watching the movement of his marvelous length pulling out and sliding back into me with such calculated precision—hitting all the right spots. His expression is full of yearning—eyebrows furrowed, lips slightly curled into a soft, pensive smile.

His other hand massages my breasts, circling my nipples with his thumb.

His thrusts become harder—more urgent. He's driving

both of us to that ultimate release. The tension builds, coiling tighter and tighter until it finally snaps, sending me spiralling. Free falling with no parachute to save me. My body writhes beneath him as wave after wave of pleasure crashes over me. I cry out his name, my voice echoing through the room. I pray that this apartment is soundproofed, and Leo can't hear me on the other side of that door.

Ace doesn't slow down, he thrusts deeper into me, his own release building. I can see it in the intensity of his eyes, in the way his muscles tense as he gets closer and closer.

His fingers dig into my hips. Heat fills me at the same time a groan spills from his lips.

He collapses, his weight settling on top of me.

"Mine," he murmurs against my chest.

"Yours."

32

Surprise

Calla

Nine tests sprawl across the expanse of the bathroom counter.

Nine.

I might have gone overboard, but I couldn't stop.

Each one reveals two distinct pink lines. Not even faint pink lines. They glare at me as vividly as the midday sun.

How did this happen?

"Well, when two people fuck like rabbits, it's inevitable," Mia remarks casually. Her choice of words barely register in my state of shock.

"But I'm on birth control."

"Come on, Calla. With everything going on in your life now, you can't tell me there hasn't been at least one day you forgot to take it."

Her words sting, reminding me of the inconvenient truth that this is far from an ideal time. "Thanks for reminding me this isn't an ideal time to be pregnant."

I divert my gaze to the mirror, studying my reflection. A whirlwind of thoughts and emotions seize hold of me. How far along am I? It could be a number of weeks or months since there's nothing to go off. I've been using the pill to skip my period for years, so the absence of the usual pregnancy symptoms isn't surprising. It's the norm. The only reason I even took these tests was because my *food poisoning* decided to return today. I haven't puked yet, but I've felt sick as a dog since I woke up.

Am I selfish for considering the possibility of growing this life inside of me and bringing it into a scary world?

Will I be able to look after this child when I'm not even set up for life myself?

Am I willing to go ahead with this pregnancy when I have no idea what the outcome of Ace's trial will be, whether he'll even be around for the first years of this baby's life?

Or should I consider other alternatives?

"Calla?" Mia's voice interrupts my thoughts, tugging me back to the present. I meet her empathetic gaze in the mirror, realizing I had drifted away for a few moments.

"What should I do?" I murmur. My voice carries a fusion of uncertainty and a flicker of hope.

Mia shakes her head gently. "I can't make that decision for you."

I sigh. "I know that."

I need to tell Ace and make that decision with him. But I already know what Ace's stance will be. He'll want to keep the baby no matter what. I run my palm over my stomach, lifting the camisole slightly to peer at my bare skin, searching for any sign of change.

There's nothing there. No bump.

Not even a bloat since I haven't been able to keep much food down. That was actually why Mia suggested taking a pregnancy test when she returned *this morning*. Though she tried to sneak in unnoticed so she could pretend she didn't spend the night at Theo's, it didn't work. I was already awake and heard her tiptoeing up the stairs.

"Anyway, fill me in on what happened last night." I want to take my mind off *this*.

She huffs and drops down on the closed toilet seat.

"Actually, fill me in on how you and Theo reconnected in the first place." I raise both brows and lean my hip against the sink. "I need to know *everything*."

She rolls her doe-like eyes, trying to make it seem like it's no big deal even though we both know it is. When a woman swears off all men because of one, it usually means he was a big deal—or still is.

"It's nothing extraordinary. No big moment. He heard I was in New York and reached out to me. That's all." She downplays it, but her face shows that even though there was no grand moment, it still meant a lot to her.

"He heard you were in New York? How?"

She shrugs. "I don't know. Ace?"

I nod. Even after all these years, Theo and Ace are still close—much like Mia and me. So it would make sense he would tell Theo about Mia staying here.

"Anyway, he reached out to me and asked if I wanted to catch up since we didn't leave things on good terms..." She allows the remainder to speak for itself, not wanting to relive their past disagreements.

"And how did that go?" I prompt. It's like drawing blood from stone.

She lowers her head to her hands and rubs her eyes. "Good," she mumbles. "We talked, lots of apologies from the both of us. I guess both of us needed time to process what happened."

Sounds a bit too familiar.

"So that's good right?" I ask, because she's acting like it's not a good thing.

"No... Yes. Kind of. I don't know." Her hands muffle her voice. She peeks out through her fingers, trying to gauge my reaction.

I chuckle, pressing for more details. "You have to give me more than that."

"It's not a good thing, because that means we don't hate each other anymore."

"Like you ever did," I huff under my breath.

She shoots me this stare that is both annoyed and kind of sad. The corner of her eyes droop, and her lower lip juts out.

"And you ended up staying at his place last night..."

"Nothing happened."

There are multiple reasons why I don't believe that. One of them being that Mia and Theo aren't able to keep their hands off each other. It was obvious a year ago when they reconnected, and I doubt anything has changed this time around.

"Yeah, right. Nothing." I begin to call her out on the bullshit.

"Calla?" Ace calls.

What the fuck is he doing here? He's usually never home at this time.

My gaze darts to all the tests strewn across the counter, and I rush for them.

It's not that I want to keep the news from him. I would never do that to him. But I've only just found out myself, and I need time to process this information before sharing it with him.

When the time is right.

As the door handle turns, my heart leaps into my throat.

Mia catches my wide eyes.

"I'm naked!" she squeals before Ace has the chance to open the bathroom door.

A brief pause hangs in the air. "Uh." He clears his throat. "Okay. Calla?"

"We're just—" I begin, but I don't know what to say. My mind blanks. I'm still in shock and can't think properly.

"Trying out some new skincare products," Mia smoothly interrupts, covering my ass.

I glance at her, raising my eyebrows because "trying out skincare products" shouldn't result in Mia being naked.

"Really?" Ace sounds skeptical. "Skincare products?"

"Yep," I respond with no other explanation.

Go, Mia mouths. She motions to the tests that still cover the counter. "I'll take care of these," she whispers.

I can't go out there and face him now. There's no way.

"Go," Mia urges me, pushing me into the bedroom.

My heart pounds, its rhythmic beat echoing in my ears.

"Right. Okay—" Ace begins just as I slip out into our bedroom through a small opening in the doorway. Ace doesn't get a glimpse inside. He isn't even trying to look.

He tilts his head, looks at me with those bright eyes of his like he can see through my soul. I offer a small smile that I hope looks genuine.

It doesn't.

"What's wrong?"

I shake my head. "Nothing," I say way too quickly. My hands tremble.

Pull it together.

"What are you doing here? Did something happen?" It's a genuine question, but I'm also trying to sway the conversation.

Ace appears to be considering pressing me further. He runs his hand through his hair, draws his eyebrows together. "My mom and Ellie are on their way here. My mom is mad at me. I guess."

"You guess?"

"I've barely spoken to her since the fight where I got the shit beaten out of me and then disappeared. After that, I told her you were okay and not to ask any questions." He sighs.

"And she just...obliged?" That doesn't sound like his mom.

"Fuck no. I mean she usually would, especially when I was running those underground clubs. She did her best to pretend like I wasn't doing anything illegal. But not this time since it involved you."

I gulp, suddenly feeling like the worst person ever. Since Logan happened, I've been trying to forget about the incident. Then Mia showed up, and it was like the sun started shining again. I was reunited with my best friend, and I brushed everything else to the side to spend time with her.

My phone was smashed when Logan took me, and I haven't had the chance to replace it just yet. Or maybe I've been avoiding replacing it.

Ace reassured me my dad was okay. So in reality, I didn't really need my phone.

I thought everything could wait.

Except it couldn't.

Reese was probably trying to reach me.

"God. I'm so sorry, Ace. I'm a terrible person." Heaviness flourishes in my chest, and tears pool in my eyes.

"Hey." He cups my face in his large hands, brings our foreheads closer so they're almost touching. The act is so intimate. It's comforting to be this close to him. His captivating cologne wafts over me, and I inhale the notes of sandalwood. "What are you talking about? None of this is your fault."

"I've been in my own bubble for the last few days. I haven't even asked how prepping for the trial is going. I hav-

en't even contacted Reese and Ellie to see how she's going."
That's not to say it hasn't been at the back of my mind.

"You've been through a lot."

"So have you," I reason. "But you've still made sure everyone around you is okay."

He shakes his head before I even have time to finish the sentence. "Everyone deals with difficult situations in their own ways. I'm used to taking care of everyone. It's second nature to me."

Of course it is. He had to step in and be the man of the house when his father left. I wish that weren't the case. When someone takes on so much responsibility at that age, it fucks with them, I suppose.

"You haven't told your mom about Logan?"

He shakes his head.

"I think you should."

"I can't. Not now. She has too much on her hands already."

I understand Ace's reasoning, but Reese is stronger than he gives her credit for. She can handle it. Not just that, she deserves the truth.

She will love Ace no matter what. But wouldn't it be a weight lifted off her shoulders if she knew her son wasn't the reason someone died?

I know what Ace is thinking. He doesn't want to trouble her. He doesn't want to give her false hope when he doesn't know the truth himself. I think she could provide advice on what to do. But it's his mom, so it's his decision. I'm not going to go against him on this one.

"She needs to be on the lookout. What if Logan decides to target her next?" The thought of it terrifies me, propelling trembles down my spine.

"I have security watching over them," he states.

My eyes widen. "How long till they are here? I could probably quickly whip something up." I've been cooking now more than ever. I'm not great by any means, but I'm able to make a simple potato bake or even a dessert.

Ace laughs. It's this sad, nostalgic laugh that pierces my heart in a way that I don't expect it to. Then, as if to cover it up, he leans down, tilts my head up and brushes his lips against mine.

"They will be here in half an hour or so. I'm sure my mom will bring some food with her. If not, we can order something. You don't need to make anything."

"Half an hour?" I shriek and begin scurrying around the room. I'm still in one of Ace's shirts that I slipped on last night after I padded upstairs with the content ache between my thighs.

I'm far from ready to see his mom and sister.

Ace watches me with what seems like humor and some fascination. As I rush past him, he catches me with his arm around my waist.

His fingers brush against my stomach. A second ago, I hadn't been thinking about the positive tests with Mia in the bathroom, but Ace's faint touch *right there* serves as a blatant reminder.

How the hell am I going to get through the next few hours without being consumed by my own gushing thoughts?

33

Family

Ace

My phone buzzes in my pocket. I swiftly tug a cotton shirt over my head and pull my phone out of my jean pocket.

Nik's name, along with a picture of his head underneath Princess Peach's from the time we played Mario Karts, pops up. He wanted to prove there was no better character to choose. I still disagree. The game requires skill, but mostly luck about what stupid item box thing you get.

No, I'm not still mad about it.

But I want a rematch, because I know I'll kick his fucking ass next time.

"What's up?" I answer, pressing the phone to my ear.

"I have news on the case against our father."

Nik has been busy with my case, but alongside that,

he's also been trying to make sure our shitty father gets what's coming to him. I don't know why. I won't give that asshole a second of my time. Karma will serve its own justice eventually. Nik is resolute on doing it himself, or at least, expediting the process.

I stride for the door and pull it closed. Calla is downstairs with Mia. I can hear the banging and clacking of pans and utensils. She's set on having something to offer my mom and sister when they arrive.

When did she get so fucking housewifey?

It's definitely making my cock hard at the wrong fucking time.

Also it's making me feel shit that I have no right feeling. Like not wanting to take the stand...or praying to whomever or whatever is listening that I'm found not guilty so I can spend the rest of my life worshipping her even though I'm not worthy.

I clear my throat along with the futile thoughts. "I'm listening."

"I have a contact, a prosecutor in the area, who is eager to take the case on."

"Does he know who he's dealing with?" Few people are willing to go against our father.

"Oh, he's well aware."

"So our father has pissed this guy off? Typical." It seems like that's all he does these days.

There's a brief pause from Nik's end. "Something like that. Anyway, he wants to see our father behind bars."

I nod to myself. Where there's a will, there must be a way. However, even if our father does end up in prison—which I highly doubt, given the corrupt connections he has—I doubt he'll stay there for long.

"I thought you'd want to know," Nik continues when I don't reply. "Also, your trial begins soon. We've been through everything. The prosecution has a good case against us—" he uses *us* like we're in this together, "—but there's a possibility that the judge will give you some leniency—"

"You don't need to do that," I interrupt, grinding my teeth at the false hope he's trying but failing to give me.

"Do what?"

"Try make me feel better or some shit. I'm not one of your fucking clients you can bullshit to soften the blow." I know the possibility of me walking away from this a free man is slim to none. Perhaps I've already accepted that.

"I don't do that usually," Nik states. "Bullshit my clients," he clarifies.

"Well, don't start now."

"Noted," he says, all business like.

Fuck. Did I fuck up this brotherly conversation that we were apparently having?

I run my hand over my face and consider my words before I say them. Weigh in the pros and cons. Decide there are barely *any* cons. It may be the last time I have a collective meal with my entire family before all goes to complete shit. "Look, Reese and Ellie are coming over. We'll probably have early dinner here or some shit. Did you want to come over too?"

There's another drawn-out pause from him on the other side. I'm beginning to think he's going to tell me he has other plans or to go fuck myself. Instead, he surprises me with a simple response. "Yeah, sure. I'll finish up some stuff and make my way over."

"See you soon."

Twenty minutes later, my mom and Ellie stand at my front door eyeing the security warily. Like I knew she would, my mom carries Tupperware wrapped in foil in one hand, and a bag packed to the brim in the other. I take the bag from her, lean down and kiss her on the cheek.

"Hey, Mom."

She looks at me cautiously and then darts her gaze over to Romeo. He stands a meter from the door. He's taller than me, with his hands at his side, still as a statue.

Perhaps I should've told my security to be more discreet—not sure if that would've made any difference. Mom doesn't say anything though.

Ellie does. "Why is there so much security here?"

I don't know what to tell her. Hopefully they haven't seen the security that's been tailing them. So, I just say, "Precautions."

I zero in on Ellie, scan her features, even though it's been less than a day since I last saw her.

Does she look sicker?

Healthier?

I always hope for the latter, but as much as I hate to admit it—it seems as though she's losing that spark. It might be her eyes that have grown dimmer, or the smile that's always plastered on her face is smaller. Something about her has changed.

My chest fucking aches. I wish there was something I could do for her. If I could switch bodies with her and give her my healthy one, I would in a fucking heartbeat. Without hesitation.

"Hey, sis." I throw my arm around her shoulders.

"Hey, bro," she mimics. "Mom's pissed at you."

"Ellie," Mom scolds.

"Moms angry at you." Ellie rolls her eyes.

"Figured," I mutter under my breath. I'm not ready to have that conversation with her. I don't know how much to tell her, how much truth to reveal. I don't want to worry her, though she'll be worried either way.

She's been asking about Calla since my fight—almost a week ago.

What happened?

How is she?

I couldn't provide satisfactory answers. I couldn't possibly tell my mom that my fiancée was fucking kidnapped by Logan, my former best friend who's mentally unstable and looking for revenge.

I brushed her questions off.

I know she knows something is up. Even more so when

Calla didn't come and see them over the last couple of days. That's why she took it upon herself to come here. Now, there's no hiding the bruises on Calla's face and body.

Calla rushes toward us in an olive-green sundress that makes her legs look like she's spent the last week basking on the shores of Santorini. A cozy knit cardigan drapes over her shoulders. Her hair is loosely tied in a bun at the top of her head, and short chocolate-colored strands shape her face and stretch to her chin.

Fucking goddess.

"Hi." She goes in for a hug with Ellie and then Reese. "Sorry, I've just been making some lunch…or trying to." She admits shyly. I love how adorable she looks when flustered. "Ace didn't give me much notice." She turns, providing me with a cute glare.

"Oh, you didn't have to. We've brought enough with us." Reese motions to the bag in my hand. "It's my fault. I didn't tell Ace we were coming until we were already leaving. I didn't want to give him time to think up any excuses."

My mother's gaze scans Calla from head to toe, her eyes narrowing slightly as they settle on the marks layering Calla's face. Calla tried to cover them with makeup—though she doesn't need that shit, she's beautiful as fuck without it—but the remnants are still visible. Not as bad as they were before, but still not healed.

I clench my fists just thinking about it. Thinking about all the marks that fucker left on my fiancée makes me want to rip his head off.

"Well, I'm sure it's a hundred times better than what I've managed to whip up. Here, let me take that into the kitchen." She takes the Tupperware from my mother's hands.

"Don't sell yourself short," Mom says kindly.

"Oh, I'm not. I'm telling you the truth." She laughs and turns to lead the way.

I catch Calla by the waist, turn her so she's facing me and looking up at me with those big hazel eyes that hold the entire fucking world in them.

"Ace," she whispers in a small voice, her eyes darting from my mom to Ellie. She tries to wiggle out of my grip, embarrassed by the intimacy in front of other people, especially my family.

I don't let her go. Instead, I tighten my arm, keeping her in place. Then I wipe her nose with the pad of my thumb. "Flour?"

Her eyes go wide. "Mia." She sighs. "She spilled the sugar powder."

"Ah." I slip my thumb into my mouth, tasting the sweetness. Calla eyes me and clears her throat. Her cheeks turn red. Her filthy thoughts stray exactly where I want them to.

I release my grip on her and follow her into the kitchen. Right at that moment, Mia pulls a pie from the oven—which has only been used a handful of times since I bought the apartment, and none of those times have been by me. The pie looks like it's seen better days.

"I think we had the oven too high," Mia admits.

"You think?" I chuckle.

She glares at me, turns her attention to Reese and Ellie and introduces herself. Have they not met before? I can't fucking remember with all the shit going on inside my head.

Either way, I zone out for a minute or so, watching my mom, Calla, and Mia move around my kitchen. My entire family (minus Nik, who's about to be here soon anyway) in one room. Talking and laughing. The picture before me sort of plays in slo-mo, mocking the fuck out of me—reminding me there's little chance I'll get to witness and experience this again.

When I zone back in, the conversation has strayed to Mia and her rising career as an artist.

"Can I see your art? I've started drawing on Procreate using those YouTube tutorials, but it's harder than it looks," Ellie admits.

"Sure. I don't have any canvases with me, but I'll get my iPad after we eat," Mia says.

Ellie beams at this.

Within ten minutes, my kitchen table bursts with more food than I've seen here before, and the apartment smells mouthwatering. Mom brought garlic shrimp pasta, some salads and slow-cooked lamb shanks. Calla managed to make a potato bake and a sweet pie that she's dusted with sugar to hide the burnt edges.

Nik arrives just as we are about to take our seats. Romeo leads him in the front door and looks at me to make sure he's welcome here. I give Romeo a nod, and Nik raises a dark brow at me like he's saying, *what the fuck?*

"Nikky, I didn't know you were coming," Ellie exclaims, her expression lighting up.

When did he become the favorite brother?

"Ace's heart finally warmed up, and he invited me," Nik replies, shrugging like it's a normal thing these days.

"Don't get used to it," I mutter.

"Wouldn't dream of it, little brother."

He removes his jacket, drapes it over the chair and joins us at the table. Nik lifts his head, searching for Calla. It fucks me off for some reason. He examines her face, not being discreet about it either.

"How are you feeling?" he asks her while staring at her forehead right below her hairline. She used her hair to cover it up, but now the strand has moved, revealing the stitches.

Calla touches her forehead. "Uh. Yeah, I'm okay."

"Now is the moment you tell me I should've seen the other guy," he jokes while reaching for the potato bake.

It also fucks me off that he's the only one who's not afraid to ask the question or make a joke with Calla about it.

She laughs, actually laughs. Not one of those fake ones she does, but a real one.

And what does that do to me?

It fucks me off.

Her eyes dart to me like she's checking if it's alright with me that she's laughing at his jokes. Like fuck. Of course it's not fucking alright. It does something to my head, makes me doubt myself or some shit. But that's my issue to deal with—not hers. She's done nothing wrong.

I give her a smile, make sure it's genuine enough. Her eyes instantly warm.

The meal passes with small talk, and that's about it. I think it's because everyone is too busy enjoying the food. Especially Nik. I thought I ate a lot, but he's an animal. Where does it all go? He's all muscle. Does he even work out?

The apple pie doesn't taste too bad actually, if you pick off the burnt crust.

"Show me your drawings," Ellie says to Mia once they're done. Mia obliges, and the both of them go upstairs.

While Mia is showing Ellie her art, my mom gets into the hard stuff. "The trial is in about a week," she states.

A week.

A week until my life is altered for a very long time, if not forever.

I hate that word. *Forever.*

It doesn't fucking exist. Don't romanticize it. Don't even flirt with the possibility of it, because nothing can be forever.

I'm not scared to face the consequence of my actions. I've been anticipating it for the longest time. I'm scared of losing time with Ellie when there isn't much left. I'm scared of not having a life with Calla as I previously imagined.

I've been trying not to think about it. I've tried to take it one day at a time, because if I'd thought about it too much, I wouldn't have made it this far.

But now?

Now there's only mere days left...

There's no avoiding it.

"Yes," I confirm. The word comes out as a grunt, that's all I can manage.

She exhales a heavy breath. Her eyes hold more than she wants me to see. Exhaustion amongst other things. There's also disappointment there, although she'd probably never tell me that herself.

"You don't have to be there," I tell her.

"What are you talking about?"

"You don't have to come to the trial. I know it's hard with Ellie." Both with her sickness and trying to shield her from it all.

"I'm your mother, Ace. I'll be there for you until the end, no matter what."

Her words stab at me like a fucking spear to the heart. Fuck. Might as well take an actual spear. It would probably hurt less.

I can't look at her.

My eyes stray to Calla instead. She hasn't eaten much. She's been playing with her fork, trying to make it seem like she's eating. She may have fooled everyone else, but she hasn't fooled me.

I know she's nervous about the trial. It's going to take a mental toll on her. I just hope she can recover. After everything I've put her through, I hate that this is happening. I hate that after all the promises and vows I've made her, it all will be for nothing. I should've stayed away from her in the first place.

"Come on." I rise from the table, wanting to lighten

the dreary mood. Might as well make the most of the days I have left as a free man.

All of them stare at me. I nod toward the living room where the Nintendo Switch sits, then I look directly at my brother, casting him a challenging look. "I'm going to kick your fucking ass, Princess Peach."

34

Stay With Me

Calla

Ace meticulously weaves his tie. His hands and fingers remain so steady they could undoubtedly rival a surgeon's. For some reason, a wave of frustration ripples in my stomach at his bizarre calmness.

"How are you so calm?" I huff, retreating from the bathroom after I've flipped the switch on the hair curler.

Is it all just an act? Is it his way of getting through today, or does he genuinely not care what the outcome will be? If it's the latter, it rips a hole in my chest. How can he not care that the worst-case scenario will break us apart? Or has he come to terms with it?

Restlessly, I fidget with the collar of my designer dress, incredibly uncomfortable. Nik insisted I buy this particular dress, and he knows best when it comes to these situations.

So all I can do is follow his lead and hope that he knows what he's doing. Hope that today's outcome will be a positive one.

I tug on the ends of my wavy hair. "Are the curls too much? Should I straighten my hair instead?"

There were times during the last few days where I wondered whether I could do this—sit in the courtroom with my head held high and listen to the heartbreaking case the prosecution built against Ace. Whether I could sit there, in the room that I'd always thought would bring me justice and watch the man I love be sentenced for a crime against my mother that I only recently came to believe he didn't commit.

I kept my reluctance to attend hidden, because I know Ace needs me there. But during the times when Nik came over to prepare us, I think he might've sensed my hesitation. He emphasized my presence is essential at the trial, as it might sway the decision in Ace's favor. It will show that if I, the daughter of the *deceased*—Nik's words—can find it in herself to forgive Ace, then perhaps the law will show mercy.

I wanted to tell Nik that Ace isn't guilty. That it wasn't him that night, but Ace made it clear I have no proof except for Logan's confession that I heard in my delirious state. No one would believe me or Ace. They would simply think we're searching for a way out.

Ace steps in front of me, blocking my view of the mirror. He stands tall, strikingly handsome, with his broad shoulders pushed back. His Adam's apple bobs up and down as he drinks me in. "Calla." He intertwines our fingers and lifts my knuckles to his mouth. His lips graze over my skin and the expensive diamond ring on my finger. It's larger than the knuckle itself. *Mine*, he seems to say.

"Everything will happen exactly the way it's meant to," Ace says.

"Do you truly believe that?"

He looks directly in my eyes, the depth of them never fails to entrance me. "Yes, I do. Don't you?"

I should, because it's been like this for us the entire time, and I've always lived by that motto. But my views on that have shifted slightly.

"I don't know anymore," I mutter under my breath just loud enough for him to hear.

"Come here." Ace wraps his long fingers gently around my small wrist and pulls me into him.

Our chests collide like opposing tides crashing against one another. A wild clash full of emotions and unspoken words.

"Your shirt will get crinkl—"

"Shh," he murmurs into my hair and presses his lips against my temple.

His warmth permeates my entire body, spreading from my fingertips to my toes.

Our breathing syncs.

I don't know how he does it, but he casts a bubble of comfort over me although I should be the one providing comfort for him.

This would be the perfect moment to tell him I'm growing a mini human inside of me. I part my lips, but the words lodge themselves, refusing to escape. I inhale deeply, yet I still can't bring myself to speak those life-altering words.

What's wrong with me?

He deserves to know, but other thoughts and pleas threaten to bubble over.

Don't do this.

Tell them about Logan.

Please.

Would me telling him that I'm pregnant change his mind about his planned testimony for this trial?

I press my cheek against the warmth of his neck, inhaling his cologne and feeling the slight stubble that remains after his shave. I drink all of him in. The rhythm of his breathing, the beat of his pulse, the soothing motion of his fingertips tracing up and down my arm.

I drink him in. Imprint him in my mind. Ensure that the memory of how he smells and feels embeds deeply in my neurons.

"We have to go," I say.

Ace lets me pull away from his embrace, but then he cups my face with both hands. He gazes down at me with those marvelous eyes that I couldn't help but fall in love with five years ago. "No matter what happens—"

"For me, it's always been you," I finish his sentence, the exact words he once spoke to me. I need him to know the outcome of this trial will not change how I feel about him, even though it may change everything else. It has always been this way.

His lips curl into a smile. "For me, it's always been you,"

he murmurs, repeating the phrase before pressing his lips to mine.

He kisses me with hunger. Longing.

He kisses me like there's no one else in the universe.

Like I'm oxygen and he's dying for air.

He kisses me like he's leaving his mark on me. With his hands in my hair and his teeth on my lips.

Finally, he kisses me like this our last moment.

And I'm scared it just might be.

Denzel drives us to the courthouse. My body moves on autopilot, but my mind races through the possibilities that await us during the trial. Only when Ace takes my hand do I realize I've been digging my nails into my knee, leaving half-moon marks behind.

Without a word, he guides my hand into his lap, intertwining our fingers.

Together, he seems to say even though his lips are tightly sealed. I manage to breathe a little easier, and a small weight lifts from my shoulders, even though nothing has changed.

I close my eyes and lean my head back into the seat. This is it. Whatever happens during this trial will define the rest of our lives. I clutch Ace's hand the remainder of the way, wondering if this is the last time I'll do this. Nik says the trial will span over a few days, but I've learnt the hard way that anything can happen when you least expect it to.

We arrive in front of the courthouse, and reporters and journalists are already gathered.

Waiting.

I expected just as much, but I'm still caught off guard by how many of them crowd the area. I used to dream of being in their shoes, rushing to cover breaking news. But now, standing on the other side of the cameras and microphones, I notice the added pressure and stress that a person experiences being in the spotlight.

"Pretend they aren't there." Ace squeezes my hand.

Having spent years in the public eye, Ace has grown accustomed to the media. He doesn't turn his head to acknowledge them as he exits the car and heads for my door. I'm already out by the time he reaches me.

Nik waits by the stone stairs to the entrance.

Swallowing what feels like a hundred times, I force my feet forward. I've finally managed to master the simple motion of taking step after step until I spot my father.

I freeze.

I knew he'd be here. He wouldn't miss the trial. He wouldn't miss witnessing justice for his wife. A million emotions flood all at once like a tsunami, and my breath crashes in short, uneven bursts. It's difficult to look at my dad without seeing flashes of my mom behind my closed eyelids.

I'm torn. Under normal circumstances, I'd be here with my dad. We'd both be rooting for the same side, but my life became far from normal the moment I met Ace.

Would I still be here if Logan hadn't confessed it was him behind the wheel that night? Would I be able to sit through trial, unsure of how I want it to pan out? A part of me, a part that is my father's daughter, would want justice to run its course. But the other part, a part that has finally found their soulmate, would want the law to show mercy for the boy I've fallen deeply in love with.

Maybe that's why I'm desperate to believe Logan, to believe that loving Ace isn't wrong. Because how can something so pure, so heart-consuming, so earth-shattering be wrong?

It all happens within the blink of an eye.

My father approaches us. His posture is stoic, and it reminds me of the time I saw him at the airport in Idaho. He hasn't tried to contact me since, and he looks different now. Older. As if he's aged a decade within a matter of weeks.

His eyes appear sunken with deep, dark craters beneath them. His beard is more salt than pepper, and he's in bad need of a haircut.

This is my fault. I chose Ace over him.

"Calla," my father speaks, his voice emerges rough, accompanied by a cough as he clears his throat.

Drawing a shaky breath, I brace myself for the hurtful words I anticipate he will unleash on Ace. His eyes, sharp as daggers, aimed at the man who he despises with all his being—the man he thinks stole everything from him and turned his entire world upside down.

If only he knew the truth. If only Ace would try and believe it himself.

I've been thinking about suggesting he try hypnosis to bring back memories of that night. I'm not sure how open he'll be to that idea, and even that comes with its own risks and consequences. I have even gone as far as Googling a reputable hypnotherapist in New York.

It might be a can of worms that shouldn't be opened, but don't we all deserve the truth after living so long in uncertainty? Or is that just me?

Before my father can unleash his thoughts, Ace swiftly grabs me by the waist and spins me around, shielding me with his body.

I stumble, nearly losing my balance in the process.

"Wh—" I manage to utter before screams shatter the air, jarring and deafening.

Mayhem erupts all around us.

People scatter in every direction. Leo sprints for us, his muscular figure slowing him down. I search for the cause of the chaos. And then I see *him*.

He stands out like an anomaly with his hooded jacket and jeans, a stark contrast to the summer-like day. He strides away, a gun clenched tightly in his right hand.

After that, the world around me seems to slow down, each second stretching into an eternity. My dad's grip tightens on his shoulder, his hand stained crimson with pooling blood.

Instinctively, I clutch my hands to my stomach, not understanding why my first thought is to protect the little life inside me. Half of me, half of Ace.

In front of me, Ace crumples onto the steps, his face contorted in pain as he clutches his stomach. Vibrant red stains his Prada shirt. At first, I don't register it—my mind and body completely numb.

Blood.

So much blood.

It pours out of him like a waterfall, painting the path beneath our feet with the color of demise. Three blinks, three heartbeats, and no one would know his shirt was formerly white.

I widen my eyes, terror seizing me by the throat and tightening its hold.

Squeezing.

Squeezing.

Squeezing until the very air escapes my lungs.

Somewhere in the background, anguished screams continue to pierce the air, but I consciously shut them out, my body trembling uncontrollably. The chattering of my teeth echoes in my ears, but I remain oblivious to the physical sensation. I don't realize it's my own screams penetrating the air as my knees hit the ground.

I fist his blood-soaked shirt. "Ace." I think I keep repeating it over and over, because all I can hear is his name echoing in my head like a prayer. This can't be happening.

Panic swells, but I still try to unbutton his shirt to search for the wound. I don't know much about first aid, but isn't pressure supposed to be applied to stop the bleeding.

There's so much blood. I can't see anything else but red, and I can't find where it's coming from. It appears to flow endlessly.

How much blood does a person have? How much are they able to lose before life begins to fade?

Ace stills my trembling hands, grasping them firmly with

his own. "Calla," he mutters, drawing my attention from his chest to his face.

His eyes, kaleidoscopic in their brilliance, seem almost otherworldly. They grow duller with each beat, a consequence of the rapid blood loss.

This isn't real. This isn't real.

I hope at any minute I'll wake up from this hellish nightmare.

"Calla," Ace repeats, and I realize I'm squeezing my eyes shut.

When I open them, his gaze pierces through me, fixating on my stomach that I'm cradling protectively once again.

He shakes his head weakly. "I wish..." He chokes out. "I wish you would've told me." There's genuine pain in his eyes. In his words.

Are they from the bullet wound? Or does the pain stem from the fact I've been keeping a secret from him? Not wanting to entirely acknowledge the news myself.

"I—" I falter, words eluding me. I never intended to keep this from him for long, but I haven't been entirely honest with him either. I wanted time to process the news myself before telling him, and perhaps my actions were selfish.

"Stay with me, Ace. Please."

Sirens blare in the background, but they remain at least several blocks away.

Too far.

I need to keep Ace conscious. I press down harder on his stomach, desperately hoping the added pressure on his wound will slow down the excessive bleeding. In the meantime, I need to keep him awake. His eyelids droop heavily as he fights against the weight of exhaustion. He's trying to stay with me, and it's taking everything out of him.

"You're going to make it through this. And we're going to start a family. You're going to be a great dad." My voice shakes and a tear escapes, tracing a path down my cheek.

The corners of his mouth twitch ever so slightly, barely forming a smile. His trembling hand reaches out, resting on my stomach. His mouth moves as if to say he loves me, but no sound emerges, and then he shuts his eyes and doesn't open them again.

"Ace. Stay with me. Please. Ace!" I cry out in desperation, my voice pleading for him to come back to me.

Paramedics swarm around us, bombarding me with rapid-fire questions. I move out of their way, letting them do their job. I try to provide coherent answers, but I can't concentrate on anything except for the paramedic who's over Ace and the words flowing out of her mouth.

"He's lost an excessive amount of blood."

"There's no pulse.

"Starting chest compressions."

35

Numb

Calla

I thought losing someone you love is supposed to render you numb, devoid of feeling. I wish it did.

I want to feel nothing. God, what I would do to feel nothing.

Every part of me is ablaze, consumed by an inferno that reduces me to ashes.

Over and over and over again.

My heart has been torn out of my chest. It's been subjected to unending onslaught and then thrown away, charred and destroyed.

I can't do this. I'd rather be dead than feel this much pain. I've already lived through it once. I can't do it again.

My head is spinning.

I'm drowning.

Someone is calling my name in the distance.

But it's not the person I need.

I fade away, become lost in my own head. I think my body hits the ground, and that's when everything finally goes black.

36

The Funeral

Calla

3 weeks later

Black dress. Black shoes.

The atmosphere is steeped in darkness and melancholy.

Standing on the wooden floor, I gaze into the mirror, carefully examining each minor detail yet not truly registering any of it. I barely acknowledge the stray strand of hair that's escaped the tight ponytail, the shadowy crescents beneath my eyes that show my weariness, or the subtle bump emerging on my stomach.

I'm only ten weeks along, almost eleven. But I've always had a flat stomach, so I guess it's why I may be showing so early.

My mind shifts to the two pink lines on the test that showed up right away. The shaking in my hands when I dialed the doctor's office number. The déjà vu I felt going into the clinic to confirm the results.

The decision that weighed on me for days...until I saw the way Ace looked at me when he realized what I'd been hiding from him. The way his eyes flashed between my stomach and the expression on my face.

In that instant, everything crystallized. The pivotal moment when my decision was made. Or perhaps I'd already known what I wanted to do. I just hadn't accepted it yet with everything else going on.

I snatch a dark-navy coat from my closet and drape it over my shoulders. Covering the bump or bloat. Today isn't the day to be making such announcements. But that's how the world works, isn't it?

One life fades away, making room for another.

It's the cycle of everything. A constant haunting reminder of the ebb and flow of existence, the constant interplay between joy and sorrow, life and death.

I slip my feet into the black heels, grab my handbag and open the door. Denzel is waiting for me. He gives me a look conveying a million words. I'm glad he doesn't use phrases such as *I'm sorry for your loss*. I've heard them too many times in my life already, and I know I'll be hearing them again today.

The words somehow feel pitiful and almost condescending. I understand the meaning behind the phrase, I do. But it seems almost insincere.

The weather is gloomy. The bright spring sun tries but fails to break out through the angry clouds.

Nik awaits us by the car. I notice him before he sees me. His sad eyes stare off into the distance.

I swallow the lump in my throat and force myself to ask, "How are you doing?"

Nik snaps out of his daze, looks at me and shrugs. "I don't know."

I nod. I'm glad he gave me the truth. I slide in the car, place my handbag in my lap and stare out the window. The world passes by in a blur. The city seems unaware of the weight on my shoulders, the gaping hole in my heart. It's hard to imagine a time when I was truly happy.

Will I ever experience that feeling again?

Without thinking, I bring my hand down on my stomach.

Moments like these make me wonder or more so solidify that everything is destined in a way. This life inside of me, no matter how small it may be, is what's holding me together.

Nik's eyes stray on me, and I quickly hide the mindless action by running my hands down the dress, and then the jacket—hoping he'll only see me just trying to smooth my clothing and nothing else.

On a normal day, that most likely wouldn't have worked. Nik is too perceptive. It might be the lawyer in him, or maybe it's just the way he is…but today he doesn't even give me a second glance. His mind is elsewhere.

Denzel pulls up to the chapel, and the car comes to a

halt. I take a deep breath, attempting to steady my racing thoughts. The gravity of the moment hangs heavy in the air as I open the car door and step out onto the pavement.

I don't search Ace out, but I feel his presence instead.

I always do.

I'm drawn to him no matter what. No matter what we are doing, where we are, or what we are going through.

He's wearing all black from head to toe, his signature *color* is the color of grief today.

He's by his mom's side, swarmed by people who are here to pay their respects. His slate eyes land on me instantly. They're broken beyond repair. Even though we haven't been apart for more than a few hours, it feels like it's been way longer than that.

The weight of the grief he's facing is imprinted in every line on his face. His features are a haunting reflection of the shattered pieces within. Pain and sorrow consume him, and I yearn to reach out, to somehow mend the irreparable damage.

How can mere words heal wounds so deep?

How can I offer comfort when his pain feels impenetrable?

I've dealt with loss before. I know all too well what it feels like. No matter the condolences anyone offers, it doesn't become easier.

"You're here," he says, approaching me and walking— no, *falling* into my arms.

I wrap my arms tightly around his waist. Careful not to touch the place where he's still healing from the bullet wound.

His body is warm against mine, and I grasp it. Trying to

inhale it into my own body. "I'm here. Always," I murmur against his neck.

He squeezes me tighter. I feel the rumble of his chest, like he's desperately trying to hold it all in. For his mom's sake.

So that's why I need to hold it together today. For him.

When we pull apart, I allow my gaze to scan the scene in front of me.

I doubt Ellie would have wanted this somber gathering. But these things are not so much for the person who's passed but for their families, for the people who need to say their final goodbyes. Those who need closure.

My heart stills when it lands on the person who shouldn't be here today.

I recognize him instantly.

He's the man who showed up at Ace's mom's house. The man who ruined Ace's life. The man who refused to be in Ellie's life, and now he has the indecency to show up here when everyone is grieving.

From here, he looks like any other person paying their respects. Dressed impeccably in black, I see so much of Ace in him.

If I didn't know any better, I'd assume his eyes are red from crying. But I *do* know better. I know this man has no emotions for others—not even for his own children. So the red eyes must be from whatever he consumed prior to coming to his daughter's funeral.

"Ace," I attempt to warn him, but he must've seen the man at the same time I did, because his entire body turns taut.

I tighten my hand around his, hoping he won't do anything irrational. I know what Ace can get like in the heat of the moment, but I also know that he'll regret giving that man any attention today.

But while I'm clutching Ace's hand, I notice Nik striding in the direction of his father. Nik's expression is stone cold. Some people, like Ace, wear their anger vividly. Others, like Nik, conceal it behind their eyes.

Those who don't know Nik, wouldn't know he's only moments from setting hell loose on the man in front of him. I've never seen the violent side of Nik, but perhaps I haven't spent that much time around him, or he keeps it buried away.

Ace pulls me along with him.

"You have some nerve showing your face here," Nik says to his father in a low tone.

From the corner of my eye, I notice Reese striding toward the commotion with her head held high. Her heels dig into the ground, but instead of looking off-balance, she seems grounded. The sorrow on her face is evident, of course. Her cheeks are stained with tears, and her vibrant eyes portray the loss that no mother should ever be alive to bear.

After all, in a perfect world, mothers grow old and watch their children grow up. But Reese will never see her daughter experience her first love, or her first heartbreak. She'll never see her graduation or prom. She'll never know what career path Ellie would have chosen.

"What are you doing here?" Reese asks, the question directed at her ex-husband.

"I have as much right to be here as you do. I'm grieving the loss of my child," he says.

"The child you abandoned when she was three years old," Reese says. "You didn't care about her then. You didn't care about her for almost a decade. Why are you here now?"

"A man can change."

Reese stares at him with broken eyes, but even though they are broken, they still hold so much rage inside. "Not you," she hisses.

He places his hand on his chest, attempting to feign sincerity. He's trying to manipulate the situation, but Reese can see through his façade. She's had to deal with it for years. She takes a step closer, her gaze piercing through his pretense.

"Change?" She scoffs, her voice laced with years of pain and resentment. "You don't get to come here now, claiming some newfound sense of responsibility that I'm sure has a different purpose. You were absent when she needed a father. You missed the milestones, the laughter, the tears. You weren't there through the hard moments, and you don't deserve to be here now."

"Reese, I…" he begins, but his voice falters. Even if he's here for the right reasons, he's done so much damage over the years that no one from his blood wants him here.

Reese raises her hand, silencing him. Her eyes, still brimming with tears, also shine with a glimmer of resilience. "No," she says firmly. "You need to leave before I call the police. I have a restraining order against you."

He snickers, grunts something along the lines of, "Can't

even pay respects to my own daughter." Then he turns and walks away somberly.

The rest of the ceremony is beautiful and heartbreaking. My face is stained with tears. Tears that manage to escape no matter how much I tried to hold them in.

Ace clutches my hand, like I'm the only thing keeping him grounded. Like I'm the oxygen, and he's gasping for breath while being suffocated.

Knowing that Ace needs me to be the anchor for the both of us is all that's keeping me from having a breakdown.

When it's time to say the final goodbye, he untangles his fingers from mine and drags his feet to the casket. Each step is a heavy burden, each movement filled with an indescribable weight. I watch him with an ache in my chest that's ready to combust.

He takes a deep breath once reaching the casket and attempts to compose himself. His trembling hand hesitates for a brief moment before he places it gently on the smooth surface. His eyes lock onto the engraved name, his lips mouthing the words as if etching them into his soul.

In that moment, there's this vulnerability carved across his face, pain that cuts through everything. I step forward, find my place by his side and wrap my arms around him, offering a silent embrace that conveys the words I'll never be able to find. I become his rock, offering the support he desperately needs.

We stand there frozen, united in grief and finding some sort of solace in each other's presence.

37

The Aftermath

Ace

3 weeks earlier

The incessant beeping of machines and muffled voices fill my ears. I open my eyes to blurry and unfamiliar surroundings. My mouth is as dry as fucking sandpaper. I try to sit up and lean on my elbows, but a sharp pain shoots through my stomach down to my toes. I groan and clench my teeth to suppress the ache.

"Hey, hey. You shouldn't do that," a familiar voice I would recognize anywhere, even in hell, says.

Concerned eyes stare at me. The warm blend of brown and green catch the light and reveal the flecks of gold. They've always provided me with a sense of ease.

I glance down at the various tubes and wires hooked up

to my body. My head throbs, and my limbs feel heavy, but I revel in the pain because it means I'm alive.

Aren't I?

Calla's hands move to my chest, gently pushing me back onto the pillow.

I let her, just so I can feel her touching me.

When she's sure I'm not going to remove any wires, she turns her back to me for a moment. I reach out and catch her hand. "Don't go," I plead, my voice hoarse.

She looks at me and shakes her head. "I'm not going anywhere. I was just going to get you some water."

I nod, releasing a breath, and even that feels arduous.

Calla offers me water, and the first sip feels like I've swallowed a million glass shards. She sets the cup on the table near me.

I survey my surroundings. The room is dim, but the blinds are up. The sky still sports dark shades of blue and is transitioning to a soft orange. A navy hospital chair is nestled into the bed as close as the machines would allow, and a pillow wedges into the armrest with a hospital sheet draped over it.

My gaze travels to Calla. "Did you stay here all night?"

"For the last three nights," she admits sheepishly. "I wanted to be here when you woke up."

Even though I'd do the same for her, a pang of guilt overcomes me. She slept in an uncomfortable hospital chair because of me.

"You took a bullet for me…" she says.

My lips turn up at the corners. I took a bullet for her, and I'd do it all over again even if it meant not surviving it. I'd give my life for her without a second thought because if she got shot, I don't know if *I* would be able to survive.

Living without her is excruciating but doable when I know she's alive and happy. I wouldn't be able to if I knew she was dead.

"It was stupid," she continues. "And reckless. And I would never have forgiven you if you died." Tears build in her eyes, and she blinks them away, hoping that I don't notice.

My smile dissipates. "A simple thank you would suffice." I try to make the conversation lighter.

She rolls her eyes. "I haven't finished."

I make a motion with my hand for her to continue.

"But…you saved my life. That bullet would've hit me in the chest if you didn't react so fast and step in front of it." She's right. Logan's aim was impeccable. "And there's nothing in this world that I can do to repay you for that."

At the thought of Logan, my blood boils, and a deep sense of responsibility knocks at my conscious. I should've taken care of him by now. I've been slack, too focused on the trial and worried how it would go, even though I've been trying to conceal my feelings around Calla. I didn't want her to worry more than she already was.

And now I know why she was overwhelmed with worry. My gaze darts to her stomach. A cream sweater covers her upper half, and I begin to doubt what I concocted when I got shot, before I lost consciousness. But when Calla mindlessly puts her hand on her stomach, she confirms it for me, even though she doesn't even know she's doing it.

"You don't need to repay me. I'd do it all over again in a heartbeat." I take her hand in mine.

"Ace—" She clears her throat. "I should've told you earlier, but I... It's just with everything going on, I couldn't find the right time, and I hadn't decided what I wanted to do."

"What do you mean you hadn't decided what you wanted to do?" I ask, my voice rough. Was she going to make this decision on her own? What happened to communication? She's the one who is always asking me to open up to her, and yet how long has she kept this from me?

"It was a shock, unplanned and unexpected. I couldn't think rationally. God, most of the time I wasn't thinking about it. Instead, my mind was on Ellie and the trial."

"It's not your decision to make alone. You should've told me as soon as you found out."

"How is it not my decision?" She huffs. "You're set on taking the stand and telling the entire world you're guilty, even though we have reason to believe that you weren't the one driving that night. And if they find you guilty, who will be left to bring this baby into the world? Me. Alone. So I took that into consideration."

"I—"

"But I was going to tell you."

That statement doesn't take away my frustration. She didn't fucking tell me because she thinks she might have to raise the baby on her own. "It changes everything."

"That's what I thought."

"I don't understand. Why is that a bad thing?"

"Because nothing else has changed your mind. Not your family. Not me," she says, quickly saying the last part, which makes me realize this is what it's about.

She thinks I wouldn't change my mind for my family or for her, but I would for a baby, and that's not entirely true.

"I thought you wanted this! I thought you wanted me up there on the stand, taking responsibility for what I did. I'm doing this just as much for you as for myself."

She shakes her head. "What part of me saying don't do this is me wanting you on the stand? The lines were blurred before. Before Logan told me what he did. But now... What happened wasn't your fault, and it's like you don't want to believe that. It's like you want to be guilty."

I swallow. My whole body radiates with pain, and it doesn't help that I'm tensing up. "After believing something for so long, it's so fucking hard to accept a different reality."

I have lived with the guilt of it for what feels like an eternity. I've struggled with forgiving myself for what I've done. I've battled with the demons that took up residence in my head and chanted that I'm not worthy of anything good because of it. It's not easy to turn my mindset around, especially since I don't remember much of that night. So how does she expect me to change all that based only on what Logan said?

"No one will believe me at the trial if I start blaming Logan for it." I'd look like I was purposefully trying to shift the blame, which is the last thing I want to do. Instead, I'm ready to take whatever punishment the system decides to give me—the punishment that I probably deserve.

"None of it matters anymore anyway," she says with a relief-filled expression.

I assess her. She's glowing with this new radiance that I haven't seen in a while, like she knows something I don't. "What are you talking about?"

"Logan was taken into custody...after Leo shot him— nothing severe, only grazed his shoulder."

I have to give that man a raise. Not only did he shoot Logan, but he made sure not to kill him, because that task is for me.

"He was unhinged. He confessed to everything. Nik says it completely kills the case the prosecution has against you."

I stare at her. It seems too good to be true—too easy. After all these years of hating myself and carrying the blame on my shoulders, I'm not going to be held responsible.

It doesn't seem right to me, even though it should feel like a massive weight has been lifted off my shoulders. "What's the catch?"

She sighs like she was hoping I wouldn't ask. "Like I said, he's unhinged, so they still have to question him extensively, and he has good lawyers. Not as good as your brother, but I'm sure they know what they're doing."

I'm sure they do. He'll be able to weave his way out of this. Plead mentally ill or some shit.

"This is a good thing, Ace. He confessed."

I still don't understand why the fuck he would do that, especially after all these years. It doesn't make sense. Seems too easy.

But maybe after everything Calla and I have experienced over the years, we're catching a break.

Maybe we deserve easy.

I've been here for two days now. My mom, Ellie and Nik practically live here now too. I was ready to leave this morning. Got up, put my clothes on—ones Calla brought for me since the ones I wore when I was brought in are stained with blood.

Calla arrived while I was in the middle of reassuring the doctor I felt completely fine, even though each step I took sliced pain through my stomach. Calla's eyes bulged open when she found me standing by the door of my hospital room. She practically tackled me back on to the bed, told me I was being a "selfish asshole".

So here I am, spending another night here. I managed to convince everyone to go home to rest and shower.

Visiting hours are almost over when the last person I expect to see walks through the door of my hospital room. I'm glad I'm already in the hospital. After this conversation, when he's finished with me, I'm probably going to need to be here either way.

Each time I see Calla's father, he seems like he's aged a

few years at a time. He's grown out his beard. It's dark with many white hairs throughout, so much so that the white looks like it's eating away the dark.

But it's the look in his eyes that holds the decades.

I don't speak at first. There's nothing I can say to him that will make anything he's been through better.

Briefly, I consider apologizing. But I quickly wash that idea away with the blink of my eyes. Sometimes it's better to say nothing at all than to apologize for something so severe, something that can't be forgiven.

"Calla told me," he says.

At first, I don't understand what he means, but then it clicks into place.

Calla must've told him about Logan. Although I'm not sure why or how her father, the man in front of me, would believe it.

"I know what you're thinking," he says before I have the chance to speak my mind. "I didn't believe it at first. But seeing the evidence presented to me... I've come to the conclusion that it wasn't you driving that night."

Spoken like a true cop.

Evidence? What evidence is there apart from Logan's confession?

"However, that doesn't mean you're innocent either."

"I know." *Innocent* is not a word I'd ever use to describe myself. I've done my share of bad shit. Shit that would for sure get me a one way ticket to hell.

"You took a bullet for my daughter. And I guess that

puts me in your debt. So if there's anything I can do for you, let me know." A pained look sets upon his face, like he doesn't want to be here.

I clear my throat, look him right in the eyes. "There is actually something you can do for me."

He stares back, surprised by my answer. Like he meant his statement more as a formality, not something I would take him up on.

"I'm in love with your daughter," I say earnestly. "I have been for a long time. And I plan on marrying her no matter what." I look him straight in the eyes as I say this. I want him to know that absolutely *nothing* will change my mind. Not him. Not anyone else. "But I've come to realize that your opinion means the world to her."

"You want my blessing," he states, reading in between the lines.

I give him a tilt of my head. "Yes."

He considers this for a moment too long. Perhaps I've misread this situation completely. Perhaps this is not us uniting.

Did Calla put her dad up to this?

Though there's no reason why he'd agree to it even if she did ask, is there?

"My daughter is the only family I have left. If she's alive and happy because of you, and if this is what it takes for me to stay in her life...in my grandchild's life, then you have my blessing," he states reluctantly.

It's clear from his expression that I'm not his first or second choice of a proper suitor for his daughter. If he had his way, she'd never see or talk to me again. But she's a grown woman, and she has decided on *me*.

I still can't believe it.

She chose me.

And for that, I'm the luckiest man in the world.

38

Shattered

Ace

It's been two and a half weeks since I took a bullet for her. I'm at my check-up, as per Calla's orders, when I receive *the call*. The call I've been dreading my whole life. I'd hoped it would never come.

Without a second thought, I drop everything and gun it for my mom's house, pushing my motorbike to its absolute limits. The mere thought of losing Ellie has been gradually killing me since the first time we found out about the diagnosis. Since we sat in that room and a professional diagnosed her with one of the leading causes in children's deaths.

At the time, it'd been devastating. But we'd known we had a chance, that *she* had a chance. During her recovery, that was what kept us going. All of us believed that it was just a hiccup in our lives, something that Ellie would be able to overcome. That she'd come out stronger on the other side. And she did.

Until she got sick again. And again.

Each appointment, each treatment dimmed the spark of hope we held on to. Until one day, we sat in the pediatrician's office and received the blow that completely darkened our reality.

"There's nothing more we can do," the doctor told us what we already knew. What all of us could see up close with our own eyes. "It's best if she was in the comfort of her own home."

We all knew what that meant.

As he relayed the information, he remained cool and collected. His expression portrayed the perfect amount of sympathy and compassion. He'd had years of practice, years of delivering bad news to a number of patients.

I wanted to jump out of my chair, pull him up by his shirt and slam him into the wall. I wanted to yell at him to do something, to help her. But I didn't do any of those things. My anger or frustration wasn't directed at the man in front of me, the man who'd tried but failed to save my little sister. It didn't have a source. It just was. So I sought a second opinion. And then a third.

They all told us the same thing.

Each time they conveyed the same words, I had that urge to knock that person against something.

Of course, I didn't.

When I arrive at my mom's house, I drop the bike in the

driveway and jog inside. Terrified of missing even a second by her side.

Calla is already here. A sky-blue dress graces her flawlessly and brings a little bit of color into the room. Her eyes soak with dread, but still, she holds a smile on her face like her life depends on it.

She might be fooling everyone else, but not me. I see right through her.

I look over to the bed where Ellie is tucked in.

I've been struggling to come to terms with how all of this has panned out. How can the world be so fucking cruel? No one believes it. No one believes it could happen to them, to their loved ones, until it does.

She looks so small, yet she still manages to have a smile on her face.

She doesn't deserve this. But what kid does?

I'd do anything to take her spot in that bed. To give myself up to the culprit that's taken over her body.

"Ace?" her voice emerges barely a whisper.

I'm at her side in an instant. "I'm right here." Her hand is cold, and I drag the soft blanket farther over her body.

"Look after Mom." Her lips move, but no sound comes out.

"You don't worry about that." I sink onto the bed by her side.

Nik rushes into the room in his work clothes with only moments to spare. Even though he hasn't spent much time with Ellie, anyone can see the love he has for her.

Ever since he found out about her, he took on the role of big brother, and I hate to admit that he might be better at it than I am.

"Hey, how's she doing?" Nik asks quietly as he approaches.

I shake my head, unable to find the words. Calla fills him in, her voice trembles while doing so.

The four of us remain in the room, silent except for the occasional word here and there when Ellie can muster it. We sit there for what seems like an eternity. My heart shatters over and over with each second that passes. There's a sinking feeling in my stomach, and it just keeps tumbling and tumbling with no end in sight, because I know what's coming, and I can't fucking stop it.

When Ellie takes her final breath, my own breathing becomes strenuous. It's like a part of me is now gone too. Losing someone you love, someone you spent the better half of your life with does something to you, changes the roots of your being.

I'll never be the same person again.

I step outside. Branches stir in the wind, a dog howls in the distance.

Life goes on while my world fucking shatters. There's no coming back from something like this. It fucks you up for eternity.

I'm seconds away from completely shutting down.

Mentally and physically.

I eye my motorbike in the driveway, and it suddenly seems

like a great fucking idea to take it for a spin. To feel the wind whip in my face and hear the roar of the engine in my ears. To feel something other than my chest contracting in agony.

A steady hand clasps down on my shoulder. In some fucking weird way, it grounds me, stops me from crashing completely. Stops my mind right before it falls into that darkness where my actions aren't my own anymore, but instead are dominated by the monster within.

"I'm here, little brother," Nik says, and I know he means it.

I nod. "I don't know if I can get through this. I'm already fucked up. I'm afraid of what this will do to me."

The words surprise me. They probably surprise Nik too, since I've never been this fucking candid with him.

"You don't have to do it alone."

39

Closure

Ace

It's true what they say about grief. In a way, it just gets worse. The more time passes, the more I fucking miss her.

The most fucked-up part is that I have no one to blame but myself. Every now and then I go through scenarios in my head. What I could have done throughout my life to save her—better doctors? Should we have traveled to a different country for another opinion? Did I do enough? Were there other treatments only in their trial stages that I should have researched? Should I have pushed her—forced her somehow—to do the treatment even though it would've cost me our relationship?

I have no answers and seeking them out won't do any good.

Instead, there are other things that still need to be taken care of.

Logan.

Yeah, that fucker still roams the planet.

While the law worked against me, it worked in favor for Logan. Since he'd remained in Idaho while the clock ticked over, and the statute of limitations ran out, there was nothing anyone could do to bring charges against him. He must've confessed knowing this.

A blessing in disguise.

Now I get to take care of him my way without relying on justice.

I can't let him live in the same world as I do. In the same world as my family. In the same world as my unborn child. I don't want to have to always sleep with one eye open. Waiting. Expecting. Guessing when he's going to come after me or the ones I love again.

That's not the future I want.

I'm also a man of my word. And I told him I'd kill him if he ever touched Calla. I'll serve justice in her honor even if it's the last thing I ever do.

Cassidy?

She's not a problem without Logan.

She's the type of person who's all talk and no action. She needs someone to take care of her grand plans. She doesn't hate me as much as Logan does. At least, not enough to kill me. And when this is all over, she'll find a new shiny toy to play with.

When I twist the doorknob, it's already unlocked. He's waiting for me like I hoped he'd be. There's nothing worse than heading into someone's home and putting a gun to their head when they least expect it. That would be cruel and cowardly act. Better that he's prepared for this. It's better that he's willing to fight.

I find him standing in the center of the room, his posture defiant.

"Finally." Logan's voice pierces the heavy silence, dripping with a toxic balance of arrogance and malice. "You're just as predictable as I thought." He sneers.

When I look at him, rage builds inside of me at the thought of what he did to Calla. Of what he *would've* done to her if I hadn't gotten there in time.

Anger eddies, ugly and vicious, and I can't help myself. I pull my fist back and deliver a powerful punch straight into Logan's smug face.

It's not enough, so I do it again.

And again—for good measure—directing all of my power into it.

The impacts reverberates through the room, a satisfying release of pent-up fury. His head snaps back each time. Blood spurts from his broken nose, and he stumbles, struggling to maintain his balance.

The toxic façade of arrogance and malice doesn't crumble under the weight of his own actions. Though I wonder if he'd underestimated the depth of my determination and the lengths I'd go to protect those I love.

I advance on him, my anger still boiling. Knowing what he did to Calla fuels my every move, igniting hell. I grab him by the shirt, forcing him to meet my gaze.

"You thought you could hurt her?" I growl, tightening my grip. "I made you a fucking promise." I shove him back.

"I've been waiting." He wipes his face with the back of his hand and spits a mouthful of blood onto the floor.

"Seems more like *running*."

He extends his hands, a gesture that mocks my impatience. He's here now, isn't he?

I reach for my gun, wanting to get this over and done with. I have other places to be. He's not worth my time.

He chuckles, his sadistic nature revealed once again. "Can't we settle this the old-fashioned way?" he suggests, as if relishing the thought of prolonging his own suffering. Perhaps he's stupid enough to believe he could defeat me in the sport I excel in.

"No," I reply, my voice steady and resolute. "This ends here."

With unwavering focus, I steady my grip on the gun, my finger inching closer to the trigger. Every fiber of my being poised for action, ready to unleash the storm that had been brewing for what seems like eternity.

"Aren't you going to thank me for my confession?" he asks. "Without it, who knows where you'd be."

I ignore him, refusing to play this game with him.

"Do you not want to know the truth?" He sneers, a cruel blend of arrogance and perhaps desperation on his face.

"No," I spit.

I've had time to think about it, to come to the conclusion that even if I came here demanding the truth from Logan, there's no guarantee he'd give it to me. Or even if he does, I won't be able to tell the truth from lies.

So there's no point. The truth will always linger as a question mark.

"Were you driving that night or weren't you?" he taunts. "Were you behind the wheel, or was I?"

"It doesn't matter." I work my jaw. *It does.* But I won't allow him to goad me any longer.

"I often thought about how you'd react when and if you found out the truth," he continues, a sinister smile playing on his lips. "I wish I was the one who told you. You know... we're no different. You're just as fucked up as I am."

"I'm nothing like you," I say, but I'm not sure how true that statement is. After all, I'm standing in my former best friend's apartment, pointing a gun to his fucking head, and I won't be leaving until I pull the trigger.

"Though I still can't fucking understand the fascination you have with her," Logan continues as if I haven't said anything. "Perhaps if I'd had the chance to find out for myself—"

The deafening sound of the gunshot explodes in the room, echoing. It sort of happens in slow motion. Time freezes as the bullet locates the target—his head.

Logan staggers backward, dead in an instant. His body crumples to the ground.

I hate how I feel when I watch the life drain out of him.

A conflicting and disturbing sensation gnaws at my conscience. I'm fucking repulsed by the darkness within, the part of me that revels in the power and control accompanying such moments. But then I see Calla's face in my mind. She's the reason why I had to do this. And I'm not going to feel bad for protecting her.

I arrive at the restaurant, my hands soaked in another man's blood.

The buzz of conversation, the clinking of glasses and the occasional burst of laughter saturates the room. Sleek wooden tables and chairs are carefully arranged, and a large window stretches across one side of the restaurant, offering a bird's eye view of New York City skyline sprawling before me.

I don't have to search for her. My body carries me to her on its own. It's as if a magnetic force guides my every step, drawing me closer to the woman who holds my heart. The woman who I killed for moments ago and would again and again if it meant keeping her safe.

She's fucking stunning. Her hair falls in gentle waves and frames her face. She has a natural glow. A long dress clings to her body, accentuating her beautiful curves and the new life growing within her. A part of me.

I can't get over that. It fucking amazes me each time I think about it.

My mom sits next to Calla, and she smiles when she sees

me. The last few months have been tough on her. I've offered her to come live with us—Calla's idea—but she straight up refused, like I knew she would. Calla and I see her on most days though.

"What took you so long? I had to order for you," Calla says nervously once I'm standing by her side.

"Happy Birthday." I bend down and kiss her on the cheek. "I'll make it up to you, love."

Her gaze drops to my hand, to my fingers wrapped around the back of her chair. My knuckles are busted, bruises already forming on them. I leave them there for a moment longer, for the truth of what I've done to sink in.

She knows instantly. Or perhaps she only suspects. "Is *he*..." Her words, barely a whisper on her lips, trail off into the distance, swallowed by the buzzing of voices around us.

I tilt my head forward in a slight nod. "You don't have to worry about him anymore."

Even though she knew his fate all along, knew from the day he took her, I'm still afraid of how she'll react. I search her face for disgust, hatred or fear. There's none. Instead, I find relief.

"Are you okay?" she asks.

I don't know. Is anyone okay after taking a life no matter what the circumstances are?

"I will be."

Her shoulders relax, and she places one hand on mine— the other reaching out, wrapping around my neck and bringing my mouth down on hers.

I love kissing her. Touching her. Being in her vicinity. It makes me fucking high.

"Hope I'm not interrupting, but are we all going to get the same greeting?" Nik chuckles.

I feel Calla smile against my lips and pull away.

Nik, along with Calla's father, Mia, Theo and Josh are also at the table. All eyes on us.

What does a man have to do to get some fucking privacy around here?

"Right. Sorry." Calla blushes.

"I mean, don't stop on our account. We were enjoying the show," Theo remarks, right eyebrow cocked.

"Yeah, I bet you—" I'm about to serve him a retort.

"I'm not paying for a dinner and a movie," Nik interjects, his grin widening.

Everyone chuckles, even Calla's father, who I think still isn't a fan of mine and probably never will be. I serve as a memory of how his wife died, but as long as he can tolerate my company in the presence of Calla, I'm happy.

"Fucking clown," I mutter to Nik, shaking my head with a grin on my face.

I take a seat at the table next to Calla, taking her hand in mine, interlacing our fingers—needing to be touching her after what I've done earlier this evening.

"So what does it feel like to know you're going to be a dad?" Josh asks me.

We've already told everyone the news. Mia was the first one to know since she was there when Calla found out. Then probably Theo, even though Mia claims she didn't tell him. Calla told her dad at the hospital, which is why he was set on making amends with me, I think. I know without her having to tell me that she provided him with an ultimatum.

"Fucking incredible," I say without much thought.

Theo's grin falters a bit, and I feel like an insensitive prick after knowing what happened with Mia and him, but then he says, "I can't wait to meet him."

"Him?" Calla raises her brows at Theo.

We haven't found out the gender. We're not planning to until birth.

"Yep, I have a strong feeling it's a boy," Theo replies confidently.

Calla looks at me with a smile. "And what do you think?"

I shrug, not wanting to make predictions. "Twins?" I joke.

She throws her head back and laughs. "Twins? Are you trying to give me a heart attack?"

Mia raises an eyebrow. "Well, if it turns out to be twins, you better start preparing for double diaper duty and sleepless nights."

"Guys, relax. There's only one in here." Calla places her hand on her stomach.

"We're not going home?" Calla asks as I drive in the opposite direction of our penthouse following her birthday dinner.

"I still haven't given you your birthday present."

"And my birthday present isn't something you can give me at home?" She tries to reach for clues.

I shrug and place my hand on her thigh. "Impatient as always. That's never going to change, is it?"

"You love it."

"I love everything about you."

Silence follows. "So it's all over?" she finally asks.

Her question is weighted. She's not asking just about Logan or Cassidy. She's asking about everything that stood in our way.

I don't lie to her. "I fucking hope so," I say, massaging small circles into her thigh.

She releases a heavy breath and relaxes into the seat.

I pull up outside a commercial building, and we take the elevator up to the top floor.

"What's this? What are we doing here?" She glances around the empty floor.

There's nothing here. No people, no furniture. It's an empty canvas.

"It's yours," I say.

"Mine?" Confusion sweeps over her face. She rests her hand on her stomach. She has a bump now, and it's incredible.

"Yours, Calla. It's going to be your own publishing company. You can run it however you want. Publish whatever stories you want. I know it's been your dream, and I want to help make it come true."

Her jaw drops in shock, and her body trembles with emotion.

"I know how much this means to you. This company is yours, and I can't wait to see all the amazing things you do with it."

"I can't—" Although words evade her, I'm prepared for it.

"You can, and you will," I say, my tone implying finality. "Look, I know our lives are going to be chaotic with this child—"

"And planning a wedding," she adds.

Yeah, there's that too. I'd marry her right here and now if I could.

"But I know that writing makes you happy, and I wanted you to have space for that." I pull her close, wrapping my arms around her.

Calla leans into my embrace. "Thank you. This is everything," she whispers.

She gave up so much for me, including the career she worked so hard for.

It's the least I can do.

EPILOGUE

Calla

one year later

It's crazy to think how all the events that happened led me to this point in my life. Some were good, and others not so much, but all have taught me something along the way.

Contrary to societal expectations, I never thought much about marriage. It's often ingrained in young women's minds as something they should think about from a young age. But I'm grateful that my parents didn't put too much emphasis on it. They were more focused on their careers and loved their jobs. Although they were married, they didn't see it as a necessity to solidify their relationship.

Standing in the spacious room of the two-story building, only a few hours remain before I walk down the aisle and say

"I do" to the man who's changed my life in more ways than I could've ever imagined. The mere thought of it makes my heart race and my hands become clammy. I try to swallow down the nerves and distract myself while waiting for the makeup artist, hairstylist and bridal party to arrive.

I have to admit, I don't have many people—female especially—that I consider more than an acquaintance. So it was a struggle to find a handful of people to be a part of my special day. I settled on Mia—of course—to be my maid of honor. I even asked her in one of those cute ways I saw on Pinterest, with a box proposal. Although I think I may have unintentionally hurt her feelings by waiting so long since she'd already started planning my bachelorette party.

Mia's voice startles me out of my thoughts, "What did I say about getting that beauty sleep?"

I look up to her standing at the entrance wearing a pink bridesmaid nightgown, hands on her hips. Her heart-shaped face is framed perfectly by her short side bangs, which are clipped back with a claw clip.

We spent last night at the venue, but Ace and I slept in different rooms—as per the night-before-the-wedding tradition. Surprisingly, he was the one who suggested it. I was taken aback by it, because Ace didn't strike me as one who was big on traditions.

Either way, whether I spent the night with Ace or not, it wouldn't have changed the current situation of me running on maybe an hour of sleep.

"I didn't get much."

"Clearly." She shakes her head in disapproval. "How are you going to stay awake today or tonight? I'm sure Ace has plans for your wedding night," she adds with a wink.

I don't doubt that. I'm sure he has wicked thoughts running through his mind on how he wants to spend our first night as husband and wife. Thinking about what Ace has possibly planned for the night ahead makes me more excited to get the anxious part of the day over and done with.

I'm still as crazy as ever about him.

The thought of loving someone so much that I would want to spend the rest of my life with them had never previously crossed my mind.

Not until I met him.

And now, I can't imagine my life without him. Ace has consumed me—body, mind and soul. There's no one else that I see myself having that connection with. Not in this life, and not in the next.

The makeup artist and hairstylist arrive promptly on time and begin working on me. My hair is pulled and tugged in every direction while my face is transformed. I emphasized that I don't want anything too crazy.

The photographer lingers by my side, snapping photos. She ducks out for half an hour to get some photos of the guys.

When the hairstylist and makeup artist finish with me, I feel like a goddess. My hair is swept back into an elegant updo with loose curls cascading down my neck. The makeup artist enhanced my natural features, making my eyes pop with just the right amount of liner and shadow, and painted my lips the perfect shade of nude.

I step into the luxurious white dress. It's everything one could want and more. Delicate lace gushes down the bodice and extends onto the sleeves, creating a subtle and enthralling effect as it gently brushes against my skin.

I never thought I'd be the type of person who'd be overly concerned with something so materialistic. And at first, I was happy with the very first dress I saw and was ready to elope. Mia almost had a heart attack at the thought.

Ace was happy to do whatever I wanted. He made it abundantly clear he wanted to be married, and the rest was up to me. But I knew Mia would never allow me to elope. There's a part of me that's thankful to her for that no matter the tears I shed while planning the wedding over the past year. And even though Ace said everything was up to me—except for one thing, he didn't want to get married in a church—he still gave me his all when it came to the planning. He went with me to look at venues, cake tasting and floral choosing. Throughout it all, he didn't complain and gave me his honest opinion, which was sometimes not what I wanted to hear, but I appreciated it, nevertheless.

As I stare into the full-length mirror, admiring the beautiful dress and feeling beautiful myself, Reese knocks on the door and peeks in. "Can I come in?"

"Of course."

She nudges the door open and enters. "My goodness! Look at you. You look absolutely stunning," she says, coming to stand in front of me. Her gaze scans me from head to toe, approval and awe in her eyes.

"Thank you, Reese."

"I just came here to say that I'm so glad that you and Ace crossed paths, even though it was through a tragic incident. You've brought so much happiness into his life—into *all* of our lives. I can't thank you enough for that." Reese tears up. "I want to give you something." In her hand lies a beautiful blue hairpin with a silver metal base and delicate detailing. The sparkling blue gemstone catches the light and glistens.

Something old, something new, something borrowed and *something blue*.

"It was my great-grandmother's. It's been passed down through generations. I was going to give it to Ellie..." She trails off, her eyes growing distant and sad. "Sorry. I don't mean to bring up sad memories today. This is your special day, and you've been looking forward to it for the longest time." She sniffles.

I go to take the pin from her, but as I do, I also cover her hands with mine. It's a simple gesture, but it's also intimate. "Thank you. I wish she was here with us today. But I know she's watching over us, wherever she is."

Reese nods and embraces me in a warm hug. When we come apart, we both fall into a comfortable silence as she helps me secure the hairpin in my updo.

"You look amazing," Mia exclaims and bursts into the room. "I can't believe my best friend is getting married."

She has my daughter in her hands. Yes, *my daughter*. Even though she's nine months old, I still find those words surreal to say. She's a clone of her dad. Dark hair with curls, mesmerizing mix of blue, green and gray eyes. Ace and I named her Astra. It seemed fitting.

Astra Ellie Blackwell.

"Thank you. For everything. I don't know what I would do without you," I say to Mia. She helped me plan all of this and was there through all the breakdowns.

Mia grins. "You'd be lost," she says, and we both laugh.

Astra extends her arms for me. "Mama," she coos in her cute little baby voice. It melts my heart every single time.

I take her from Mia and place her on my hip. "Hi, baby."

She's wearing a light pink dress with a puffy, flared skirt. Her hair is long enough to have two tiny pigtails. She reaches out and tries to grab my hair, and I laugh and lean back to avoid her fingers.

"Is he out there?" I ask Mia.

"Who?"

"Ace!"

"Where else would he be?" Mia asks. "Of course, he's out there!"

With her words, my heart begins to beat faster. Everything sets in. I'm about to walk down the aisle to marry the love of my life.

Excitement and nerves mix as the moment approaches.

There's a clearing of a throat by the door. I look up to see my father standing there clad in dark tux.

"Uh, everything is ready for you," he says, breaking the silence.

"I'll give you two a moment," Mia says, reaching for Astra.

Mia and Reese leave the room with my daughter, and it's just my dad and me.

I'm grateful to have him by my side on this special day, despite the tension between him and Ace that still lingers when they are in the same room. I know he's trying his best to be present in my life and to be a good grandfather to Astra, and I appreciate that. I won't force him to accept Ace entirely and without reservations. Time may help heal those wounds.

As my dad's eyes fill with tears, he takes a step forward and tries to offer me a compliment, but his words get choked up. "Calla—" he begins before wiping his eyes. There aren't many times I've seen my dad shed tears before. Probably only once. At my mom's funeral.

"You look beautiful. Your mom would've been so proud of you."

His words mean more to me than he could imagine, and a gush of emotions surface. Then he pulls out an envelope from his pocket and hands it to me. It's yellowed with age, and my mom's cursive handwriting on the front reads:

To my beautiful daughter on her wedding day.

My eyes widen in surprise.

"She wrote it years before she passed," he says.

I take it from him, open it and begin to read.

Dear Calla,

Today is a day that I have been anticipating and prepar-

ing for, both in my heart and mind, since the day you came into this world. It feels like yesterday when I held you in my arms, your tiny fingers wrapped around mine...

I stop reading, knowing that I'll burst into tears if I continue.

"I can't cry, I can't cry," I chant, trying to convince my tears to go away. "I have a few hundred dollars on my face." I delicately dab at the corners of my eyes with a tissue that my dad passes to me, careful not to smudge my makeup. I fold the letter and vow to read it after the ceremony.

"Right, sorry," my dad says and wipes his eyes again with the back of his hand. "Ready to be married?"

I inhale a deep breath and nod, weaving my arm through his.

Mia walks down the aisle holding my daughter in her arms, playfully peppering Astra's shoulder with kisses. Astra giggles, and her little feet in white sandals flail. Mia guides Astra's arm toward her basket of petals, and Astra grabs a handful, throws them up above her and stares in wonder as they drift away.

For someone who doesn't want children of her own, Mia is incredible with her. She hasn't gone back to Switzerland. As it happened, an apartment in my old building—where Betty lives—became available, and Mia signed a year lease. Since then, she's renewed it for another six months.

She's been here since Astra was born and every step of the way since. She was the first person I called, no matter what time it was, even though she was as lost as I was on how to look after a newborn.

As the music changes, it's finally my turn to walk down the aisle. I gulp in as much air as I can, feeling nervous for reasons I can't explain. This won't change anything except my last name, but I'm still trembling. My dad takes the lead and pulls me along with him. When we finally step onto the white aisle banked with roses on either side, it hits me that in mere minutes, I'll be Mrs. Blackwell.

Ace's wife.

Bound to him in every way possible.

Memories of our first encounter and all the moments in between seep in as I make my way toward Ace.

I lift my head, and my breath catches in my throat. Ace stands at the end of the aisle in front of a magnificent arch of garden roses intertwined with wild green grasses.

I'm lost for words.

He's strikingly handsome. When isn't he? But today, there's this electric charge about him. He's in a tux with his hands clasped together as he looks up at the sky. He shifts nervously from side to side, and wow, *nervousness* looks so hot on him.

Nothing around me matters anymore.

As I move closer, my speed increases. I remind myself to slow down so I don't trip over in front of all these people whose eyes are glued to me. I know the moment that I'm near him, all my nerves will fade.

I think my grip tightens on my dad's arm, because he smooths his other hand over mine, reassuring me.

When I meet Ace's gaze, the world stops, falls away. We both smile, and then our smiles turn into full-blown grins. He chuckles, drags his hand down his face and turns away from me for a second.

When he turns back, I'm done.

Gone.

Dead.

Ace's eyes glisten with tears. They're more vibrant now, more green than blue, like two shining emeralds in the vast darkness of space.

Aws echo through the crowd when they realize.

When I finally reach Ace—after what feels like the longest walk in my life—my dad gives him a handshake, because a hug is too much, right?

I gently cup Ace's face in my hands. "Why are you crying? Did you have a change of heart?"

He snickers, places his own hands on mine. "No fucking way. I'm crying because you look so beautiful. You walking down that aisle and choosing *me* kind of fucks me up."

The officiant begins the ceremony. When it's time for the vows, Ace rights himself, puts his shoulders back and takes my hands in his.

"Calla Maven. You came into my life like a meteor, unexpected but beautiful. You were everything I was running from. At first, you reminded me of my past, of my appalling actions that led me to you. I thought the universe sent you to punish me, but I was wrong. I tried not to fall in love with you, but that's exactly what I did. I was an asshole back then,

I still am, but I'm glad I have you to call me out on it now."

There's laughter from our friends and family.

"You drive me crazy—" he says and I roll my eyes playfully. "And I fucking love it. I wouldn't have it any other way. We've been though lots of lows, more than most couples have to endure, but we came out the other side stronger than ever. I vow to take care of you and Astra and all of our future children. For the rest of our lives, I'll live everyday trying to be worthy of you. Because for me, it's always been you."

Tears run down my face. There's no stopping them.

"You may now say your vows, Calla Maven," the officiant instructs.

Unlike Ace, I need my vows written down. Mia quickly hands me a piece of paper with my vows.

"When we met, I didn't have very nice thoughts about you," I admit. "That was a lie. I thought you were nice to look at but a total asshole."

The crowd chuckles, and I smile at Ace, feeling a rush of love and warmth in my heart.

"When you showed me the *real* you, that's when I was a goner. I was done for. There was no way out for me. And even when we were apart, I think there was a part of me that knew the universe would somehow bring us back together. Ace, you're my best friend, my soul mate. I love you, and I can't wait to share the rest of my days with you. I know we'll probably fight and argue, you'll be an asshole, and I'll drive you insane, but there's no one else that I'd rather spend my nights under the stars with. I love our little family, and

I vow to be the best wife and mom that I can be."

When I finish my vows, Ace has the biggest smile on his face. It's beautiful and mesmerizing. I want to keep that smile there every day.

"The rings?" the officiant asks.

Ace looks over at his best man. Nik approaches us and pats his pockets.

Once.

Twice.

A panicked look floats on his face.

"Are you fucking shitting me?" Ace blurts out. He shakes his head, but I can tell he's slightly amused.

Then Nik doubles over in laughter and pulls out our rings from his pant pocket. "Hah, did you really think I lost the rings on your wedding day, little brother?" Ace goes to elbow him, but Nik swiftly moves out of the way.

The officiant clears his throat in a way that implies he's not impressed, and he's probably got other places to be.

Ace takes my ring—a stunning gold band with little diamonds, like shimmering stardust scattered throughout it, perfectly matching my engagement ring—and slips it onto my finger. As my engagement ring and the newly added band unite, a breathtaking transformation occurs. The two rings merge flawlessly, creating a celestial spectacle, like a constellation formed in the heaves.

The combined rings look like a sparkling star.

Ace gazes into my eyes, and it's just us. We're in our own little bubble again.

I take his ring—a simple, classic band—and slide it onto his finger, feeling a surge of emotion as our skin touches.

"I now pronounce you husband and wife. You may kiss the bride."

Ace has me in his arms before the officiant has even finished speaking. He leans me back like they do in movies, gazes into my eyes and whispers, "My wife." Then his lips are on mine.

Our first kiss as husband and wife feels like sinking into soft bed sheets after an exhausting day. Or that feeling you get when you look up at the stars on a clear night and feel like you're a part of something that's bigger than yourself.

I don't want it to end, but the sound of whistling, cheers and clapping reminds me that we're not alone. Far from it.

Ace threads our hands together, and the weight of his ring on my finger is a reminder that we have each other. I can't wait to spend the rest of my life with him.

The reception is filled with our friends and family celebrating with us. There's an embarrassing speech from a tipsy Mia, who even compiled a presentation full of videos and pictures. I was ready to strangle her.

Sitting behind the main table, I look up to see Ace on the dance floor with Astra in his arms. My heart bursts with so much love and happiness, and I can't help but smile at the sight. Astra is giggling and babbling while Ace makes her feel like the center of the universe.

Moments like these are a reminder that in a world full of chaos and darkness, there's still beauty and happiness to be found.

A few hours later, I stand on the deck outside of our room and stare out into the darkness. In the distance, there are a few laughs and shouts. I'd wager it's Theo and Josh. Apart from that, the serenity wraps around me like a tight blanket. My hands run along the wooden railing, and I stare at my finger, which now has two beautiful rings that symbolize my love and commitment for Ace.

I think they symbolize so much more than that too.

It shows how much we've overcome, and how much we're willing to sacrifice. How much we're willing to go through to end up together.

I feel the atmosphere change, and my body electrifies like a thousand fireflies lighting up inside of me. I don't have to turn around to know that he's here.

"I've been looking for you, love." His voice is low and so unholy that I have trouble concentrating on anything else.

"You found me."

I hear every footstep as he moves toward me. "Have I told you that you look absolutely beautiful?"

"About eleven times. Give or take."

He chuckles, and the rough sound of his voice soothes me. When his knuckles brush against my bare back, my knees tremble.

"Make it twelve then."

"Astra?" I ask.

"Sleeping in the cot."

Ace is a great dad, just like I thought he would be. He's a natural with her. During those early days, when we were both surviving on next to no sleep, and Astra would do nothing but scream her little face off, Ace would take her from me. She'd instantly calm down. I used to hate it. Hate that he was able to make her stop crying and I wasn't. Like that somehow made me a shit mother.

Eventually, I came to realize that it wasn't the case at all.

"She'll be awake in a few hours." I sigh.

"My mom offered to look after her tonight," he says with a cheeky glint in his eye.

Those words and everything his look conveys goes straight to the apex of my thighs, leaving me yearning for more.

"Talk dirty to me some more," I joke, but I'm also kind of serious.

"Being my wife has its perks," Ace says.

"So you've been holding out on me?" I raise both brows.

I doubt that's possible.

Ace chuckles and pulls me closer into him. "Maybe," he whispers, his breath warm against my ear. "But I promise to make it up to you tonight, Mrs. Blackwell."

You don't wait for the stars to align. You push with every ounce of your soul. You make them align. Make the universe see that this is where you belong. That this is your life, and you won't settle for anything less.

The most at peace I've ever felt in my life was in Switzerland with Ace, but there's a part of me that craves more. More adventure, more exploring, more discovery. We've decided to remain in New York for the time being but to move into the suburban part of it—near Ace's mom.

No matter what she says, she needs our support more than ever.

As a mother, I can't begin to comprehend the pain of losing a child.

Ace sold his infamous penthouse where we'd made many memories over the past couple of years. We bought some land and built a house. That was stressful.

I don't recommend trying to plan a wedding and build a house while being pregnant.

Not all stories have a happy ending, and those that do are still interwoven with tragedies.

I hope that after everything, this is finally our chance at a happy ever after.

Or whatever one may call it.

The sky lights up for us. "A shooting star," I murmur. "Make a wish." Because that's what you do, right?

"Fuck the stars. I have everything I need and more right in front of me."

Acknowledgments

To my readers—From the bottom of my heart, thank you for riding out this journey with me. I'm so lucky to have been able to share this universe with you.

To Hilary, Sonali, and Praveen—Your feedback, comments, reactions and messages are everything. Thank you for being my beta readers.

To J, my fiancé—Thank you for being with me every step of the process.

About the Author

Genicious is a #1 bestselling author from sunny Australia who writes new adult romance. With love for heart-fluttering moments, spicy encounters, and unexpected plot twists, Genicious writes stories that will leave you hooked.

When not writing, Genicious can be found sipping on lattes (or wine) while reading novels that spark her imagination.

Beyond writing and reading, Genicious spends the remainder of her time with her little family—travelling, enjoying walks on the beach during sunsets, and browsing the markets for a new plant to bring home.

Also by Genicious

Sins for Cigarettes

A standalone, new-adult, romance novel

One steamy summer
Two hearts
Many secrets
And countless sins